Pure Life

by

Benjamin Cullen Yablon

Apple Tree Publishing

100 Fillmore Street

Denver, Colorado 80206

ISBN 13: 9780615677194 (soft cover)

ISBN 10: 0615677193 (soft cover)

First printing July, 2012

Printed in the United States of America

Visit Apple Tree Publishing online at
www.AppleTreePublishing.com

Writing is a labor of love, most of which comes from those that support the writer. I would like to thank my family, my wonderful wife Kara and my beautiful daughter Charlotte. A special thanks to Marshall for making *Pure Life* a reality.

Bon Voyage,

Benjamin C. Yablon

1 *Pura Vida* Oil Tanker, Atlantic Ocean

"I'm not going to hurt you," Abigail lied. The boy in the sterile lab before her remained motionless. None of the others had survived this long. "I want you to tell me about your work on Wall Street," she said.

Noah stared at his reflection in the mirrored wall in front of his gurney, but said nothing.

"Do you remember working on Wall Street, Mr. Smytheson?" she asked. Still nothing. She clicked the microphone off and told Brian, her oversized lab tech, "Increase transistor frequency by twenty-five percent."

Noah shrieked and collapsed back onto his bed. Abigail's hand shook as she clicked the microphone back on. "Do you remember your work on Wall Street?" she asked.

Noah only stared blankly at the mirrored wall and pulled his knees up to his chest.

"Increase the voltage?" Brian asked from behind her.

"No—" She caught herself. "Not just yet."

"We have clear parameters in place. We are to increase voltage to the neural implants until host subject six-oh-nine is able to recover donor memories or becomes unresponsive."

She ignored his statement. "I tried this experiment on the rats. The failure ratio is too high."

"What do you mean, you tried this on the rats?"

"I needed more empirical data and that was the best way to get it."

"You know Mendelbaum has a standing order on animal experimentation. Nothing that causes pain to an animal without his prior consent. I assume you didn't get his consent, did you?"

Abigail looked at the man for a moment. "Do you know why he opposes animal experiments?"

"I don't care," he said, turning his back to the chirping control panels. "He doles out the ship credits; that's reason enough to do what he says."

"He got his medical ethics in Venezuela, from his German father. Does that ring a bell for you?"

It was his turn to remain silent. He turned back toward the long bank of gleaming controls, double-checking calibration settings for the experiment she had repeatedly re-scheduled.

Noah, their nine-year-old test subject, sat behind the glass, staring into his own sad reflection, but it felt to Abigail like he was focusing on her. She shook it off; she had her own child to think about.

"Reduce sedative by half, and initiate secondary sequence," she said.

Brian's thick fingers played over the dials before she'd finished speaking. The boy closed his eyes. Abigail turned her head and dabbed at her eye so the tech could not see. She cleared her throat and spoke into the microphone attached to the monitor before her. "Try to stay calm," she said. "It won't be as bad." Her voice echoed in the chamber and the boy recoiled from it. A snort from the tech sent a squirt of acid into her throat. She bit at her inner lip to avoid screaming at him. He cared little for human life; less for the life of another clone that would be harvested for useful organs should the RYE Project fail to upload.

She inhaled slowly before she said, "I'm in charge of this disgusting lab. You will follow my orders."

"Perhaps I should take my concerns to Dr. Mendelbaum?" he asked evenly.

The threat was not the least bit veiled. Abigail knew Brian's fortunes aboard the ship hung in the balance of his work on the RYE Project. Short for Restoring Your Essence, the RYE Project was the *Pura Vida's* most ambitious plan to upload the recorded memories of the ship's clientele to cloned hosts. Dr. Mendelbaum had already docked Brian's credits and he was unlikely to be able to afford much leisure time this quarter.

"Shall I adjust the voltage," he asked contemptuously, "Doctor?"

She looked at Brian and recalled that he was also known as "the Beast" by some of his friends. He placed his hand on the voltage dial. Abigail took a deep breath, and said, "I will remove you from this program if you—"

But it was too late. She heard only the shrieks from the cold room behind her as the voltage spiked to fifty percent. She spun back toward Noah and saw the horror on the boy's face. He clutched at his ears, a thin trickle of blood visible beneath his pale fingers. She turned on Brian and swung an open-handed slap into his face. It was like smacking a statue. Brian grinned back at her and licked his already swollen lips, enjoying her feeble attempt to harm him. She opened her mouth but chose silence as Mendelbaum strode confidently into the lab.

When no one spoke, she said, "I can't work under these conditions. I want this man off the project immediately."

"Doctor, I can explain."

Mendelbaum was not looking at either of them. Instead, he was smiling through the glass at Noah. The screaming had stopped. Abigail turned, expecting to see him dead or unconscious, but was stunned to see that he was standing on the other side of his cell, writing on the dry erase board. They had tried for weeks to get him to use it.

"What is it?" Brian asked.

"His account numbers, I suspect," Mendelbaum said.

He reached out and massaged Abigail's shoulder, staring deeply into her eyes. She fought the urge to pull away from him with every fiber of her being. Her son, Edvard, needed her to be strong.

2 CHAMONIX, FRANCE

Mendelbaum paused before entering the high, alpine retreat owned by Heir Bernhard Schnell, where he was to greet his potential clients. Stable ground felt strange under his feet and he missed his quarters desperately. He hadn't drunk a decent meal since leaving the *Pura Vida* and his stomach was cramping. The soft breeze brought pollen to his sinuses that he hadn't been exposed to in months, which forced him to dab at his eyes and nose every few moments.

Mendelbaum had not been off his ship for several years for longer than a day. He had grown quite fond of his home's subtle motions, but coming here meant that this would be the last time he'd ever have to leave it. Once this final piece of long-term funding and investment was established, his ultimate goal for the RYE Project would be within reach. The breakthrough with the boy, Host 609, hadn't come a moment too soon.

The elaborate chalet sent a brief wave of nostalgia over him. His father loved to describe the Fuhrer's mountain retreat, known as the Kehlstenihaus, to him as a boy. This replica had been built by Dietrich Schnell, an influential member of the Vichy regime; Hitler had used him to manage occupied France. His son, Bernhard, was now the director of the French Safety Authority, or ASN, the nuclear subsidiary of the Ministry of Environment, Industry, and Health that regulates nuclear safety and radiological protection in France.

Hitler had only used the real Kehlstenihaus a few times, but it had become a symbol of the regime and was open to the public and was nothing more than a tourist attraction. This new estate, located high in the French Alps, was an exact replica. His father's descriptions of the place helped him regain his focus on the task at hand. Mendelbaum's father, Reinhart, and Josef Mengele's experiments had been a wonderful jumping-off point for his own project, but he had accomplished much more in the sixty years since the Allies had stolen the research. The dirty little secret of the modern medical community, Mendelbaum mused, was the reality that so much of today's science was based on discoveries the Nazis made during the Holocaust.

It was time to meet the moneymen. Mendelbaum strode through the mudroom of the chalet, removed his coat, and walked purposefully into the great room. He looked around at his guests and fought a wave of nausea. He missed his ship. The feel of the open ocean under his feet calmed him. “Ah, welcome friends,” he said thinly as he walked past the assembly to the head of a long, dark table and sat. He began talking at once, launching into a conversation with his startled guests that seemed like he’d already begun. “The long-term survival of the human species is linked to its ability to weather the coming global catastrophes. Global warming, terror attacks, and treatment-resistant disease will all play their parts in the approaching die-off.”

“My father had it all wrong with eugenics; the only thing that really matters is isolating genes that are free from defects. The ‘white race’ is a lie. Hitler was a visionary and yet a pathetic failure. Every race can create a superior human. We have proven that aboard the *Pura Vida*. The treatments we’ve developed on the ship are indispensable to the long-term health of the species. As you know, all avenues of research are pursued on the Pura Vida—cloning, organ re-growth and transplant, stem cell therapy, live embryo harvesting, and of course, cryonics.” Mendelbaum was the least fond of the cryonics research but it brought in the most investors.

Freeze me today, thaw and cure me later. That was the idea.

Most of those present had been hooked on the idea of cryonics. They were from all over the world and shared only one common characteristic: vast wealth. Almost half of those present were Arabs. Great oil wealth had put them in a position to doubt the accuracy of their clerics' claims that paradise and seventy virgins awaited them. Many of them had dedicated their money toward creating paradise on Earth. But now that they had paradise they wanted a way to keep it. They were all acutely aware of their own mortality. Several prominent heads of state were present, too, hand-picked by Mendelbaum. Men like them had proved particularly useful in preserving the autonomy of the *Pura Vida* project. What they lacked in liquid capital they made up for in political backing.

Mendelbaum realized that he had not spoken in several seconds and his guests were shuffling nervously. He cleared his throat as he rose from the ancient cherry table. It was time to focus this meeting and get it over with. "The *Pura Vida* holds the promise of eternal life for the one-percent." And with that, Mendelbaum had their attention once again.

These high-level fundraising opportunities were tiring, but necessary. His ship had been at sea for nearly twenty years. The 'Vida was a retrofitted oil tanker, the only ship of her type. She housed one of the most advanced—and certainly the most ambitious—medical treatment facilities in the world. Treatment was available only to the *right* sort, of course—the sort that surrounded him now, high in the Alps, enjoying the hospitality of his original benefactor, Sheik Abdul bin Jabara. The aging sheik believed in his work. He had entrusted Mendelbaum and his doctors to treat his beloved wife, Rafiqua, and had provided the initial capital to retrofit the treatment center. It was on the Sheik's referral that many of those present today had been selected.

Mendelbaum clicked a small button set into the wall to activate the home theater system. The window glass slowly faded to a dark brown, blocking out the clear morning light. A rare, life-sized oil painting of the Fuhrer slid into a housing in the ceiling, revealing a giant, high-definition television screen.

"You have all taken the virtual tour of the ship by now, but I thought it would be worthwhile for you to have a chance to chat directly with one of our success stories."

He glanced at his watch and noted that he was exactly on schedule, as usual. "Are there questions before we begin?"

He had decided against using his satellite phone to communicate with the ship. Too many intelligence agencies were trying to listen. Instead, he'd arranged for one of his patients to be available for a Webcast at this exact time.

"How do you protect secrecy?" The question had come from a small Arab man in his mid-fifties, an Iraqi-born oil contractor—Khalid Sharif Akbar. "You claim that the patient list is strictly confidential, but I find it hard to believe that you can keep the ship itself a secret."

Mendelbaum had not been expecting the question even though he got it all the time. This group was supposed to be better informed than most of those he had to suffer. He sighed, knowing that his perfect timing was ruined, and launched into his stock answer. "You are correct, Mr. Akbar, the patient list is strictly confidential. Even so, my staff rarely knows whom they are treating, and on the rare occasion when a recognizable celebrity is aboard, detailed non-disclosure statements are prepared for those assigned to the patient. No major media outlet has to date been able to put together a story on the *Pura Vida*. We operate in the shadows of the waves, outside the realm of popular news coverage—"

"But it seems that this kind of story would be juicy," Akbar cut in.

"Yes," Mendelbaum said slowly. It was like speaking to a child, "but without hard evidence of the ship's existence, nothing truly publishable has ever come to light. A few print articles here and there, but no TV. And TV is everything. This is why we operate at sea, far from any cable news outlet's reach. Our patients pay a fortune to be treated and to be kept anonymous. Like the senator with HIV we treated last year. There was no way he could go to a regular hospital. The right wing of his own party would have destroyed him."

The point was made and the room had fallen silent, but Mendelbaum continued. "The care aboard the *Pura Vida* is so good that patients don't want to risk their chances of coming aboard again if they need help. We make it clear to them all that they are never to discuss their stay. Besides, patients are kept medicated and isolated from the rest of the ship's crew except when they require treatment. And of course the crew is hand-selected and overpaid. I keep a detailed dossier on every employee aboard. I prefer crewmembers with a great deal to lose if they were ever to leave out of turn, like a family member who needs our help. In reality, we have a very low turnover. Most crewmembers stay aboard for years at a time, only taking the occasional week off. All their needs are taken care of aboard the ship. They are paid in ship credits which technically can be converted into hard currency, but the exchange rate is not very favorable." This drew a few snickers from the assembly. "Now, on to more important matters. We are here to discuss the long-term financing goals of our patients and to provide a display of our highly successful stem cell therapies."

Mendelbaum typed a series of numbers and characters into a recessed keyboard and hit enter. The screen flashed blue and then focused into an overhead shot of a very clean, modern hospital room. Several nurses and doctors scurried around the bed in the middle of the room, finishing their last-minute preparations for the interview.

"I'm sure you all remember our esteemed Bernard Schnell's father, Dietrich?" Mendelbaum asked.

Heads nodded in acknowledgment, but not in understanding. Schnell's father was presumed dead. No one had seen the family patriarch in six months, not since his devastating horseback-riding accident. It was widely speculated in the French press that he had gone into an upscale hospice somewhere to live out his final days. The Webcam zoomed in on the bed, and the assembled group realized what they were looking at—*who* they were looking at.

Bernhard Schnell was seated nearest the monitor. He gasped at the image of his father, relaxed and quite alive, and looking up into the camera. A wry smile spread across the old man's face as he greeted his son in German.

The desired effect had been achieved, but Mendelbaum let father and son speak for a few moments longer than was necessary for his purposes. The Webcast was scheduled for one minute, far too brief to allow the NSA, FSB, or DGSE to intercept it. Father and son said a joyous farewell, and the screen was once again covered by the dark-hued oil portrait of the Fuehrer.

"We extracted DNA from Wilhelm Schnell and created the genetic material we needed to treat him."

Several faces swung back toward him, a modicum of understanding beginning to spread through the group.

"Yes, we cloned him," Mendelbaum said. "The technology to create viable human clones has existed for years; it is only because arbitrary rules have been enacted that such practices are not commonplace. Not only is there a ban on human cloning, most nations outlaw the use of embryonic stem cells as well. We cloned and harvested the embryonic stem cells we required for treatment and went to work. Heir Schnell's treatment is a complete success, and he will be discharged from the Pura Vida within the month."

Mendelbaum let his words sink in before moving into more important territory. The reason for the meeting had not been broached; it hung thickly in the air like cigar smoke. There was no reason to assemble this many members of Europe's elite bankers and their Middle Eastern clients to show them a stem cell success story. They were here because he needed their banks. The Pura Vida could only carry so much gold.

"The treatment Heir Schnell received aboard the *Pura Vida* hardly touches the outside edge of what we are capable of. The real work being done aboard the ship is nothing short of extraordinary."

Only one man in the room seemed perplexed by the statement. Akbar cleared his throat and raised his hand. He had been invited to the retreat because it was well known that his wife was gravely ill. Mendelbaum stared across the table and raised his eyebrows rather than verbally acknowledging him.

"Are you saying a human embryo was cloned and then destroyed to facilitate this treatment?"

Mendelbaum was shocked he had asked the question. Those in attendance had all been carefully vetted. No one present should have had any moral hang-ups regarding something as trivial as the abortion of a fetus. Far more intense human testing and harvesting were undertaken aboard the *Pura Vida*. If this gave Akbar pause, he was in for some rude awakenings.

"Perhaps you would like to be excused?" Mendelbaum asked.

The small man stood up too quickly, knocking his chair to the floor. As he walked toward the door, Mendelbaum nodded to his chief of security, Fawwaz al-Barq. Mendelbaum thought it excellent that this man's Arabic *laqab* so matched his characteristics: lightning. Al-Barq was indeed fast. Fast and dangerous. He opened the door and followed Akbar into the waiting area, pausing to look back toward Mendelbaum for instructions. Mendelbaum gave his chief of security a slight nod of the head, indicating that he wanted Akbar to remain alive for the time being. Al-Barq closed the door and Mendelbaum returned to his assembled guests.

“As you can see, there are certain among us who do not fully understand the depth of the advances we are achieving aboard the ship. Their path does not lie with ours.” The fifteen men remaining in the room stared at him expectantly. He continued. “As you all know, the work we are doing is already well capitalized. We have been treating patients and running an active cryogenics lab for the last decade, and our results are excellent. We have extended the lives of nearly a thousand patients far beyond what modern science—with its ethical and financial limitations—could have ever done. I am not here to offer you empty promises. I am here to demonstrate the reality of our undertaking. The *Pura Vida* works and the bullion aboard the *Pura Vida* keeps us beyond the reach of any government. We are our own government.”

“As you all know, we require our clients to pay us in gold. This has kept us out of reach of any particular government’s meddling. But we are reaching the end of what we can reasonably store aboard the ship. We need a physical bank to house our surplus and to allow our clients’ investments to grow, so that when they are re-animated from their cryonic states in fifty, a hundred, or even five hundred years from now, their wealth not only remains, it has grown and is waiting for them. Banking regulations do not allow this kind of dead-hand control today. Switzerland has always been the best place for these types of specialized financial undertakings. When the Fuhrer fell, we didn't *all* lose our lederhosen. The Swiss were instrumental in keeping us afloat all over the world; I myself relied on a trust established just before the Reich fell. Your privacy laws and immigration polices guarantee that Switzerland will far outlast America."

A representative from one of Switzerland's most private banks, The Morval Kantonalbank, had heard enough. "If I may, Mr. Mendelbaum?"

"Of course, Heir Austerlitz, but only if you call me Doctor," Mendelbaum said mildly.

"*Doktor*, these financial instruments are all interesting, but they seem highly unnecessary. You must have billions of dollars of gold aboard the ship."

"Financial planning for their inevitable wake-up is a key factor in which our clients must feel secure." Mendelbaum crossed the room to stand directly before the massive hearth. "They come to the *Pura Vida* because we are going to safeguard their bodies and their money. Governments may change, but this ship will not. We are designed to stay at sea forever, if need be. America is nearly lost to socialism already. The government is supervising their banking system. Some of your own colleague's banks—*Swiss* banks—were forced to disclose the names and account details of Americans to the IRS. You will note that none of those banks are represented here today. Their services will not be needed."

"Well, we are happy to set up the trusts you have described. But having a client name himself as the beneficiary while he is in a cryogenic freeze seems like a lot of trouble. What if there is never a cure found? What if the person just stays frozen forever?"

"Then your financial institution will always have the account. From today until the world ends. Our clients understand the risk they are taking. It is well worth it to them. Either they wake up or they don't. Besides, we are typically only talking about a small portion of their net worth being transferred into the trust accounts you will establish. The one thing my clients are all sure of is that if they *do* wake up, they don't want to be poor. A mere fifty million dollar investment today, earning a reasonable eight percent rate of return will be worth two point three billion in fifty years and a staggering two hundred and forty trillion in two hundred years. So, to conclude, I would like you to know that I have arranged for those of you who wish to see the ship to accompany me on a tour of the *Pura Vida* next week."

3 Washington D.C.

Senate Candidacy Announcement

"So how do you want to introduce me?" Jim asked.

His father took a step back and looked him up and down. "As James Lantana, a decorated CIA agent steeped in foreign policy and the intricacy of international relations."

"How about as a professional thumb-twister?"

Lawrence Lantana ignored his son for a moment before saying, "I know that it's been awful since we lost Sharon. I'm sorry I didn't do more to—"

"There's no time for that now. Get out there and introduce me, future Senator Jim Lantana."

"I have it on good intel that you have not resigned from the CIA yet."

Jim smiled without humor and held his gaze for several seconds. Then, "I don't need to resign just yet. This Senate bid is still in its infancy. Besides, I keep getting interesting briefings. The last one concerned you, Dad. Something about a kid with computer files uploaded into chips in his brain. He knew your name, any idea why?"

It was Lawrence's turn to remain quiet. When he spoke he seemed to search for the right words. "I'm retired. There's always a bit of residual intel that comes in after one of us calls it quits. Once we're done here I want you to get away for a few days. I have a cruise booked for you aboard Owen Tiberius's prized vessel, the *Marquis*. It'll do you some good before the main fundraising campaign begins."

"I don't know how you talked me into this, Dad. I ought to be in Iraq scaring intel out of Muslims."

"You served your country with distinction, but that part of your life is over. It's time for the next chapter. It's time to move on. You've lost your course."

"Lost my course? You say it like she was a puppy."

"Lantanas always find a way," Lawrence said.

"My wife died, Dad. She died and I wasn't here for her. *You* were supposed to . . ." Jim couldn't finish the sentence.

"What can I do, son?"

"Make me understand why I wasn't brought home when you knew how ill she was. Explain why you've retired in the middle of your career."

"It was time for a change. I can't explain it. It's just . . . not that easy." Lawrence turned away and walked onto the brightly lit stage where the audience of donors had been waiting patiently for over an hour. Lawrence had been distant since Jim's mother passed a decade earlier. But this was different; he seemed to be forgetting things. Jim took a deep breath and steeled himself for the night of hand-shaking that lay ahead.

The next night Jim stood on the deck of his private suite aboard the *Marquis* ocean liner, wide awake at 3:00 a.m., a glass of vodka in one hand and the rail in the other. He stared out at the moonlit waves and replayed his last conversation with his wife.

She had looked frail. Frail but determined. She was always so stubborn. Her small fist on the pillow was white with anger.

"I can't leave you, not now," he'd said.

"I'm fine," she'd lied. "It's just the chemo that's making me so tired. If you don't go back and finish what you started, innocent people will die. Another Bay of Pigs."

"It's not that bad. Someone else can finish for me."

"No." She'd inhaled a ragged breath before she could speak again. "I love you. You'll never forgive yourself if you stay here and let someone else try to finish up for you. I am going to be fine; it'll take more than cancer to knock out a Drake."

The tone of her voice meant the conversation was over. He would never convince her and she would never let him stay. She was worse than her father.

He didn't remember the man, but his own father had served with him in Vietnam. Samson Drake had been awarded the Medal of Honor posthumously. His father could only talk about Samson after a night of intense drinking, and only then in a sort of off-hand and distant way. He would always talk about the stubbornness of the man. The unwavering commitment he showed in the face of overwhelming odds.

He had martyred himself during the Tet Offensive, keeping enemy forces at bay behind the spray of a .50-caliber machine gun, allowing most of his men to survive. He had pulled the trigger even after he had been mortally wounded. His lifeless fingers held on long after the gun emptied of ammo.

If Jim's father was impressed by the man, there was no question Jim would have been. Jim idolized his father, even after he had failed him. Lawrence Lantana had promised his son he would look after his wife. He would make sure she was okay and he would contact him if he needed to be pulled back from Iraq, regardless of where he was or what he was doing. Lawrence had the power and connections to move mountains. He could get his son out of Iraq with a phone call. But he had failed. For the first time in Jim's life, he had seen his father fail. His call had come too late. Sharon was already too sick.

It had been three years since she had gotten sick and a year and half since the disease had taken her, and the emptiness only felt like it was growing.

He could have gone back to Iraq if he'd pushed hard enough. The work had been all-consuming. "Who knows," he said aloud from the deck of his private VIP suite aboard the cruise ship, "maybe somebody will put me out of my misery."

The idea, once hatched, wouldn't leave him. They hadn't had kids; there was no one to leave behind now. He couldn't look at his father these days; the man had failed to save her. High-risk intel missions—that could be the cure. It had been the reason he was away from her in the first place. He had been away from her and they hadn't started a family, and then it was too late. She was already sick.

Jim stared at the water one hundred feet below and thought about jumping overboard. *Water grave, just like bin Laden. Terrible way to go.* He stared out at the calm ocean horizon where it met the black sky and let his eyes go out of focus. That was when he saw it. It was an oil tanker, steaming directly toward them. He didn't know why, but something about it held his gaze. It was the way it shimmered and seemed to almost disappear for a second, like a ghost ship. Was it possible? He had been briefed on a new cloaking technology being developed by the Navy that looked remarkably similar to the visual distortion on the tanker. *What the hell was it doing on a tanker?* The ship was still several miles away. Jim raised his binoculars to get a better look. Maybe it had just been the moon reflecting off the water.

As soon as the visual apparition had registered in his mind, it was gone. The ship looked like any other oil tanker again. *I'm losing it.* There was no reason for it to be utilized on an oil tanker. It was intended for attack ships and it was not scheduled to be deployed for another two years at the earliest. With the new administration, it could be even longer. The idea was to cover a ship in tiny fiber optic cables. The cables displayed the images captured on the other side of the object, essentially creating an optical illusion.

But he knew he had seen it. The short video that had circulated on the secure CIA network showed the same visual effect, a kind of shimmer that could still be seen when something very large was being cloaked. But the best the CIA had done so far was to cover a thirty-foot cutter with the cables, and even then the effect was far from perfect. This was an entire oil tanker. It was a fifteen-hundred-foot-long vessel, two hundred feet across. Crewmembers rode bicycles across ships of its size.

Jim took a deep breath and realized he could be dealing with something new. It was new and possibly very dangerous. He would have to talk to the boss about it. Great. Then he realized a small chase boat had been launched from the *Marquis*. It was headed on a course to meet up with the oil tanker.

4 Washington D.C.

James Lantana Fundraiser

Christiana dabbed at the wine stain on her gown as she watched Jim Lantana move across the room. She fought the urge to call out to him. He would see her soon enough. His dark-tanned skin and the deep lines around his eyes made her question the answers he had given about his work in Iraq. "Consultant," he had said. "Yeah, right," she had replied. She had come off as coy and had tried to smile and take a sip of wine at the same time. She had ended up with a ruined cocktail dress and the strong desire to duck out of the party early. Then he had excused himself to find the podium at the front of the room to give a few brief remarks. She had hung on every word. It was just like being back in high school with him. Star athlete, quiet and modest 'A' student. Rich, well respected family. Jim's father had been a big help in Christiana's career, and she had been more than happy to attend the fundraiser as Jim's date when Lawrence requested she do so.

Her attention was distracted by Owen Tiberius' approach with Jim's dad; the crowd was parting like the Red Sea as Admiral Lantana moved through it. *Retired* admiral, she reminded herself. He and Jim looked alike, but Lawrence wasn't nearly so tanned.

The three men met in a semi-circle around her. The admiral smiled at her warmly, then turned to Owen and said, "This is my son, James, and his date, Christiana."

"It's Jim, Dad."

"Yes, Jim. How good to see you again." Owen said. "I was so sorry to hear—"

"It's been a tough eighteen months," Jim said. "I wanted to thank you for the hospitality I was shown on the cruise."

"It was my pleasure. Your father has been an invaluable friend to me. How did you like the *Marquis*?"

"Truly an exquisite vessel. Her crew, however . . ."

"The crew? You had a problem with the crew?"

Lantana senior looked at him briefly, his smile fading. "Owen, this is Christiana Facchinetti, a dear family friend in spite of her job."

The comment momentarily deflected Owen's attention from Jim's comment. "Charmed," he said. Then, turning back to Jim, "Was the experience less than exceptional?"

"I just found it odd that the *Marquis* had a brief rendezvous with an oil tanker," Jim said, staring into Tiberius's face for a response. Owen's expression was not one of shock; it was more akin to embarrassment. The set of his jaw was no longer relaxed when he looked at his father's friend.

"An oil tanker, you say?"

"Yeah, the *Pura Vida*," Jim said.

"James, this is hardly the time," Lawrence said. Jim frowned at his father. Neither spoke for several awkward seconds. Finally, Lawrence said, "And you're ignoring Christiana." All eyes moved to her and she felt her pulse throb in her ears.

She nodded to Lawrence, and then locked eyes with Jim. She opened her mouth to speak at the same time he did.

"You look nice tonight," they said together.

"Thanks," they said, smiling.

"Sorry to hear about Sharon," Christiana said.

"I was just about to tell Tiberius that the cruise he and my father arranged helped a lot. It gave me some perspective for the first time this year."

That was not the vibe she was getting from the exchange, but whatever. She wanted to talk to Jim, to hear his voice. "How about another drink?" she suggested.

"We'll leave you two to chat," Lawrence said with a pat on Owen's shoulder and a wink at her.

"Don't leave on my account," Christiana said. "I was hoping to hear about your son's nightclub business, Mr. Tiberius."

A cloud passed over Owen's face and he glanced away. "I don't have anything to do with that. My son chose his own his path." He turned on his heel and walked away. Her interest was piqued. This would be her next story whether her news chief wanted it or not. Besides, she might even get to see Jim because of it.

Lawrence Lantana locked eyes with Christiana and smiled at her. "You sure know how to get a man's attention," he said.

Christiana smiled in spite of herself. The Lantana men charmed her too easily.

"I'll go and try to calm Owen down. I'm going to promise him that you are not going to include him in any planned story about his son."

"For you, Lawrence, anything," she said sweetly. She meant it, too. She would do anything for the Lantanas.

Jim and Christiana stood awkwardly in the crowd for a few moments. She finally broke the silence. "So, you gonna tell me what you do for the CIA?"

"Officially? Not the most exciting work, but it pays the bills."

"You look healthy," she said, smiling in spite of herself.

"You, as well," Jim said. "What was that about with Tiberius?"

"His son is a nightclub owner and a pimp in France. I am going to do a story on him and his father if I can find a connection to the ship building business. So far I can't find one." She sighed. Jim was staring after his father and Owen Tiberius, lost in thought.

She was perfect for him and he had never made a move. She wasn't bad to look at, she knew that. Even at a boring Senate fundraiser men were gawking at her. She was tall and athletic with short red hair and pale skin. The pink highlights in her cheeks needed almost no makeup to stand out. She had a tiny, heart-shaped birthmark on her left cheek that looked as if it had been drawn on, such was its symmetry. The mark had not proved fatal to her, through she fought the urge to try and rub it away.

Seeing Jim Lantana made her want to touch up her makeup just in case, though. She remembered how awful it had been for the Lantanas when they lost Jim's mother. She had been in a coma for nearly a year after the car accident. It had been just before Jim entered his freshman year of high school that they finally took her off life support. Christiana, and many other girls, had wanted desperately to help him through his grief. He was sad and withdrawn but had always stayed calm and quiet. He seemed unflappable and it made him irresistible.

She realized that she hadn't felt nervous like this in as long as she could remember. Jim looked different to her. It was more than the passage of years. She had agonized over him in high school, and if anything, he was far more handsome today than he was then. He had possessed an innocent demeanor in high school that had driven her crazy. Now he looked as though he had seen more than he wanted to, and she wanted to hear about all of it.

Her cheeks blushed as she recalled the night their senior year when she had thrown herself at him. She'd had too much to drink and made an advance. He had just smiled and given her a hug to diffuse the awkwardness. She could have died from the embarrassment. But he had not said a word to anyone, not even his future wife, Sharon.

She had thought about that night for years. She had gotten over it, of course, and was now a successful journalist. She all but ran the international desk at CNB. She had dated many good men since high school, but never found the time to marry. Here he was again, though, twenty years later, and she felt her knees tremble when he spoke to her. God. He had filled out since high school; even in a suit, he looked like a coiled spring. She guessed he had added fifty pounds of muscle to his 6'3" frame. He moved carefully, like a prowling tiger. He was unaffected by the nervous chatter around him. And there was the unmistakable grief etched around his eyes. Sharon had died, she knew that. She felt instantly guilty for her intense attraction to him, but reached out anyway and put her hand on his forearm.

He glanced up, his eyes a long way away. "Maybe we should get out of here," Christiana said, shocked at her own boldness.

"Why?"

She nearly died of embarrassment on the spot.

"Oh, sorry." Jim said. "I thought maybe you weren't feeling so well."

“Well, I’m not feeling well now,” she said. She fought the urge to rub at her cheek.

“Maybe we could get together for coffee sometime. I have all kinds of stories for a good reporter,” he said, smiling.

Jeeze. He actually didn’t know what she had meant. That was worse than his knowing and blowing her off. “Sure, coffee.”

5 Atlantic Ocean, *Pura Vida* – First Quarter Gala and Award Dinner, Great Ballroom

"My friends," Mendelbaum said from the polished ebony podium, "Welcome. We have several honored guests with us this evening." He motioned toward the newly arrived donors from Saudi Arabia and China. "As you all know by now, an additional allotment of a thousand ship credits will be given to the group members of the table responsible for the most significant breakthrough this quarter—as decided by me and the other council members."

Phineas Kostopoulos moved uncomfortably in his chair from one large cheek to the other and prepared for another long-winded monologue. His diarrhea had gotten worse with the additional stress. He tuned out the drone from the podium and went over his mental checklist once again: *Upload data to Noah, inform Dr. Valquist of my plan, destroy active camouflage fiber optics, jump overboard.* He couldn't wait to be off the ship and away from these unending pep rallies.

"Hey, Fatty, pass the bread," Brian the Beast said from across the large, round table.

"What?" Phineas asked.

"You heard me, Tubby."

Phineas picked up the breadbasket and slowly dumped it on the floor. With a shake of his head he turned back toward the podium and Horst Mendelbaum. Brian would now begin to have difficulties aboard the ship; Phineas would see to it. His stomach grumbled at the thought of the feast which lay on the other side of Mendelbaum's dry monologue. Phineas had gone to great lengths to improve the quality of food aboard the ship. The dreadful state of the cuisine before his arrival had nearly driven him to seek a watery death.

Mendelbaum lived on vitamin cocktails and ate a calorie-restricted diet of some kind of kelp; Phineas had seen the offensive greenish-brown slime in the massive kitchen and thrown it away at once. Phineas was sure it smelled like feces. Mendelbaum was forced to eat like a normal person for a few days before enough of the green algae could be reproduced in his private tank. Although his diet was a ship secret, Phineas had bribed it out of the head chef: Once a week, Mendelbaum ate a mega meal and then slept for twenty-four hours straight. The rest of the time he drank only his foul-smelling kelp shakes. The strange diet was part of a life-extension theory based on medical studies of Asian cultures that produced the longest living humans.

The only contribution to the ship that Phineas was proud of was the proper training of the cooking staff. It had taken months to bring them up to speed, but it made life bearable. It was between meals that his mind wandered to dark places. He had gained nearly fifty pounds in the last six months. Mendelbaum chided him to work out and threatened to dock his credits, but never followed through. Phineas was too important.

Now that the food was in order, he'd run out of excuses for Mendelbaum to keep him from carrying out the work he'd been hired to do: perfect the process whereby memories from wealthy donors were transferred into their cloned hosts. The algorithms he'd perfected were ephemeral works of art, beautiful only until Mendelbaum molded them into another piece in his ambitious life-extension program. The results were undeniable, but the cost was staggering. Phineas would never remove the image of the first screaming infants he watched his "upload" program applied to. He repressed a shiver in the warm room and thought of more pleasant things, like Abigail Valquist.

". . . it is with great pleasure that I have welcomed our guests onto the *Pura Vida*. For the benefit of our guests, will each table head please rise when your section is called," Mendelbaum said.

This was an unusual step and it would delay their meal. Phineas took a deep breath and held it for a moment. It did nothing to quell the nervous rumbling in his stomach.

"You are equally aware that the group which has achieved the *least* this quarter will forfeit half their allotment of credits for the coming quarter," Mendelbaum went on. "I will provide a brief overview of work your teams are charged with and review the results submitted by each of your table leaders. And then I will allow you to enjoy your dinners. I assure you a winning team will be announced before dessert is served. Now, for the benefit of our guests, I'll point out that Table One, the Cryonics team, is charged with preserving the patients we are not yet equipped to treat."

Phineas looked at the table on the far side of the room and repressed a shudder. Cryonics was the least objectionable research area of the ship, but the idea of all the frozen bodies aboard made him ill.

"This quarter they have perfected the use of silicone gel in their cryonic tanks." Mendelbaum said. "This has proven invaluable in creating the proper atmospheric conditions inside the tanks to reduce cellular damage to almost zero by preventing the formation of ice crystals in the blood. Several specimens were frozen for a period of three hours and were then reawakened with minimal damage to their nervous systems. Well done, Table One."

There was polite applause that hadn't quite died down when he began again, "Table Two, the RYE Project team, has successfully uploaded donor memories into a host and stimulated the host's neural implants to awaken partial memories. We expect a lower mortality rate as the process continues to improve."

Phineas felt his face grow hot as Mendelbaum stared across the room at him. The gamble he'd taken on Noah was working so far. He had manipulated the death records to show Host 609 as another child who'd died in testing. The truth was that he and Abigail had set the terrified child off on his own aboard a self-steering rescue pod the week before. He just hoped the automatic GPS performed as he'd designed it and guided him to Italy.

"Table Three, the Stem Cell Research team, has developed concepts for attacking cardiovascular disease and cancer, mitochondrial rejuvenation, stem cell therapies and regeneration, tissue reconstruction, extra-cellular rejuvenation, artificial DNA repair, and the full deployment of nano-scale drug delivery systems. They have perfected several highly valuable cloning experiments while working on their stem cell research, which are being actively used by Table Five. I will discuss the details of their work momentarily . . ."

Phineas tuned out the rest of the explanation as his eyes wandered across the table to where Abigail sat. She was looking at her watch, cycling through its various modes when he caught her eye. She looked away almost instantly.

"Table Four, the Biogerontology Group, studies the social, psychological, and biological aspects of aging. It is to be distinguished from geriatrics, which is the branch of medicine dedicated to the study of the diseases of the elderly . . . Bio is the subfield of gerontology dedicated to studying the biological processes. Their group has an updated sirtuin-modulating pill available for human trials. Sirtuins have been implicated in influencing aging and regulating transcription, apoptosis, and stress resistance. Their work has yielded nothing new this quarter outside of the theoretical. Very promising work, however. Nice job."

"Table Five, the Telomere Maintenance group, draws their research from the 2009 Nobel Prize in

Physiology or Medicine for the discovery of how chromosomes are protected by telomeres and the enzyme telomerase. Telomeres have been compared to the aglets on the ends of shoelaces that prevent fraying. The possible relationship between telomeres and human aging is viewed as a crucial piece in understanding how to slow or even reverse the process of biological aging. This quarter, the group perfected several vitamin treatments which have been added to the kelp supplements of several test subjects. The results are impressive so far."

"Table Six, the group working on the prevention of immunosenescence, which refers to the measured deterioration of the immune system brought on by natural age advancement. It involves both the patient's ability to respond to infections and the development of long-term immune memory, particularly by vaccination. This age-associated immune deficiency is omnipresent and found in both long- and short-living species as a function of their age relative to life expectancy, rather than chronological time. It is a major causal factor of the increased occurrence of morbidity and mortality among the elderly. Their team is the most active user of cloned embryos developed by Table Three and the Stem Cell research program. This quarter, they have shown beyond doubt they can produce viable clones of several high-value donors. They have successfully used a clone of a high-value donor to grow a complete set of viable replacement organs. Our orders for the procedure have tripled since we released the news to prospective clients."

There was more polite applause for what Phineas knew would be the group to be rewarded this quarter. Creating valuable medical processes was the principal focus for every team.

"And of course, last but not least, our very own Nuclear Reactor Crew at Table Seven." There was no applause. Mendelbaum cleared his throat and said, "Their tireless work to keep the ship's reactor running smoothly allows the rest of our research teams to maintain their massive power consumption needs, all the while minimizing our ecological impact." Mendelbaum smiled broadly at the group at that table, genuinely proud of the emission reduction his nuclear reactor caused.

Phineas fought to avoid looking at the table, but his eyes were drawn to it nonetheless. Once his gaze had found them, he couldn't look away.

There was Guillermo, Mendelbaum's younger brother, who had chosen to attend the gala tonight. He was, as always, clad in his customized full-body survival suit. He required the hydraulic survival suit to move on his own for more than a few steps. Phineas had worked on the design and fabrication of the carbon fiber and titanium suit himself. He had hated adding the supposedly defensive weapons to the design, but the choice was not his. Mendelbaum had insisted that his brother be supplied with a reasonable level of protection. The pale, shriveled form inside the mechanized walker wore a pouty expression as he stared out at the room. He was rarely seen outside his lavish quarters and was not required to attend ship functions. Mendelbaum had publicly threatened to revoke his brother's casino privileges if he were involved in any other altercations. Guillermo had most recently broken the arm of a card dealer after he lost a hand of poker; a relatively minor transgression in comparison to some of his other misdeeds.

Next to him sat Jacques, an even less attractive man. Mendelbaum had brought him over from the ASN, the arm of the French government responsible for regulating their massive nuclear program. The *Pura Vida's* reactor had come over from them as well. Bernhard Schnell had objected to losing the man, but Mendelbaum had won out.

"Without further ado, please enjoy your meals and our casino this evening," Mendelbaum said. The words still hung in the air as the *Pura Vida's* team of waiters appeared from the kitchen and began serving each person their pre-selected gourmet meals.

Phineas turned back to his table, picked up his napkin and tucked it into the front of his shirt. He had assumed that Mendelbaum was going to bore them with his usual twenty minutes of hyperbole before allowing them to eat, but tonight had been particularly brutal.

"Hungry, Tub-o?" Brian sneered.

Deliberately ignoring him, Phineas set about devouring his dinner. Dealing with morons added to his general discomfort, but meant little in the scheme of what he had set in motion. They had succeeded in freeing the boy, Noah. That was step one. Step two would necessitate a favorable weather pattern.

Shortly after the final dessert dishes had been cleared away, the lights of the massive chandelier overhead began to dim. On cue, the reinforced steel ceiling peeled silently back, exposing the thick glass panels and brilliant starry night above.

Mendelbaum strode to the ebony podium once again. "After long and diligent consideration, this evening I have decided that Table Six shall receive an extra allotment of a thousand credits per team member. Congratulations!" he bellowed.

There was earnest applause from the other tables and a bit of hooting from the men at Table Six. The applause quieted down immediately as the dreaded announcement of the table whose team members would be forfeiting 1,000 of their own credits was expected next. "I am pleased to announce that the work of our other teams has been exceptional on all fronts. To penalize any one table for the exemplary work of the past quarter seems unjust. So, for the first time, no table shall be docked!" The announcement drew passionate applause.

"As you all know, the ladies who have been our guests this quarter must depart in the morning. Please enjoy our casino this evening."

The divider wall at the back of the room slid away, opening a fifty-foot-wide passageway into the lavish casino. Phineas had been to Las Vegas many times. He loved the release of gambling. But this casino was nothing like the places he had visited. There were no garish lights or strobes. There were no winding passageways flanked by mirrors intended to disorient and confuse. This was an exact replica of the Grand

Casino in Monaco. As the prostitutes filtered in from their private suite, the only other place on the ship they were allowed, the dinner tables quickly thinned out. There were nearly two hundred doctors, support staff, and researchers who would gamble and fornicate wildly for the next twelve hours.

Phineas winked at Abigail, who merely nodded in reply and sat still at the table. He grabbed his wine glass and made his way to the roulette table. At least gambling would keep his mind off the rest of the ship.

6 Pleasure, Pain, Pills

Jim drove toward his office in Virginia slowly; he was in no rush to sit behind his desk today. His phone chirped from inside his breast pocket and he guessed it was Christiana. He knew that his father was trying to set them up, and the thought of companionship seemed worthwhile for the first time in as long as he could remember. He fished his phone out of his blazer pocket and glanced at the phone number. He didn't recognize it, though. "Hello," he said.

"Mr. Lantana?" the female caller asked.

"Yes?"

"This is Doctor Jagovich from the National Naval Medical Center."

Another call was coming in as well. "One second," he said to the doctor as he glanced at the phone. This time it was Christiana. He pressed a button on his phone to send her to voice mail.

"Yes?" he said to the doctor.

"I have some bad news. It appears that your father, Admiral Lantana, has made an attempt on his life. He is presently stable but unconscious."

Jim said nothing.

"Hello?"

"I-I'm on my way," Jim said as he hung up. He was only ten minutes from the hospital but he made it there in six. He was escorted to the room where he sat for several minutes, staring at his father's immobile form. After what felt like an eternity, the doctor finally briefed him: His father's housekeeper had found him early that morning, a bottle of pills spilled out next to him. His prognosis was neither good nor bad; there was simply no way to know when he might wake up.

Several hours later, Jim shook hands with Doctor Jagovich and left the hospital. He made a stop on the way home to pick up something that had been nagging at the back of his mind. He dropped off his package, showered, and packed himself an overnight bag before heading back to the hospital where he stood guard over his father all night. He had screened several more calls from Christiana. He wasn't sure what to say to her, so he finally just turned his phone off.

Twelve hours after the attempted suicide, he was no closer to understanding it. His mind reeled as he thought back through the fundraiser the night before and the events of the last few hours. His father had been acting strangely but Jim had ignored it. Neither of them had been right since Sharon had died. But this? An attempted suicide?

There was something else, something he was missing. His father was trying to tell him something. A fucking pill overdose? Lawrence Lantana was an *admiral*, a decorated military veteran. He would have shot himself if he'd really wanted to die. But the evidence was clear: he had chosen a coward's death. He had looked Jim in the eye at the fundraiser and there was a deep sense of calm. Like he had completed something.

And he had made Jim talk to that insufferable Owen Tiberius. Why? Lawrence had been trying to tell Jim something but Jim had been distracted by Christiana. She still wanted him very badly. Jim repressed another wave of nausea, not so much at the thought of Christiana—she was pleasant, just not his type—but at the fact that his mind was wandering to the utterly trivial when his father was lying in a coma in the bed behind him.

What had he wanted Jim to understand? Jim firmly believed there was clearly much more to this.

It was Tiberius. Of that he was sure. But what?

His father had left the party after Jim had spoken to Tiberius, been forced to make eye contact with the man, if he could call it that. Tiberius had been furtive and even evasive, but Jim had ignored it at the time. Jim took a deep breath and closed his eyes, recalling each detail about Tiberius the night before. His shirt had been rumpled in the front, like he'd been grabbed. And he had a cut under his nose where he'd nicked himself shaving. He'd been distracted or moving too quickly, or both, while he got ready. And his father had wanted details about the cruise that he had insisted Jim take.

Jim usually took no pleasure in torture. He had garnered some of the most useful intelligence the U.S. had ever come across in his early days with the CIA and had rarely needed to resort to physical violence. The psychological wounds were worse than the physical ones. The key was to understand who you were interrogating. Muslims were in fact quite easy to break. Even the hardest Al Qaeda operative had certain mental pressure points that could be massaged and worked, psychological levers that never failed. The real trick was convincing the detainee that you would act on your threat. That was the fulcrum.

Slaughtering a pig in the detainee's cell and draining it overnight into a bucket near them was a usual starting point; water-boarding them with the pig's blood was typically unnecessary. The smell alone had many ready to talk, but for the tougher-minded, a bit of Hollywood trickery usually sufficed. Jim would soak a bullet in the pig's blood with his bare hand, load it into his long-barreled chrome .357 and shoot one of the detainees in the head, leaving him in the cell floating in pig's blood. All this before he even asked a question.

The men knew they were sure to die; the question was could they die in a manner that allowed them entry into Paradise? It was not death they feared; it was the callous manner in which the giant American would surely condemn them to roam eternity alone and defiled, never entering the Kingdom of the Prophet. The only part of the interrogation that was real was the slaughter of the pig. The rest was a masterful piece of deception involving exploding blood packets taped to the agent's head and blanks loaded into his gun.

Breaking Owen Tiberius wouldn't be tough. Jim had sequestered him in his apartment for the last twelve hours—to allow Tiberius time to think about things.

Tiberius shook himself awake when he heard a key turning in the lock. A moment later, a large man walked into the dark apartment. He recognized Jim's purposeful gait and felt a surge of terror. He had clearly gone insane over his father's attempted suicide. Poor man, losing his wife to cancer and then, in all probability, losing his father to a sinking, pathetic, fear-inspired act. It surprised Tiberius, really. Lawrence hadn't seemed the type. James couldn't know what a blessing it was that his father had chosen this path; he would need to be dealt with delicately.

"What am I doing here, James?" Tiberius asked, twisting his wrists inside the nylon rope.

"Call me Jim."

"Of course, Jim. So . . . what am I doing here, Jim?" Tiberius asked again. Jim said nothing. Tiberius watched as he carefully took off his coat and hung it in the front closet, revealing a shoulder holster strapped to his thick torso. A long chrome revolver caught the light from the kitchen. The gun looked fairly average until he looked closely and realized how large a man Jim Lantana was. The pistol had at least a nine-inch barrel, but hanging below Jim's armpit it seemed proportional.

Tiberius tried to follow Jim's movements across the room, but couldn't turn his head far enough. He twisted in his chair and heard the same crinkling sound under him that had been there all night. He'd had a long time to look down at the carpet beneath his feet, but it was only now, with the light from the door that he could see that he was positioned over a square of clear plastic, like the kind he had seen at construction sites. Why in the world would Lantana have tied him over a sheet of plastic? What could the man have planned? Surely he didn't plan to murder him? He would be caught. And what did he hope to *gain* by killing him? He'd been over it a thousand times in the last twelve hours and always came to the same conclusion: Jim knew nothing of substance. If he did, Owen would already be dead.

Tiberius tried to keep his voice steady when he asked, "What's your father's condition?"

Again Jim didn't respond. Instead, he walked slowly across the dark room to the kitchen table and lifted a chair by its back. He placed the chair behind Tiberius and sat down heavily.

Tiberius was not sure, but he thought he heard Jim remove something from his pocket. He realized with a reflexive clench of his sphincter that he had probably just pulled the large gun from his shoulder holster. His suspicion was confirmed when he heard the telltale sound of the gun's cylinder being opened and the cartridges being emptied onto the plastic sheeting. A bead of sweat formed on his forehead as the sound of one round being reinserted into the gun seemed to echo off the walls. From across the room, Tiberius could see his reflection in a small mirror next to the door. He could make out Lantana's silhouette behind him; he appeared to be crying noiselessly.

Tiberius screamed at the seemingly deafening sound the gun made as Jim snapped the chamber back into the body of the revolver with a flick of his wrist.

"James!" he screeched. "You don't have to do this!" He heard the hammer click back and lock into place, then felt the barrel pressed roughly into the back of his head. "What do you want from me?" he howled.

Jim said nothing. He simply sat still, applying increasing pressure with the pistol.

Nearly a minute passed and Tiberius began to regain his composure. His sobs began to subside and he regained a bit of mental clarity. "J-James?" he asked.

Jim pulled the trigger, dropping the hammer home with a dull click of metal on metal.

Tiberius's bladder let go. He heard Jim reopen the gun, spin the cylinder and snap it back into place. The barrel was against his head again.

Finally, Jim spoke. "Tell me about the oil tanker, Owen."

When Tiberius got himself under control, he realized that this was not going to end well. James had figured out more than he should have. “Stop it, James. Enough,” Tiberius said at last. “I know what you want to know. But I don’t know what you’re after. There is nothing to be gained from this.”

“Why did he do it?”

“Your family is connected, but you’re not rich. He couldn’t afford the treatment Sharon needed.”

“I know who I am, Owen.”

“Your wife was waiting for treatment. This didn’t sit well with your father. He was here to see the pain she was in. He had to do something, so he traded the only thing he had—his influence—to get her the help she needed. I showed him the way, yes, I did. But the decision was his.”

“Why did he come to you?”

“He knew that our daughter was ill; she’d been diagnosed about the same time as Sharon. But he knew that we didn’t treat her in the States. He knew that we’d sent her somewhere else.”

“So?”

“He was my friend, Jim. When he asked me, I had to tell him what we did. I had to tell him about the ship.”

“What ship?”

“I had to tell him how we saved her.”

“What ship?!”

“Sharon was being treated at the National Naval Medical Center; she was on a wait list. Your father couldn’t wait for the bureaucrats to catch up with the disease. He wanted to stay ahead. He used what he had.”

“All he had was his honor.”

“It was enough for the doctor. It was a long shot, but it was just enough to get her onboard. The doctor agreed to waive his normal fee if your father was willing to help him.”

“Help him do what? And who is this doctor?”

“Imagine, James, an admiral! The information he had, the protection he could offer. It was all he had, Jim. It was the only way to save her.”

“But my wife is still dead. What’s the doctor’s name, Owen? I have to have the details if I’m going to let you live now. If you tell me what I need to know, this can just be an unpleasant day for you, not the last day you spend alive. It's up to you. Killing you will bring me no pleasure, I think you know that. But unless you help me understand what my father did, I'll have no choice. You have to give me something big. Something that proves to me that you can be trusted not to discuss our time together today. Do you know what I mean?"

"I know what you mean. Blackmail. You're just like the doctor, you know?"

"What fucking doctor?" Jim screamed.

Owen took a deep breath and seemed to sag down in the chair. "We took our daughter to a ship."

"I know that, you told me that already, remember?"

"She was too ill to be treated in the States. She needed a procedure that was awaiting FDA approval. But on the ship, there is no wait time. They saved her there, and I can't talk about the ship. That's the whole point of what he makes you do, what he makes you give him to keep you quiet. Don't you see? My daughter is safe now. If I tell you what you want to know, he'll find out. He won't treat her if she goes into remission. Anyway, I doubt you'd believe it anyway."

"Try me," Jim said evenly.

Owen took a shaky breath. "The ship is called the *Pura Vida*. Your father contacted them through me. The ship is a cutting-edge hospital at sea. Only the super rich or super powerful, or both, can have access to it. They work miracles, Jim." He looked at Jim's reflection in the small mirror and realized his mistake. "Usually."

"So my father arranged to have my wife treated aboard the ship, but they were not successful. Why did he try to kill himself?"

"I . . . I just don't know, Jim—"

"Not good enough Owen," Jim said, ripping the pistol from its holster and cocking it in one motion. He stepped around Owen to face him, leveled the gun slowly onto his forehead and got the response he had hoped for. Jim stepped off the plastic square and reached for a roll of paper towels. He spooled several onto his hand and threw them at the mess before it ran onto his carpet. He allowed nearly a minute to pass and still said nothing. He just stared at Owen.

Finally Owen cleared his throat, and said, "There's a boy that escaped from the ship."

"And?"

“The doctor told me about him. He told me that the boy would try to contact your father. If you find the boy you find the ship.”

“Why would they tell you that?”

“They wanted me to help your father find the boy. They wanted your father to come back to the ship.”

“The name, Owen, what’s the doctor’s name?”

“M-Mendelbaum, Horst Mendelbaum.”

7 CIA Analysis of Noah

"Where did we find him again?" Freddy asked. He knew the answer, but he had to hear the bizarre story again to believe it. He had been in his office at CIA headquarters since the call came in from J.C. the night before. He needed a shower and a better explanation.

"He broke into our embassy in Italy," J.C. said.

Freddy liked J.C. He was a competent admin, but he didn't have nearly the drive needed for a real promotion.

"He still won't speak?" Freddy asked. He knew the answer, but thought he would ask just in case. You could never be too analytical or repetitive with J.C.

"No, but he likes to write. We gave him paper and pen, and he hasn't put it down since yesterday."

"What's he writing?" Freddy asked. He sat back in his chair and closed his eyes.

"Numbers. Nothing but line after line of numbers. We thought it was weird so we plugged them into the code breaker and it came back as some kind of narrative."

"This kid gives me the creeps. Any idea who he is?"

"None. He isn't on any missing children reports. We were going to turn him over to the authorities in Venice, but then the numbers started making sense because he was writing in code."

"Freaky."

"Yeah, and then he dropped a real bomb. He wrote out all of Admiral Lantana's personal information and a request that the admiral be brought to him. How the hell he knew that name doesn't make any sense. But now that he seems to be some kind of security threat, we aren't letting him go anywhere."

"Admiral Lantana? Jim Lantana's dad?" Freddy asked. "It's a bit late for that; the man tried to off himself."

"Yeah. Read some of what the kid has been writing, though. It's scary shit."

Freddy opened the file on the desk in front of him and began to read.

Pura Vida Treatment Facility – goals and objectives. Life extension, disease prevention, memory transplantation.

Patient list:

Bauer, Adalwolf R. – Germany

Chesterson, Shara V. – America

Drexel, Wilson P. – America

Dyson, Charles F. – Canada

Freddy looked up from the list. "This thing is hundreds of pages long," he said.

"Yeah, there are thousands of names there. But what's interesting is this description," he said, flipping to a marked page. Freddy began reading again.

I want to run away from him like I have all the other times but the woman doctor with the pretty hair tells me over the radio not to be scared. She says that if I relax the pain won't be as bad. She's right about the pain, but if I don't run, the fat man can get close to me again. When I close my eyes he's there, inside my head, smiling with lips like wax. He reaches for me. His hands are damp and cold. If I run from him, the pain inside my head is worse, like fingernails digging out through my ears. But when I stop running, I can feel him seeping into me. I can hear him talking to me but his mouth is not moving. His words are in my head, like I'm the one saying them. It hurts. I scream and scream until I fall down and finally it stops. It always hurts like this but he's never gotten so close before. It's over for now and I can sleep. I'm so tired. I know they'll start again soon. They always do.

"What's chasing him?" Freddy asked.

"I asked him the same thing. You're not going to like the answer," J.C. said. "He thinks that he's being chased through his dreams by a stockbroker's memories . . . that were uploaded into him. I assumed it was some childish delusion until we deciphered the binary code he wrote out that gave us the list of names and the rest of the data."

Freddy scanned the notes the boy had written for the CIA caseworker. "I have to get this to Jim."

"This is good, Freddy, real nice work," Jim said.

"Sure am sorry to hear about your dad," Freddy said.

"Thanks," Jim said. "Are you sure this is the same ship, though?"

Freddy stretched his skinny arms over his head before answering. "I've been up with this project all night, sir. It has to be the same ship you told us to keep an eye out for yesterday. Too many similarities. The one we try to keep an eye on uses active camouflage technology that rivals what we are able to deploy. Every few weeks we pick up a trace signature of it and can pinpoint where the tanker is, but then it drops off again." There was a reason Freddy was such a sought-after CIA analyst, he was hard not to like—and he always got results.

"How do you know it's the same ship?" Jim asked.

"They put out a distinctive radiological signature. Goddamn thing is nuclear-powered; as far as I can tell it's the only non-governmental nuclear-powered ship in the world. We'd love to track her down and have a look inside if we could. Problem is, we only find her for a few minutes at a time before she disappears. The ocean is a big damn place. By the time our sensors can pick up the signature of the reactor, we don't have long enough to deploy our assets to their area. They know we are watching them."

"This has to be the same ship I saw. It was a rusted-out oil tanker that moved like a cutter."

"That sounds right to me, sir. I've tracked the movements of this ship for the last two years. It moves so fast we can't get a decent read on where it will end up next. They must know that we will try to investigate if we get the chance. She never gets close to our fleet; she's always in deep, open waters."

"If the ship is nuclear it would never need to go in for refueling. They must have smaller ships they take out to restock their supplies."

“Or planes. The tanker you saw is easily long enough to land a plane.”

“What about the kid?”

“We saw that he had some kind of surgical scars on his head and neck. We did an MRI and found small pieces of metal implanted in his brain. They appear to be computer chips that have small rechargeable batteries attached to them. Their power has drained away and he seems better every day. As long as we keep him away from any electrical fields, he’ll be okay. It was after the MRI that he wrote all those pages of code. But at first--man, was he full of codes and strangeness.”

“I’m glad to hear he’s doing better. Any idea why this kid would have chips implanted in his head? Do they serve any medical purpose?”

“None that we could figure out. They are highly sophisticated and aren’t in a place that we’d dare remove them. It could kill him.”

“What else ya got, Freddy?”

“The data stream the kid gave us was unbelievable. We have patient lists, pricing information, ship’s crew, the whole deal.”

"This is great. Complete ship complement, nice work. How big's the operation out there?"

"Fifteen cooks, fifteen janitors, twenty-five security personnel, fifty doctors, seventy-five research assistants, and two hundred and fifty patients, give or take."

"So that's what, four hundred or so aboard at any given time?"

"And none of the crew appears to be female."

"Hmm. They must not want any romantic entanglements, you know. I bet they have too many bulls aboard to give anybody free reign. Kinda like a submarine in the old days. No female distractions unless you're on shore leave. You've outdone yourself, as usual. Time to run this intel up the flag pole."

"I'll tell you what you ought run up that flag pole . . ."

"I know it, Freddy, but he's the boss now."

"It oughta be you, and you know it. Why you keep passin' up jobs, man?"

"Goodbye, Freddy."

"Who fucking cares, Jim?" Carmichael MacHale asked. He didn't bother to look up from behind his thick mahogany desk. “It’s a ship in the middle of fucking nowhere playing with chemistry sets. I’m not dedicating any more resources to tracking it down. You know what they just did to my budget? This is not a priority. Al Qaeda is a priority. Somali pirates are a priority. Fucking Russians are a priority. Again. Do you know what that goddamned Putin is doing?” He motioned to a stack of paper on his cluttered desk. “And don’t get me started on Iran and North Korea. I’m buried in priority intel and you bring me this shit?”

“With all due respect, sir, I’ll contact the president myself on this one.”

“You’ll fuckin’ *what*?” McHale was the new assistant director of the CIA and he hoped to stay that way. He cleared his throat and tried to adjust his tone. “I was sorry to hear about your dad. How’s he doing?”

“No change, sir.”

“Look, Jim, your dad’s an admiral so you’ve played golf with the big guy, is that it? You know I don’t give a shit about his blessing. Besides, how did you come by the intel on the ship in the first place? You didn’t by chance extract info from a U.S. citizen by force, did you?”

Jim ignored the question. "According to Freddy, the ship was first used as an oil transport in Venezuela. Then it dropped out of sight for several years. It showed up again flying the flag of Saudi Arabia six years ago," Jim said. "We've been tracking her for two. I have reason to believe that the data from the boy is referring to the same ship."

"The Saudis?" Carmichael repeated.

"Yeah, it's known as flying a flag of convenience. Countries with the best tax and wage laws attract shipping interests to register with them. No inspection, no environmental mandates."

"No rules."

"This ship scares me. Have you read the accounts that we got from the boy of what they're doing? They may not be breaking the laws of any nation, but they sure are creepy bastards."

"I read the file," MacHale said, pointing toward another haphazard stack. "What do you hope to accomplish?"

"If I'm right about the nature of the human experiments, we can take him before the International Human Rights Commission." Then, "But that may not be enough."

Carmichael looked at him over the rims of his reading glasses. “You’re looking for a green light to take him out, aren’t you? I didn’t think you had the stones for wet work,” he said, smiling humorlessly. “I know about your military service, but straight assassination is a little below your pay grade. You’re on track to replace me someday, not shoot a silenced .22 into a fucking eye socket.” He sucked a breath through his teeth and raised his eyebrows. “When was the last time you shot a man? Jordan? Dubai?”

“Look, I don’t know what I want out of this. I just know that if the boy’s stories are true, this thing is too terrible for us to allow it to exist. It’s right out of the concentration camps. This guy’s work is based off Mengele and the other Nazi doctors, including his father Reinhart. His father worked at both the Dachau and Ravensbrueck camps in 1942 and ‘43. He was renowned for his work on bone regeneration and transplantation on female prisoners at Ravensbrueck and for his freezing experiments at Dachau.”

“You are a crusading prick, aren’t you?”

“Wrong is wrong, Carmichael,” Jim said. He left out the details that Owen Tiberius had shared with him. There was no need to bring *his* father into this now.

“What do we know about the owner of the ship?”

"His name is Horst Mendelbaum. His father fled the allied advance on Nazi Germany with several other high-level doctors. Reinhart was smart; he set up new identities years in advance. They made an easy move to Venezuela, instead of Brazil with the others. He married into the political class and had another son. Reinhart died of natural causes as an old man. The Israelis got the stepmother with a car bomb in the early eighties. His original financing came from Saudi Arabia, but judging from the information we got from the boy, his investors are everywhere now."

"Sounds like a real sweetheart. So, what do you want from me?"

"Agency sanction to investigate the ship, nothing more than a three-man team. From the data we've collected from the boy, we know where the ship is going to be."

"And where is that?"

"Off the coast of Saudi Arabia in approximately three weeks. They have to submit to a brief inspection once every year to maintain their flag of convenience. The team will make contact with the ship disguised as Somali pirates. That way you can show the Senate Finance committee that you're taking the pirate threat seriously. All I need to do is get close and document what they're doing."

Carmichael MacHale leaned away from his cluttered desk and took a deep breath. He said nothing for several seconds. "You want to lead a team to investigate a wild goose chase that could end your career? Done. Now get out."

8 ABIGAIL AND PHINEAS - *PURA VIDA* TREATMENT CENTER, ATLANTIC OCEAN

Phineas shuffled around his cluttered lab table and knocked over a pile of papers with his stomach. Cursing, he picked the papers up and dragged his elbow over the dry erase board Abigail had left on the table with her most recent calculations.

It was not easy being fat on a ship. At least in this laboratory the ship's stabilizers worked properly. Conducting delicate research in an ocean-going craft would not have been possible without the massive pistons that the surgery center and select labs were outfitted with. The entire room was sandwiched between two liquid-filled chambers that adjusted to the roll of the ship and minimized the effect of all but the toughest waves. Each room moved up and down in the massive tubes without the occupants feeling a thing.

The system required nearly constant maintenance but worked quite adequately. Phineas had designed it quickly and easily, amazing Mendelbaum and further cementing his fate as an indispensable part of the blasted ship. Other doctors and staff were allowed to rotate on and off the ship, but he and Abigail were among those who never left, not even for a day.

Phineas knew that he never should have ended up aboard the *Pura Vida*. He was here because he'd been a fool and trusted his colleagues at Berkeley. That prick Johannes had stolen the patent out from under him. He had been the foremost expert in the fields of applied mathematics and computer technology at Stanford before leaving for what he thought was the opportunity of a lifetime at Berkeley. But he would never see a penny for his breakthrough. Even now the technology languished in the clumsy hands of his former colleagues. Mendelbaum had given him the tools to use the technology again and he was supposedly earning one million dollars a year for his work. But the money was only good aboard the ship until Mendelbaum released him and allowed him to exchange the credits for currency. He was a rich, seasick prisoner, whose work disgusted him. At least Mendelbaum didn't enforce the exercise requirement for him.

Phineas straightened the pile of papers that he had knocked over, but still couldn't find the list of calculations he had been working on. Mendelbaum hated that he insisted on using paper printouts of the data stream to review the algorithms that ran the RYE Project. But looking at the numbers on the screen had always given him a headache, even back in his Berkeley days. Mendelbaum saw it as a sign of weakness.

Phineas felt his heartbeat increase as the door slid open and Abigail stood, backlit and unaware of her impact on him, waiting for the RF scanner to grant her final access to the lab. The scanners were above the bulkheads of every space on the *Pura Vida*.

Only Mendelbaum had full access to every part of the ship. Phineas had more access than most, Abigail much less. She was allowed into this lab, her quarters, the main hall where meetings and meals were served, the massive workout room, and of course, Mendelbaum's private quarters.

She had told Phineas about the time she spent each week on his private balcony, the pale, silent man fingering his Nazi charm and watching her. Freak. Phineas knew exactly what the charm held. He had designed the master override switch himself and fixed it inside the hollowed-out relic. When Abigail mentioned the charm to him he knew they had an opportunity.

Abigail walked into the lab and logged into her screen. "Good morning, Phineas," she said without looking at him.

"Hello, my lovely," he said, blushing.

"*Lovely*," she said over her shoulder.

"That's right," Phineas said seriously. "Do you know the effect you have on men?"

"I'm thirty-two, Phineas; I'm well aware of the drooling morons all around me."

"I beg your pardon."

"All but you, of course. You would never drool on me, would you?"

"On you, no—but over you?" Phineas replied. He had never flirted with her openly and he hoped he wasn't going too far.

"Have you heard anything else about Noah?"

"Not a word," he said seriously. This was dangerous. Every movement aboard the ship was recorded and studied. Mendelbaum had personally designed the program that stored and sorted every conversation for key words. There was no safe place to talk about what they had done. Abigail picked up the dry erase board and frowned at it.

"This had my latest results on it," she said.

"I know, sorry."

She drew a smiley face on the board and faced it toward him. Her meaning was clear. Mendelbaum was listening and the conversation needed to stay positive.

Passing notes was the best they could come up with to communicate covertly.

"The test data on the newest subjects is promising, but not progressing as quickly as six-oh-nine," Phineas said.

Abigail's cheeks brightened thinking of Host 609. They had named him Noah, but they knew they could not show their feelings for the poor child. "Host six-oh-nine was an enigma. He progressed so fast and then cratered within hours of the full upload," she said. This was a carefully crafted lie for Mendelbaum's ears.

The dreams that Noah had written down had chilled them both to the bone. No child should know what he knew. His memory donor was a monster of the worst kind. He was a child-molesting Wall Street tycoon who'd been shot nearly to death by one of his victims' mothers. No matter to Mendelbaum—the man was a billionaire.

The RYE Project had succeeded, but Mendelbaum wasn't yet aware of it. He couldn't be allowed to know that Noah had recalled in horribly vivid detail the key personality elements of his donor. Another session or two and Noah would have been gone, replaced with the personality of the pedophile stored deep below in the communal tank of super-cooled gel, alongside hundreds of other corpses.

They couldn't hide the success forever. If it had worked once, it would work again. After hundreds of hours of rigorous neural implant stimulation, Noah had recalled his host's implanted memories. The memory upload therapy sessions had gone on Noah's entire six years of life without success. Then Mendelbaum had ordered the dramatic increase in drug dosage and intensity for all of the two hundred young hosts involved in the RYE Project. Nearly half had died within the first week of enhanced therapy. Abigail and Phineas knew that they needed to do something.

They could not tolerate the depravity any longer, but Abigail was not in a position to anger Mendelbaum. Abigail could not give Mendelbaum a reason to hurt her own son. Nine-year-old Edvard Valquist was all she had to live for and Mendelbaum's only leverage over her. The boy provided a more than adequate fulcrum to bend Abigail to Mendelbaum's will. At least that's how it had been working. Now she knew she had to risk everything to save them both—or destroy them all.

Phineas locked eyes with her and knew that she was as committed as he. Abigail fidgeted with the buttons on her watch, a clear sign to Phineas that she was checking the barometric pressure. "It sure is nice out today," she said.

They wore matching Suunto dive watches equipped with highly sensitive barometric pressure gauges. When the right storm came, they would have to act fast.

"Don't even get me started on the weather again," Phineas said as he checked his own watch. The millibars had dropped over the last hour, but they indicated nothing more than a small tropical depression. Not at all what they were hoping for.

Abigail turned on the monitor next to the door. Every lab and almost every room aboard the ship was equipped with a 20" LCD touch screen that could be used to communicate with the rest of the ship via video chat or just to browse the approved TV stations. She watched the weather report with obvious frustration. There were clear skies for the next ten days without even a hint of inclement weather. Everything hinged on the weather. When the storm came she would move Edvard to the one place Mendelbaum wouldn't think to look for him. Then the rest of the plan went into action. It had to work; Mendelbaum would gladly kill Edvard the moment he suspected she had betrayed him. The timing was everything and they needed a storm—a big one.

Phineas felt the blood drain from his face as a fresh wave of nausea swept over him. He took a breath. If she could be brave, so could he.

Getting Noah off the ship had been the first and certainly easiest step. It was a long shot, but the boy had all the data he'd need locked inside his brain to set them all free. Phineas had uploaded more than just the required donor memories. He had given Noah the complete schematics of the ship, its financial records, its navigational history, and a few choice words about Mendelbaum for good measure. If the boy lived through his solo escape-pod trip to Italy, they had a shot. Phineas looked at the printout of the coded message and hoped that the CIA could make sense out of the data he held. He sensed that they had been quiet for too long and changed gears.

"What was he like?" Phineas asked, picking up on a conversation about her murdered husband from the day before. He knew that if he were listening, Mendelbaum would not object to this line of questioning. He liked her to remember.

"He was a Nordic skier. All he cared about was making the Swedish Olympic team."

"Was he beautiful like you?" Phineas had been alone aboard the ship for a long time. Homosexuality was tolerated aboard the *'Vida*, but not encouraged.

"I suppose, yes."

"Did he?"

"What?"

"Make the team?"

"Oh, no."

"What did he do for money?"

"I supported the family."

Phineas sucked in a breath though his teeth. "He must have been even prettier than you."

"It wasn't that bad, Phineas," Abigail said.

"We don't have to talk about it if it bothers you."

"No, I like to talk about him. You're the first one I have spoken to about him since . . ."

Phineas put an arm around her before the tears came. They stood together in the sterile room for several minutes without speaking. Abigail wept for only a portion of the time, then relaxed for the first time in months and nearly fell asleep, standing in Phineas's soft embrace. He felt the tension drain from her shoulders and seem to seep into his.

It had been dangerous, but worth it. Standing with his arms around her, he felt more energized than he had in over a year. Her perky breasts jabbed into his floppy-man chest and he hugged her tighter. He knew that their danger would only increase, and she couldn't know what he had planned.

9 GUILLERMO AND JACQUES – OZONE POOL

Guillermo opened his eyes in terror and fought to keep his face above the waves of mist that rolled toward him on top of the liquid. His thin arms flailed madly as he struggled to regain his bearings. He spun around madly in the fluid, searching for something, anything to hold onto. He heard a familiar nasal voice from far away and he shook himself fully awake. He cursed and realized that he had fallen asleep in his ozone tank again. The freedom of motion he felt in the tank allowed him to forget his severely weakened state. Having a nightmare in his holy place left him panting in the misty waves of liquefied ozone. He looked across the dark surface of the tank - nearly the size of an Olympic swimming pool - and recognized Jacques standing near the brightly lit entry to his quarters.

Jacques was looking down at him, concern etched across his pale face. "You okay?" he called out. "Dream about drowning again?"

"Certainly not," Guillermo said with added emphasis on the beginning of the statement. His heart was beating hard and he was annoyed that Jacques had seen his moment of weakness. "Have the new girls arrived?"

"I am going to get them in ten days, remember?" Jacques said, smiling. "Will you be coming to the next award gala?"

Guillermo rolled his eyes and relaxed back into the ozone.

"Your brother loves it when you come voluntarily; it helps build morale for the crew to see you there."

Guillermo began a slow backstroke across the pool. The liquid was warmed to one hundred degrees and could be heated to suit his mood within minutes. The ozone conducted heat fifty times faster than water. Guillermo ran his hands over his hairless chest and stomach, relishing the smooth feel of his skin. Pools were the only place where he could move on his own without his suit. He would never admit it, but he was embarrassed by how skinny he had become and so would never use the public pool attached to the main workout facility. Mendelbaum had added the pool to his quarters, retrofitting half of one of the former oil holding tanks for the purpose of housing Guillermo's private treatment center. It was a hospital within a hospital.

Guillermo's quarters were by far the largest aboard the *Pura Vida*, taking up nearly ten times the space Mendelbaum had allotted for even his own luxurious quarters. Guillermo rolled onto his back and swam away from Jacques with short, weak strokes.

"How's the pool today?" Jacques shouted from the far end.

Guillermo ignored him, but did run his hands over his body again, calming away the last of the nightmare. The ozone aided the body's natural immunity and did wonders for the skin. An ultrasonic current flowed though the bottom of the pool to heat it and also soothed his aching body and calmed his raw nerves. Guillermo was most at peace in the pool, his private sanctuary. This was the place he spent most of his time, especially when he was sedated. His illness required extensive therapy and this pool was the centerpiece of it all. His brother had not been able to treat his HIV as aggressively as he would have liked until several years into the disease's progression. By then, Guillermo had lost most of his muscle mass and was at constant risk of infection. His immune system was severely compromised and he required high doses of medicine to fight off infections. In turn, he needed massive steroid doses to combat his loss of muscle mass. Sedatives were the newest addition to the daily cocktail to keep his steroid-induced rages within manageable proportions.

“Unhook my walker,” Guillermo said. “I am bored with this pool.”

In truth, he didn’t want to leave the pool, but he didn’t want Jacques to leave yet, either. He was miserably bored since Mendelbaum had confined him. Guillermo flushed, just thinking about the fact that his own brother had limited his access to the rest of the ship made him want to lash out. Horst and Jacques the Worm were his only guests now. He wasn’t even allowed a full-time hooker. The walking suit was fully equipped with life-saving devices should anything happen to him when he was away from his quarters, but he hadn’t felt like going out since his last unsuccessful attempt to bed the petulant whore called Angela, and there was no reason to wear the suit around his private quarters when he was alone.

Guillermo swam to the side of the pool and slithered out. Jacques had his suit waiting. He climbed into the harness and sat down. The heart rate meter began to chirp as it stabilized to him. His thin neck had a surgically implanted hook-up for his IV tube. It snapped easily into place and began testing his blood. A small menu screen was projected before his eyes. It indicated that his antibiotic levels were low and requested permission to dose him. Guillermo slipped his arm into the Kevlar and tungsten sleeve and felt the small actuators and motors whir to life around him, allowing him to easily raise his hand to select the MEDICATE command from the menu.

He glanced longingly at the offensive weapons list. His brother had only let him use the full features once and the accident had not been his fault.

He pressed another series of keys and began scrolling through the list of drugs he could self-administer. There were dozens of low-dose downers, but very few uppers. There was an adrenaline dose he could take and he greedily selected it from his list. His brother limited him to one measure of cocaine per week, and he had cut the dose significantly. He had an alarm clock set to the exact time each week when the coke became available to him. He would select the dose from the list of available drugs and try to remember what it had been like before he got sick.

He felt his heart rate increase and his eyes open wider as the adrenaline coursed through him. The smile spread across his face and he took several deep breaths. He was glad now that Jacques had come to visit him.

"What are our plans today, my friend?"

Jacques sensed the change in his mood and smiled back at him. "Your brother has allowed me to purchase you some more time with Angela."

"Ah, how grand! My bastard of a brother hasn't taken that privilege from me yet."

Guillermo flexed the articulated arm of his suit and finished clamping his legs into their restraints. Horst had deactivated several of the best features of the suit. Guillermo flicked the small switch next to his right thumb and his spring-mounted shotgun snapped into position next to his hand. He pointed the attachment at Jacques and winked.

"Brother still hasn't let you have the use of it again?" he asked.

"Not unless he's with me," Guillermo said. "He likes to shoot skeet off the main deck. Fucking boring, if you ask me."

The suit had a breathing apparatus attached for times when he went into respiratory failure. He clicked the appropriate key on his LED master screen and felt the breathing tubes snake out of their holes behind his head. They traced a route around his neck and up into his nostrils. The flow of oxygen felt wonderful along with the adrenaline shot. He selected a dose of nitrous oxide and instantly smelled the sweet gas flowing into his nose. His eyes glazed over slightly until Jacques asked, “You ready?”

Angela couldn’t wait to get off the ship. Things had been pretty good working for Jean-Pierre at the club. She usually didn’t mind the assignments he gave her. At least until now. She still didn’t know where she was. Not even the fat queer Phineas would tell her. She knew she was on a ship because the place seemed to move a little bit. Maybe some kind of cruise ship for sex freaks. She had agreed to meet Guillermo in his private quarters the first day she was cleared. That was four days ago now. She had been forced to service the cripple six times already. She cringed, just thinking about him, and rubbed at the bruise on her arm.

Guillermo was foul-smelling and didn’t seem to care a bit. Without his suit on she could have bested him physically. But he never took it off completely, and when he was in it, his strength was terrifying. He could have taken the suit off and laid on the bed, allowing the girls he chose to do the work for him. But this was not his style. His limp penis could be artificially inflated, but he had only achieved orgasm once in their meetings. He was increasingly rough, ill-tempered, and nasty. He had grabbed her the day before and nearly broken her arm.

That was when she decided to seek help from the fat man. She sensed that he could be trusted. Phineas told her not to worry; it was against policy to force women to have sex. They might have been hookers, but they were afforded protection here. That was Mendelbaum's rule. She had never met Mendelbaum; none of the girls had. But they all knew that it was his place and that he made the rules. One of the rules was that they couldn't be forced to fuck. They had to agree to do it. Guillermo had lied to her. He said that he would have her thrown overboard if she didn't do what he wanted. She had believed him, but she still checked with Phineas.

It was Phineas who suggested she meet with Guillermo a final time in the public bar to tell him that she would not see him again. Then she had received the page from Jacques the Worm that Guillermo wanted to have a drink with her. It was perfect. Phineas was going to meet her in the bar to be present when she told Guillermo that she was done servicing him. Her guard opened the security door to the massive room and escorted her in. He left and sealed the door behind her. She entered the chamber and headed toward the bar at the far end, the same one that had been in use during her first night aboard when they had done the fancy dinner and casino night.

As she approached the bar, she saw Guillermo sitting with Jacques. They turned toward her in unison. Jacques said nothing, but Guillermo smiled and waved her over.

"I want you in my quarters in ten minutes." Guillermo said, still smiling. She counted six empty beer bottles in front of them and several shot glasses. The bartender was busy ignoring them.

Jacques stared at the large bruises on her neck and arms and snickered. "Looks like you left some bruises on the meat," he said.

Angela had heard enough. "I asked Phineas and he says I don't have to meet you. He says the girls are allowed to pick who they want."

Guillermo's smile faded. "That faggot doesn't make the rules."

"He told me that Mendelbaum has rules and that one of the rules is that the girls can't be forced." She looked around for Phineas but didn't see him among the other five or six men in the huge chamber. No matter, he had promised to join her. Still, Angela thought about waiting until he arrived to say more, but when she looked back at the two men smiling at her she couldn't help her next words. "I'm done suckin' your stinky meat. You're nasty."

Guillermo's pale face began to splotch red. Angela felt better. Phineas was right and Guillermo knew it. He wouldn't look so upset if it weren't true. She looked over her shoulder in time to see that Phineas had finally entered the room. She waved to him and never saw the blow coming. It caught her on the top of the shoulder. She felt her clavicle break and a searing pain spread though her body. She crumpled to the floor, her head facing the door Phineas had entered. He was not looking at her; he was yelling something at Guillermo. His hands were up in a gesture of pleading. She turned her head back toward Guillermo in time to see his titanium encased boot streaking down toward her head. Then there was nothing.

10 CATHEDRAL OF HORST

Mendelbaum stepped up to the polished ebony podium and cleared his throat. He waited for the subdued chatter to die down before he began. "Today's sermon will pick up on several threads we have covered in earlier meetings and hopefully tie them together for you in a cohesive manner."

Mendelbaum conceived the weekly service when he had realized that many aboard the ship needed a religious outlet. Attendance was not mandatory, but extra ship credits were awarded for those who chose to rise early on Sunday and join the congregation. Mendelbaum did not tolerate public drunkenness, but the pub was always filled to capacity for casino night on Saturdays. The cocktails were on the house; no ship credits needed to be spent. But getting so drunk that you missed the Sunday ceremony was frowned upon.

Zakar ibn Faisal al-Rashid was always in the back row, sleeping. This irritated Mendelbaum but did not rise to the level of an offense he would investigate. The man had to earn extra ship credits somehow; his uncle, Sheik Abdul bin Jabara, had sent him here as a kind of punishment. The sheik was the *Pura Vida's* original benefactor and anything he asked for, Mendelbaum was inclined to provide. So he overlooked Zakar's general uselessness. Besides, his chief of security, Fawwaz al-Barq, came as part of the package. Fawwaz was the son of the sheik's second cousin. His family was not wealthy or influential but he had proven his worth in the Saudi Secret Police. Fawwaz had been a gift to take the sting out of housing the lecherous Zakar. He cleared his throat into the microphone much harder than necessary and saw Zakar's head pop up. Good.

Conducting a weekly sermon had forced Mendelbaum to come to terms with his own religious beliefs, if they could really be called that. He rarely wrote anything more than a few notes, thoroughly enjoying his gift for expository. The services were conducted in the Great Room, as were all important ship events. During normal vessel operation the Great Room was sealed beneath airtight steel armor, but for the Sunday ceremony the massive panels could be drawn back into the superstructure of the tanker to reveal the sky above.

The warm ocean breeze flowed into the room, replacing the casino atmosphere of the night before with a pleasant but somber mood. Only the massive crystal chandelier hanging from the high, domed ceiling remained from the casino night. The tables were gone and pews had been brought in and anchored to the floor. The sun streamed through the fifty-foot-square openings left by the security panels in the ceiling, refracting through the cut crystal and spilling a dizzying array of dancing light on the worshippers below. Flanking the open panels were a matched pair of thirty-foot-long Italian stained-glass panels. They threw shafts of color around the chamber in a random pattern, creating a distinctly cathedral-like feel to the converted oil tanker.

Mendelbaum looked over his left shoulder and up past the bottom edge of the panels that hung from the ceiling seventy feet above him. The flowing silk banners moved in the breeze, drawing the congregants' gazes up and down the rows of religious symbols of every faith. Even the Star of David was mixed in. Mendelbaum had no particular hatred of the Jews; it was quite the other way round. His father had chosen the last name Mendelbaum when he fled because it was a Jewish surname; one which he hoped would add a layer of protection to his new life. But the Jews had stalked the family relentlessly, finally catching up with and killing his stepmother in Venezuela when he was fifteen. He couldn't blame them for wanting to kill his father, the infamous Nazi doctor. But the man had died in secret years before the Mossad bomb attack had taken Francesca away from him and Guillermo.

Even if he had hated them, consistency demanded that their religious symbolism be displayed along with all the others. Not that any of the symbols meant much to him, they were more a way of focusing attention onto the truly noble—and dare he say holy—work the *Pura Vida* did. Mendelbaum clicked a button on the front of the podium and small trap doors in the floor of the room in the four corners slid open. One-inch-thick gold-plated steel tubes began a slow journey toward the apex of the dome high above. A moment later the assembly was surrounded by the only symbol he found moving: a gold pyramid whose four arms came to a point at the base of the chandelier on the dome. For Mendelbaum it encompassed the entirety of the religious symbols displayed around the room.

He cleared his throat into the microphone again. "You are all here this morning of your own free will, and you shall be rewarded with two hundred and fifty ship credits."

Zakar sat up, eyes alert for the first time all morning. Good. The normal allotment for attendance was 100 credits.

Nearly half the ship was present that morning; Mendelbaum estimated the head count was at one hundred and twenty-five. Excellent. “What is the nature of good?” he began. “Is it the will to help those less fortunate than us? Certainly not. Is it to redistribute wealth from those who have created it to those who have sat idle?” he asked, gazing over the heads of the restless assembly. “Clearly, it is not. Is it to create the most happiness for the largest number of people?” Mendelbaum paused and made eye contact with several individuals sitting in the first pew. “Perhaps. But how do we create that happiness? Or more precisely, can we create that happiness at all, or is it up to a higher authority? God? Perhaps we are simply required to get out of the way so that the largest number can be happy and leave the rest to chance and divine providence. That is not for us to know. What we can know in this life is what conditions create the highest likelihood that the largest number of people will be happy.

We cannot lose our focus on the current state of the world and its interminable suffering, greed, and hypocrisy. We can only focus our energy and strength toward the future, onto the generations that will follow us. We may be able to guide them with our experiences, and even be there in some way to help them. That is why we are on this ship together. For the future generations and the possibility of creating the most happiness for the largest number of those who follow us." Mendelbaum stopped and dabbed at this forehead. He took a long look around the Great Room before he began again.

"We are, for the first time in history, in a position to live forever." He looked for Guillermo, knowing all the while that he would not be here. He never came to the Sunday sermon anymore. Mendelbaum could try to force his attendance, but that would only make his behavior worse. This latest incident with the hooker was too much.

Phineas was also missing from the congregation this morning. Mendelbaum had heard enough whining from him and had exempted him from all ship activities. His skill sets were varied and he had become indispensable to the ship. His skill in data base management alone justified the latitude he was shown. He was by far the most important member of the crew, and he was treated as such, yet he behaved like a petulant child most of the time.

Mendelbaum took a deep breath. Phineas was gentle and harmless and had been unhinged by Guillermo's brutal attack on the whore. Mendelbaum knew that he needed to take a hard line with Guillermo for the murder, but he loathed the idea of confronting him. Perhaps he would have al-Barq handle it for him. He realized that he had not spoken in several seconds.

"And what will we do with this gift? That is the question that we must each answer for ourselves. We won't tolerate Free Boaters here. If you don't perform, you are of no use to us. The technology is not perfected yet, but the RYE Project clearly points the way for those lucky enough to afford a shot at living forever," he said.

On days like this the immensity of the room helped to remind them of the colossal undertaking they were all a part of.

"The ship could not function without each of you. You are the key to its success and the seeds of its potential failure. Through your hard work and attention to detail, our fortunes will be decided. Each of you has earned enough ship credits to cash in and retire in comfort, yet none of you have. You know that your chance at immortality is connected to the ship. You could convert your ship credits into gold bullion at any time and be left at the nearest port. But you know that you don't have nearly the money necessary to purchase your own membership in our little club. You are the hired help. Only through service to the *Pura Vida's* higher goal will you be given the right to be added to the rolls of the immortal. You, too, could earn a place in the data banks and cryotanks of our super-ship. Several doctors and researchers already have. I have rewarded Jacques and Phineas with the chance to have their minds uploaded into new bodies, just as our paying customers will, because of their breakthrough work. They may live forever. Immortality is available for all of you. Exemplary services shall be rewarded," he said to polite applause.

Sweat trickled down the back of his neck and his hands shook with the excitement he felt. Perhaps Zakar ibn Faisal al-Rashid would finally wake up to the reality of what the ship could mean for him. Mendelbaum mentally snorted at his *laqab*—"the Righteous." At least al-Barq fit his; al-Rashid's was ironic. He was decadent—lecherous, even—anything but righteous. Would he finally understand why his uncle had sent him here? This was the time to make his life worth something. Mendelbaum found al-Rashid's eyes in the last pew and could tell that he was getting through to him for the first time. This was his best sermon yet. He felt breathless with excitement.

"Yet even as human beings are acquiring ever more extraordinary knowledge, we are storing it in ever more fragile and ephemeral forms. If our civilization runs into trouble, like all others before it, how much of our remarkable breakthroughs would survive? We are the answer. We have invested in massive amounts of hard storage aboard the *'Vida*. Our internal network is kept uncontaminated by the lies and half-truths that make up the World Wide Web. When the inevitability of the world's destiny catches up with it, the *Pura Vida* will be here as the backup drive for mankind. We will be protected by the vastness of the ocean from the corruption of the landlocked zombies. Science and technology have come together in mankind's darkest hour to allow us to cure the sick and prolong the lives of those in our society that must survive. Much of what we have learned over the last sixty years has been distilled into one cohesive set of treatment parameters aboard this ship. It is fair to think of our ship as a holy vessel, a Grail even, one that must survive to complete its work at all costs."

Mendelbaum finished the sermon feeling very good. The congregants left slowly after Mendelbaum had bowed politely to them and exited through his private door to his quarters.

Now Mendelbaum knew he had to face the problem his brother had created. He would need to publicly punish Guillermo, but what punishment would suffice for his crime? Anyone else would have walked the plank for such an act, but this was his brother. The ship only existed because of him; it was built to save him. Phineas was right to be disgusted and angry, but missing the Sunday sermon hinted at something far worse. He would probably insist on leaving again. And that could not happen under any condition. Without his constant supervision, the ship's complex systems could grind to a halt within weeks. Phineas had already proven this to Mendelbaum when he refused to work unless the kitchen staff was augmented by three classically trained chefs.

First the doors had stopped working properly, then the water filtration system. The cryonics coolant system began to fail, and enough was enough. He had allowed Phineas to forego the mandatory exercise required of all ship personnel and had agreed to hire a team of gourmet chefs. Phineas's demands were childish and easily met. He had a dubious constitution, though. Mendelbaum did not revel in the idea of having to hurt the poor man, but he surely would have if the strike had gone on any longer. But this time he was completely withdrawn. He performed his duties normally, but he was absent from all the activities that had once seemed to give him pleasure aboard the ship. The only person he still spoke to was Abigail. That was normal; they were each other's only friends. But things were starting to go offline again.

He summoned Phineas to the surgery center as he left the Great Room.

Phineas knew why he was being summoned and he didn't care. He had done nothing wrong by missing the sermon. He couldn't stand the idea of listening to Mendelbaum. The idea of enduring the hypocritical drivel that would flow from his greenish lips was just too much to bear. He couldn't ignore the summons to the surgery center, though.

"Would you care to explain this latest computer insect?"

He knew that Mendelbaum meant computer *bug*, but Phineas ignored it and instead shifted uncomfortably in his small seat. This was the second time in a month that the ship's artificial intelligence had produced unacceptable results. "We are dealing with highly sensitive programming issues. For the most part, the system works very well. There are always a few glitches with a program of this scale," he lied.

Phineas had created a highly sophisticated RFID system that tracked each person's movements at all times. Radio Frequency chips, known as RF chips, were one of the most popular ways to track everything from freight to lost pets all over the world. They were used aboard the *Pura Vida* to determine who had access to which parts of the ship, how often various areas were visited, and where each person was at any given time.

Each crewmember was implanted with a unique chip during his medical screening. Doors were designed to open automatically when a person with proper clearance approached them. The RF system was designed to increase ship efficiency. And it would have if Phineas had not programmed in an algorithm designed to hinder members of the ship that he found undesirable.

The first mishap had involved Guillermo. He'd tried to walk into his secure bedroom at a full trot and the door hadn't opened as he had come to expect. He had walked full force into the closed door and damaged the sophisticated hydraulics powering his survival suit. He had been so angry that it had taken a dose of benzodiazepine to calm him down.

Phineas fought the urge to smile at the thought of the sick bastard flying into a rage and having to be sedated.

The algorithm was designed to learn from each action of the crewmember. A file of common behaviors was compiled on everyone aboard, and the smart machines in their personal quarters and around the ship would behave according to their likes and dislikes. The results were compared to a master list of parameters of moral behavior Phineas had created over the years. Phineas had added something special to the overly complex code: His own testing matrix that evaluated the behavior of an individual and caused him to have problems completing ordinary tasks if he earned low scores.

Guillermo, for instance, had murdered a girl for sport and was given the lowest marks the program could offer. Phineas had hoped that the system would make life more difficult in somewhat intangible ways. Doors would not open as they were supposed to, toilets would not flush automatically and might overflow, showers would only provide very cold water, automated room cleaning parameters would miss key areas, and so on.

The system worked very well for the most part, but it was beginning to overreact to the ship's most morally outrageous members. Mendelbaum, of course, had to be exempted from the scoring system to avoid suspicion, and Phineas knew the smarter decision would have been to exempt Guillermo from the scoring system as well. But he couldn't bear the thought of the bastard living in relative comfort—not after the way he had killed that girl.

The latest incident was not as easy to disguise as Guillermo's door crash. Jacques the Worm had been scalded by his shower so badly he had needed medical attention. Mendelbaum knew something was awry.

"I will look at the program again, but I assure you, this must have been some kind of freak accident," Phineas said.

Mendelbaum seemed mollified for the time being. "Very good, check on it and let me know what you turn up. Now, as to more pressing issues, the RYE Project appears to be working properly for the first time. When can I expect to see more verifiable results?"

Phineas knew the question had been coming. He and Abigail had delayed the test results as long as they could. They would have to release the newest findings shortly, and the results were sure to make Mendelbaum very happy. It appeared that the ship's masterwork was coming together as he had planned. The so-called RYE Project referred to the experiments into mapping and recording human memories through detailed MRI scans into complex sets of algorithms that were stored aboard the ship's mainframe. The storage of the memories had been achieved years earlier. The real breakthrough was the second step in the process, the upload.

"We should have another host ready within the week," Phineas said.

Mendelbaum smiled broadly, exposing his dark gums. "Excellent. How are we progressing with mapping the memories of deceased patients?"

Phineas's brow furrowed. "Not as well, actually. The results don't appear as promising as we had hoped for patients that have been stored outside the ship for any stretch of time. Their neural connections degrade too quickly. Our best results are still with patients that are brought in either barely alive or very recently dead."

Phineas looked past Mendelbaum at the Plexiglas wall covering the colossal electromagnet he had designed to keep the surgery centers suspended in their liquid-filled tubes in all but the very roughest seas. The tropical depression they were entering was starting to create rain and some wind-driven waves. Abigail would be pleased that the storm was larger than it had first appeared. Phineas adjusted a dial on the magnet's control panel and felt the world around him stabilize once more. The magnet was designed to automatically adjust its current to counteract the rocking of the sea, but his computer algorithm had caused it to shut down. The magnet was the first major innovation Phineas perfected after Mendelbaum brought him aboard. With unlimited power from the nuclear reactor, his imagination soared with the possibilities the ship presented. But that was a long time ago. Now, nothing made him less happy than the work he was doing. When Mendelbaum had found him, the high-paying job offer had been a godsend. Mendelbaum knew it, too. He knew everything about the people he recruited. It had been far too late for Phineas to leave by the time the true nature of the ship, and Mendelbaum, had become apparent.

"What's eating you, Phineas? Didn't you like that last lad we brought in for you?"

Phineas only smiled in response. As usual, Mendelbaum was projecting his own problems. That was fine. Phineas couldn't let on to the true depth of his unhappiness. There weren't any other gays aboard because Mendelbaum forbade it. He had brought in a male prostitute last quarter, but that was not at all what Phineas wanted. He wanted companionship. Thank god for Abigail. He would have thrown himself overboard months ago if not for her. She was the only island of sanity he could cling to in this ocean of cruelty.

Mendelbaum sensed, though, that there was more to his mood. "I know that you are unhappy with my brother. His actions were deplorable and I have confined him to his quarters indefinitely."

"Thank you," Phineas said without making eye contact. Like that was justice. No matter now, though. At least he could push his advantage. "I must insist that my cabin either be outfitted with stabilizers like the surgery centers or be given permission to move my quarters into one of the unused rooms here. I just can't live another day aboard this awful ship. The constant movement is too much to endure for another second." This was, of course, a carefully planned ruse to get him close enough to the labs to steal the Norovirus strain he would need.

Mendelbaum nodded.

Phineas and Abigail had secretly and painstakingly engineered the Norovirus and its antidote over the last several months. It had been brutally slow work, but it was their best chance at escape. When completed, it would allow them to escape using the ship's private yacht, the *Eir*. The idea was that if everyone else aboard was sick, a minor distraction would allow them the time they would need.

Once they were aboard the yacht, they would just have to hope that they went undetected long enough to get out of range. That was the plan. As Mendelbaum left him, Phineas knew it was hopeless. But he couldn't let Abigail down. He knew that he would have to provide the proper distraction to give her time to escape. Dying to save her would be worth it. She was the only one left aboard with any decency. Mendelbaum had proven that when he refused to punish Guillermo for murdering that poor creature, Angela. Life was worthless to them. He had been able to believe for a while that Mendelbaum actually believed in the code he made them all live by.

But the truth was that he would bend and break his own principles to protect Guillermo.

He always would.

11 Jacques' *Eir*

The night was off to a decent start at the Parisian strip club *La Boheme*. The usual clientele were coming in, a few Russian high-rollers, several drunken college kids, an Arab, and right on cue—Jacques the Worm. The furtive little man moved in the shadows of the main stage, surreptitiously eyeing the new redhead, Kayla. Kayla was not for sale tonight, though. She had only just arrived, and Jean-Pierre Tiberius would have to taste her himself before he could let the likes of Jacques paw her over.

Jean-Pierre walked behind Jacques, his footfalls hidden by the overwhelming base pounding out of the newly renovated sound system. He leaned in and yelled, "Hello my little friend."

Jacques snapped his drooling mouth shut, startled by the intrusion. "You shouldn't sneak up on me like that," he yelled back without turning away from the stage.

Jean-Pierre had become aware of a change in Jacques over the last year. Something about having so much disposable cash really made the little man arrogant. His bad breath and greasy hair offended Jean-Pierre more than ever.

“I want that one,” Jacques pointed at Kayla.

Her name was surely something else, but she had introduced herself as Kayla when she appeared the week before. She was a sweet piece of meat to have wandered in off the street. She claimed to know his father, Owen Tiberius. “Out of the question,” Jean-Pierre said as he walked away.

Jacques stalked off after him toward the private office above the main stage. He slammed the door behind him and glared across the room. This would not do at all. This pale, putrid little man needed a lesson. Jean-Pierre turned toward him calmly and pretended to stretch his arms in a slow yawn. At the zenith of his movement, he snapped his right arm back down and caught Jacques’ cheek with his palm.

The blow nearly knocked Jacques to the floor. He staggered backward to the door, an angry mark slowly blooming over the side of his small face. Jacques opened his mouth to speak but only produced a squeak.

Jean-Pierre laughed openly at the quivering little man. “Do you have something you want to say?” he asked at last.

“I want the redhead and ten others for a month,” he said meekly.

That was more like it. “I already told you, Kayla is not yet on the market.”

“I’ll pay double for her.”

Jacques instantly had Jean-Pierre’s attention. He wanted to taste Kayla first, her pale skin and red hair were striking, but business was business. “After this last accident with Angela, you’ll pay triple for her and post a fifty-thousand Euro security deposit. If she is less than perfect when you bring her back, I will take it out of your filthy hide.” He would, too.

He never liked to subcontract his girls, but Jacques was too weak to be a threat to him, and he paid twice market price for the product. Dealing with the greasy little man over the last year had earned him nearly two million tax-free Euros. That was twice as much as he could expect to earn from his normal clientele. He couldn’t pass that up.

Jacques remained an enigma to him, though. He had known him for more than a decade, first as a low-level government employee with shabby, off-the-rack suits—a man who couldn’t get his dick wet if he fell in a pond; then as a well-dressed private-sector sex freak who picked up ten girls at a time. He must have gone to work for one of the super-rich assholes that his father built mega-yachts for. The change had come almost overnight. Like clockwork, he was in *La Boheme* every four months to pick up new girls. They were returned a month later, always a bit worse for the wear. But that was unimportant. Jean-Pierre could get new girls from the Russians with a phone call; he never struggled to keep his stables full.

"When can I expect delivery?" Jacques asked.

"Tonight, of course." Jean-Pierre pressed the page button on the phone atop his large desk. "Send Kayla up."

A moment later Kayla strode through the door and both men eyed her greedily. She rubbed at the tiny, heart-shaped mark on her cheek and smiled.

Jean-Pierre Tiberius could tell that Jacques was alone on the boat. Goddamn, she was a sexy hunk of fiberglass and steel. This was a truly state-of-the-art machine that could be steered with nothing more than a joystick. He no longer spoke to his father, Owen, but he recognized touches that his father put on high-end yacht refits like the spiral staircase and ebony inlaid railings. So, Jacques was aboard one of the finest yachts in the world. As long as you had the maintenance crew to keep her clean and running, she could be piloted by just one man. And that man was Jacques? There was just no way. That little bastard must have stolen the boat and killed her owner. He couldn't be on the title to this thing. Half way down the dock, men were loading crates of food and fine wine. Jean-Pierre saw that one entire crate contained Beluga caviar. He could smell money. More than the fucking few million Euros that Jacques threw his way for the whores. This was *big* money.

Jacques smiled at him from the top deck and gave a wave. Arrogant little fuck. He waved back and fought to smooth the wolfish grin spreading across his face. This boat had a helicopter on the back. A fucking helicopter. "Permission to come aboard?" he called up as obsequiously as he could.

The Worm seemed pleased with the request. Fool. "Granted," he called down. Jean-Pierre stepped onto the gangplank, the group of fresh women following subserviently behind him. He pointed to the lounge area where the girls were to wait and headed toward the spiral staircase amidships. The mahogany steps were perfectly maintained, a coat of fresh varnish gleamed off them. Colored sand had been sprinkled onto wet varnish to spell the name of the ship, *Eir*. If he were not mistaken, that was the Norse God of medicine.

He stopped at the top of the staircase, scratched at his chin, and looked around for Jacques.

"I have the money for you if that's what you're worried about," Jacques said from the inner salon. "It's on the table on the sun deck,"

"Worried?" Jean-Pierre said innocently. "Certainly not. A man of your refined tastes and infallible pedigree is always to be trusted in matters of sex slavery."

Jacques said nothing but gave a dumb grin. Good. He moved into the salon, away from the sun deck, and Jacques called out, "I said the money was over there,"

"I was hoping for a bit of a tour," Jean-Pierre said, turning his back to Jacques and looking out to sea.

"I'm afraid that's not possible. I have strict instructions." Jacques said. He sounded serious. Perhaps he *hadn't* murdered anyone to take possession of the ship. But who would trust him with a boat like this? And there was no one here to protect him. Jean-Pierre had to know more about Jacques's newfound fortune. He was sick of the little man throwing around money. He had decided after the display the night before that he was done with Jacques taking his best ass out of the club whenever he wanted and bringing it back worn-out without explanation. Jacques was behind him now. "I said—"

Jean-Pierre didn't wait for Jacques' hands to touch him; he spun around with surprising speed for a man of his size and grabbed the outstretched wrist. Jacques stared at him, eyes wide with surprise.

"You can't do this to me—"

But it was too late. He jerked the arm forward and hooked Jacques's ankle with his foot. He let the Worm fall into a pile on the carpeted floor of the master suite. He outweighed Jacques by easily sixty pounds. This was more fun than tossing around a mouthy whore. Jacques turned himself over as quickly as he could, but Jean-Pierre was already on top of him, pinning his skinny arms to the floor under his knees as he plopped his large ass squarely on Jacques' chest. He rested heavily and laughed a bit at how easy this had all been.

"You are not a man, Jacques. What are you doing with a man's boat?" There was no answer and he realized that he needed to let him breathe.

"Chhhhhh…" Jacques wheezed. He was looking a bit purple.

Jean-Pierre moved his rump down onto Jacques' hips and kept him squarely pinned.

“Agggg, you bastard!” Jacques finally managed.

That was rude. Jean-Pierre carefully pinched Jacques’ thin face between his thumb and forefingers, tuning it one way and then the other to admire his handiwork from the club the night before. He selected the same bruised cheek and swung his meaty hand cleanly into a resounding smack.

Jacques fell silent, anger building in his face again.

“Who gave you this boat? Where is your cash coming from?” No response. “You will give me what I want or I’ll rip your little balls off,” he said, fumbling around behind his own large ass for the space between Jacques’ legs. Jacques squealed and wriggled but couldn’t free himself. The feeble movement was vaguely exciting and made Jean-Pierre chuckle as he squeezed Jacques groin and yelled, “Where!”

“Stop!” Jacques screamed.

Jean-Pierre didn’t. He located one testicle and pinched it violently between his fingers. Jacques screamed like a woman, and the sound made Jean-Pierre laugh so hard he lost his grip. He needed to do this more often. He looked back down into Jacques contorted face and smiled. “Whose boat is this?” he asked innocently.

“F-fuck you,” Jacques screeched.

Jean-Pierre turned his head as he heard someone coming up the steps. It was the new girl, Kayla.

“I heard a woman screaming,” she said. Her mouth stopped moving when she saw what was going on. She rubbed at the mark on her pink cheek, and said, “Oh, sorry.”

“No, stay and watch,” Jean-Pierre said. But she was already moving back down the stairs. He looked back to Jacques, who was no longer squirming. Tears were streaming down his cheeks. “She thought you were a woman,” he said.

That was it. He could see that there was a change in Jacques; he seemed to have made up his mind about something. His body relaxed and he said, “The main ship is called the Pura Vida.” That was more like it. “This is just a tender ship for her,” he whispered. “When I tell my boss w-what you just did—”

“What?” Jean-Pierre said. “He’ll ask me to take over for you?”

“He’ll let your sister die, you bastard. She’s been treated on the Vida and she needs more gene therapies *every year*. Your father Owen brought her to us five years ago. The doctor saved her. I'll see to it that he'll never treat her again!"

Jean-Pierre stopped smiling. The little Worm had hit a nerve. His sister had been very ill and she had been treated at a secret location. His father had never told him where, a point of major contention between them. There was no way Jacques could know that. He felt his heart beating very fast. He looked back down at Jacques and realized that he was smiling up at him. "You can take the girls for free this quarter," he said as he climbed off Jacques and pulled him to his feet.

"Goddamn right," Jacques said. "If you whisper a word of this to anyone I'll throw your sister in the ocean myself, you fat fuck. Now get off my boat!"

Jacques idled the engine of the *Eir* for a moment before pulling out of the slip. Mendelbaum had named the yacht for some Norse god; Jacques would have called her something else. *Whoremonger*, perhaps. He smiled at the thought. With the amount of credits he had earned, perhaps he would buy his own, just like her, one day. Well, probably not as big as the *Eir*.

Mendelbaum had paid just under 40 million Euros for her and entrusted her to Jacques as a reward for his "precise and invaluable work on the ship's reactor." Jacques had a plaque with those words engraved on it from the last gala. He had worked tirelessly to learn to pilot the yacht and helicopter. The helicopter eluded him, but the highly sophisticated boat was essentially maneuvered using a simple joystick. The knife-hulled boat had been acquired through Owen Tiberius's French shipbuilding conglomerate. Mendelbaum had wanted an even more impressive vessel to bring VIPs aboard, but the hundred twenty-foot *Eir* was the largest that could be safely docked inside the *Pura Vida*.

The entire stern section of the tanker folded into a flooded chamber that had once housed crude oil, creating a massive internal dock. Mendelbaum had explained to him that all modern oil tankers are designed with storage chambers independent from one another. The design prevented the oil from sloshing around inside one giant compartment and potentially capsizing the ship. This provided endless customization possibilities to fit the needs of the treatment center. Owen Tiberius had dedicated his entire shipyard to the retrofitting of the *Pura Vida* twenty years earlier. It had taken 'round-the-clock work to complete the massive project and to move the necessary parts for the reactor into the superstructure in secret. The key was making sure that no one but a select few actually knew what they were working on. It had cost ten times what it should have, but it had been well worth it. Mendelbaum had doubled the yearly profit for Owens' company and now all maintenance work was completed at sea. A specialized nano-paint, developed onboard at an astounding cost, had been used to seal the hull. The clear paint was infused with carbon particles thinner than a human hair. The rusted exterior of the ship had been coated with the solution and barring an accident, the *'Vida* would not need to dry dock again for as long as twenty years.

Jacques looked to the stern of the boat at the beautiful helicopter. He was not allowed to fly it until he passed the pilot's test. He hated that he had failed and that that Muslim bastard al-Rashid had passed. Al-Rashid would have been allowed to fly whenever he wanted, if he could hang on to any ship credits or provided a single useful contribution to the ship.

From the captain's nook high above, Jacques looked down at the roiling, egg-shaped hot tub set into the newly stained teak deck. The hookers seemed accustomed to this kind of wealth and appeared quite at ease. Jacques had given them specific instructions to stay at the end of the boat and dance together. They were allowed to smoke and to drink, but any drugs they carried had to be either thrown overboard or turned over to him. If they were intoxicated when they reached their destination they would not be paid and would be sent back to their humorless pimp boss.

Jacques set the autopilot from the upper deck on course back to the *'Vida*. He stuck a cigarette in his mouth and winced. That prick Jean-Pierre had really mashed him good. He lit the cigarette carefully and swiveled his chair around to get a better view of the new girls. He had insisted that they strip down to their bikinis to get some sun before they were taken aboard the *'Vida*. The girls would be quarantined in the massive "Hooker Suite," as it was known, and would never be allowed to leave it without permission until they were taken back to the mainland aboard the *Eir*. They could visit the ship's Great Ballroom to entertain their men, but only at preselected times. Once the girls had passed their physicals and the bidding was resolved, their visitors would be assigned times and rooms.

The system had been established by Mendelbaum and worked fairly well at keeping order. The penalty levied against crewmembers for nearly any infraction of ship policy was a loss of ship credits. It took nearly a month's worth of credits to purchase adequate time with a girl.

Jacques took out his digital camera and zoomed in on the blond woman nearest him. She was swaying a little too drunkenly to the Caribbean steel drum music, but looked healthy nonetheless. Jacques snapped several photos of her from different angles, and then trained his lens on the brunette next to her. But the brunette didn't hold his attention. Kayla, the pale-skinned redhead behind her looked out of place. She held a glass of flat champagne and danced only haltingly. An amateur? Jacques zoomed in on her and began snapping the photos that would be used by the crew to select the women they wanted.

He wasn't sure what it was about her, but he snapped several more photos than he needed before training the lens on the other girls. As was often his habit when up in the captain's nook, he sat completely naked. As soon as he was done taking his photos, he prepared for more pleasurable pursuits. He stood at the rail and waited until several of the women realized that he was naked before he began masturbating vigorously, enjoying the warm sun on his genitals. His display was met with some looks of dismay from the prostitutes below, which he ignored until he climaxed over the rail into the water below. He liked the idea of his seed floating on the waves.

Mendelbaum probably had this part of the ship under closed-circuit camera like everything else, but Jacques was allowed certain liberties. He was always polite about his little ritual, being sure to clean up with the towel he had brought if his shot missed the ocean. He knew that if he cared to, he could have any of the girls he wanted once aboard the ship, but not before—never before. Mendelbaum insisted upon full medical work-ups on them before they were released from the Hooker Suite and were cleared for service. There was a mandatory ten-day waiting period to be sure they were clean.

Jacques had been given a nearly unlimited supply of ship credits for his work on the reactor. His pay alone was over 200,000 credits per year. He had banked almost a million with his bonuses. He smiled, in spite of himself. He rarely used more credits than anyone else. That was probably why Mendelbaum had given him so much authority. Besides, he didn't really like sleeping with the stupid hookers anyway.

He felt nervous and awkward with them in private, and always needed several drinks to work up the nerve to approach them. Not like that miserable little Arab fucker, al-Rashid. That nasty drip would burn through all his credits and then try to bum extras. Just like the rest of the Arab scum Jacques had come to hate in his old Parisian neighborhood. Mendelbaum turned a blind eye to the sharing of credits for al-Rashid, a fact that infuriated Jacques. Some of the girls would even give the little bastard free ones. For Jacques, it was a fine line between getting drunk enough to boss the filthy bitches around and still being able to perform. It was sometimes easier to just watch Guillermo or Brian the Beast do it.

Jacques knew that al-Rashid was only aboard because his uncle, Sheik Abdul bin Jabara was a key *'Vida* financier. The sheik had insisted on putting al-Rashid aboard, a fact the overtly promiscuous greaseball surely hated. That was really the worst part of al-Rashid: He didn't even want to be aboard the ship. Jacques, however, had found his calling here. He would rather die than leave—that was also probably why Mendelbaum gave him so many ship credits.

Jacques was proud of the job he had done. This new batch of girls was the best yet. Thinking about Kayla excited him and he rubbed at his still erect prick as he maneuvered the super-yacht back toward the *Pura Vida*. She had seen him humiliated. He wanted to stop the boat and have her right away, but his window to get back was tightly monitored. Mendelbaum relied on him to keep the reactor working, but he trusted no one. He would certainly lose his privileged job as lead pimp if he disobeyed the cardinal rule: Be on time.

Mendelbaum was precise in everything he did. He was likely monitoring Jacques' progress via GPS transmitter. He had to know at all times where he was and why. Jacques could say the boat had broken down; that would give him the time he needed. Just five minutes alone with her, that was all he wanted. The yacht had room for sixty guests.

Jacques never saw himself as much of a ladies' man. He had only screwed a few women before he came aboard the *'Vida*. No one had liked him at his old job for the French Nuclear Facility, especially his female co-workers. He had once been told that he had the smile of a pedophile—which was why his boss gave him to Mendelbaum. Jacques smiled to himself. He remembered the conversation as if it were yesterday, although his journey to the *Pura Vida* had begun fifteen years earlier.

He had overseen a mid-sized reactor outside Paris for ten years when he'd been summoned to his boss's office. He had been shown into the office without being forced to wait, the first time such a gesture had been extended to him. When the old leather chair swiveled around, he was shocked to see that his boss was not in the office; rather the head of the nuclear agency himself was sitting behind the desk. Jacques was too curious to be nervous. The man was a legend. He was nearly eighty-five years old and still had an active role in the daily oversight of France's massive nuclear power program. It was even rumored that he had been a member of the Vichy government that ruled in France during the War. Jacques was humbled just to be in the great man's presence. He knew immediately that he was not being fired. If he were being fired, he certainly wouldn't have been given a formal meeting with a member of the French Cabinet.

He was told that he had been handpicked by the minister himself to be part of a new project. It was non-governmental and he would be handsomely compensated. The minister slid a piece of paper across the desk. He explained that it was a non-disclosure agreement. Jacques signed without even reading it.

What followed next was an explanation of the *Pura Vida* and the special work it did. A civilian ship with its own nuclear reactor? Jacques hadn't even considered saying no. He felt like he'd just won the lottery. All these years later and he still felt that way. He loved every part of his life aboard the ship. He had authority oven fifteen men in the reactor, his team. He ruled them with an iron fist. But even better was the fact that his mentor, the esteemed Dr. Horst Mendelbaum, treated him with deference, routinely singling him out at the ship galas to congratulate him and his team on the work they did. Everyone on the ship knew who he was and how important his work was.

All but one, anyway.

As the *Pura Vida* grew, the power it needed went up exponentially. The new fiber optic cloak required massive amounts of energy to work properly. The sophisticated, radar-jamming technology, combined with a full service hospital, five-star restaurant, luxury spa, and workout facility, all meant that the *'Vida* could not run without Jacques. This gave him considerable latitude. It destined him to receive far more ship credits than he could ever spend. He got first choice on the newest hookers. He drank fine champagne every night and only had to eat in the ship's main galley if he wanted to.

The fact that al-Rashid enjoyed considerable freedom aboard the ship in spite of his complete lack of any meaningful contribution took a measure of the joy away from Jacques, though. Maddeningly, Mendelbaum still required him to fulfill the exercise requirement. Only that fat piece of garbage Phineas was exempted. The queer claimed that he might have a heart attack. Liar.

Mendelbaum viewed the hookers as a good way to keep the crew in line, but he didn't care for the added scrutiny they brought to the ship. He only allowed the girls aboard when he was sure the ship was in protected waters and free of any kind of outside influence. At first he only brought them aboard one quarter out of the year. He quickly realized that it wasn't nearly enough. Since ship romance was strictly prohibited, there had to be another outlet. Jacques had proven his ability to keep a clean supply of girls coming in from Jean-Pierre, so now every quarter he brought in a new batch of women.

When there weren't women aboard, the crew needed other entertainment. In a moment of inspiration, Jacques and Guillermo decided to start the underground fight club. Security staff and even doctors loved the idea of it. Doctors would help procure the best kinds of steroids and other necessary drugs to facilitate the matches.

The bouts were held in the restricted section, just off of the reactor and Jacques's office. The ship held a massive amount of enriched uranium. Jacques had helped procure the fuel. It had supposedly been lost at sea while in transit to a nuclear plant outside of Montreal, Canada. It had been Jacques' big test, a mission he had to complete before he could start on the ship. Minister Schnell had succinctly explained the two-fold purpose of the mission at their first and only meeting.

"You will be part of a team that will infiltrate and secure uranium headed for a reactor in Montreal. The uranium will be enough to power the *Pura Vida* for a thousand years, a feat to please even the Fuhrer. Your participation in this clandestine activity will prevent you from divulging the nature of your work, and solidify your place in history," the Minister had said.

He had again agreed readily. He and a group of mercenaries managed to overrun and sink the ship. Jacques was disgusted by the murder of the crew, but also strangely turned on by it. He hadn't killed anyone himself; he'd only been along to secure the uranium.

A chime on the control panel alerted Jacques that he was approaching the *Pura Vida*. He clicked off the autopilot and engaged the intercom. "Please be seated," he said. He would have to study the helicopter materials another time.

12 Pure Fitness

The humiliating nylon pants clung to Zakar's legs. If he exerted any real activity, they sealed themselves to him like plastic wrap. "I hate these fucking workout sessions," he said. His tracksuit's puffy shirt was bone dry even though he had been in the pristine workout room for nearly an hour. He was doing his best to ignore the terrible techno music Mendelbaum played in the background.

His cousin glanced at him, arched a dark eyebrow, and focused back on the free weights in the rack before them. Row upon row of spotless equipment filled the vast room. There were at least twenty others working out, all many yards apart, watching themselves in the spotless, floor-to-ceiling mirrors circling the room. The facility was open twenty-two hours a day to all residents. The other two hours were reserved for Mendelbaum's personal sessions.

Zakar had learned that the best way to avoid a hard workout was to partner with his cousin, the head of ship security. He would have skipped the mandatory workouts with the sanctimonious fanatic, but he needed the ship credits if he were going to have any time with one of the girls. He loved his cousin, but the constant praying and the vaguely concealed scorn he radiated every time Zakar spoke of the Hooker Suite had grown tedious. He faced Mecca with his cousin at least once a day, but he rarely managed the five prostrations per diem that Al-Barq always completed.

Zakar had nightmares about this workout room. It was too brightly lit and it always felt like he was being watched. He knew that he was, of course, being watched by the cameras that were in every corner of the ship, but this gymnasium felt worse than the rest of the place. It was state-of-the-art and massive; every conceivable piece of workout equipment was here. Everything was wrapped in soft white rubber, the floor, the free weights, even the seats.

The cavernous room had its own clean and cheery smell, an odor that turned his stomach since he inhaled it for the first time nine months earlier. It made him crave a cigarette.

Zakar scratched at the razor-burned skin under his chin. His thick facial hair was noticeable by three in the afternoon every day. He hated shaving it, but Mendelbaum insisted that crewmembers appear presentable at all times or risk being docked. You could wear a beard if you chose to, but it had to be well maintained. Zakar hated wearing a beard more than he hated shaving. One of the few bright spots about being aboard the stupid ship was that he couldn't be forced by the family's mufti to grow his neck beard. If it were up to him he would shave once a week at the most, and only after a long session in the steam room to soften up his skin. Shaving every day like this left his face dry and itchy all the time. He stopped picking at the skin on his chin and looked at the rippling muscles in his cousin's back. The man was built like a racing camel.

The spa attached to the locker room was the only area he really liked. It was dimly lit and had massive stone slabs lined up against the wall with waterfalls erupting over them. He would spend hours in the spa if it were free. Of course the only thing that didn't cost him any credits was this fucking gym. And there were far better places to spend the few credits he did have than the spa.

Zakar's uncle had insisted that he accompany his cousin, Fawwaz al-Barq, aboard the ship. Fawwaz was here to run security. Zakar was here as more of a punishment. The sheik didn't see it that way, but he was a crazy old man. His uncle was the one who'd first allowed him to enter the harem, and as a result, always felt responsible for his nephew's vice. He had told him as much before packing him off to this cursed ship.

Fawwaz had, of course, been *honored* to be given the *opportunity* to *serve* Zakar's esteemed uncle. Kiss ass. Fawwaz was destined to become one of the highest-ranking officials in the Saudi royal family's security network. He was the sheik's second cousin by marriage, and as such, was not in line for any special handouts. He worked very hard to get the sheik's attention, and the appointment to the *Pura Vida* was a major responsibility. He had confided in Zakar that it was one he had never wanted because it took him away from his beloved wife, but he would nonetheless serve obediently. God, his cousin was boring.

When Zakar had learned that there were hookers aboard the ship things had really looked up, at least until he was briefed on his allotment of ship credits. Because he had no real job aboard the ship, he had no way to earn extra credits. He depended on the allotment he had been given, haphazardly, by his senile uncle.

He soon discovered that his vast family fortune was not worth anything aboard the ship. Only ship credits purchased anything worth having. A one-hour session in the Hooker Suite was 250 credits. His job requirements were sketchy; he was required to aid his cousin in general ship security. His cousin had always had a soft spot for him and didn't push him to do much, though. Besides, ship security was ultimately up to Fawwaz, and he knew that his cousin might make a mess. Fawwaz took his duty seriously, like everything else he did.

They had very little to talk about. Zakar's whoring disgusted Fawwaz. The only time Zakar sought him out was when he needed extra ship credits. There were two surefire ways to get them from Fawwaz, but he hated both. He either had to exercise with him or pray with him. At meal times, when he really needed credits, he would sit with Fawwaz and eat a bland traditional meal. He, of course, avoided pork when Fawwaz was around, but bacon was one of the few things he could get his fill of aboard the ship. Crewmembers would always trade him their bacon rations to curry his favor. It was widely known that the girls loved Zakar, and all he had to do was put in a good word for a crewman to guarantee an extra-special time.

So here he was, an hour and twenty minutes into another miserable workout session with Fawwaz. They would pray next. Zakar had been raised according to the strictest tenets, but his uncle had allowed him to attend college in America. It was the least he could do for the boy after he had lost his parents.

Nothing would ever be the same for him, though, after living in Southern California. He had quickly lost any true desire to pursue Islamic tenets, but he knew that praying with Fawwaz brought his cousin a deep measure of solace aboard the hated ship. Zakar knew how badly his fanatic cousin missed their home. This whole assignment was fucking cruel. Fawwaz surely knew what Zakar was doing but didn't care. They were each other's only friends aboard the ship. Fawwaz knew his cousin was not a Believer, but the sheik had been clear about Zakar's safety. Fawwaz would not let harm come to him in any way. An angry Fawwaz al-Barq was like an all-consuming sandstorm.

Zakar wished he had remembered to wear his sunglasses in the gym. It was so bright that he felt like he was working out in a giant tanning bed as he picked up ten-pound dumbbells and began swinging them back and forth. He used as little effort as he could. Fucking miserable.

Mendelbaum required all ship personnel to work out at least six hours per week. Less than six hours resulted in a mandatory fine. Crew members were paid based on their jobs aboard the *Pura Vida*; doctors earned the most, ship security slightly less. Everyone was entitled to eat the common meals served in the

Great Room, but if you wanted something special brought to your room, like a nice bottle of champagne, you could use your ship credits to purchase it.

Zakar burned through his monthly allotment of credits within days. He had never been able to save any in his interest-bearing account.

"Spot me," Fawwaz said, grasping the barbell above his head. Zakar gladly replaced his small weights and walked behind his cousin. He had upped his weights this month, two of the rubber encased forty-five-pound plates on each side of the bar raised gently into the air and down to his broad chest. Unlike his cousin, he was drenched in sweat. The puffy shirt fit snugly. This was already his third hour in the gym today.

At ten repetitions he began to slow and Zakar encouraged him. "Come on, two more," he said. "Nice." He helped his panting cousin replace the steel bar in the rack. It was then that he noticed Jacques staring at him in the mirror. He bit his lip and looked away from the ugly Frenchman. Jacques wore the same tracksuit that every man aboard was required to use. Like Zakar's, his was also bone dry.

But Jacques' credits were never docked.

He was allotted as many as he wanted because Mendelbaum needed him. He ran the reactor. And he was in charge of bringing in the new girls. He had an ugly welt on his cheek that Jacques couldn't help but smile at. Jacques seemed to sense what he was looking at and flipped him the bird.

Fucking prick, that French dog was. And his credits never got docked, even though he walked around with that stupid little growth of hair on his lower lip.

But he ran the girls, the lovely girls. And he and Guillermo had a stranglehold on the cigarettes. Everything about the ship that made it bearable was controlled by this smarmy Frenchman. At least Zakar knew he could win some credits in the upcoming fight club match. He had inside information on the Beast. And he was going to do the unthinkable: He was going to bet against Brian the Beast this month.

"I'm a bit low on credits. Do you think I can borrow a hundred?"

"Again? I gave you two hundred last month," Fawwaz griped.

"But the new girls are coming in, and I just thought—"

"You are out of control with these infidel whores," Fawwaz said. "The sheik would not approve. We are here to monitor his investment, not fall prey to their . . ." he searched for the word, "decadence."

"I know, I know. But even Abdul bin Jabara likes to have a good time now and then. I am just getting it out of my system."

"You have been getting it out of your system for the last nine months," Fawwaz said. "Just make sure to get your prayers in." He handed his younger cousin his monthly credit card. "Don't spend them all this time."

"I won't, Fawwaz. I just get so bored here." He removed his own card from his pocket and held it next to Fawwaz's. He entered the number 200 on the card, pressed the small green button in the center, and watched as his card beeped in response. His pulse quickened, thinking of the girls waiting.

"We don't have to stay much longer." Fawwaz said. "Mendelbaum has promised to deliver verifiable results to the sheik by the end of the month."

"I've heard that before," Zakar said. He regretted it before it was all the way out. His cousin said nothing. He just looked very tired.

Fawwaz stared at the mirror in front of them at length and said, “I will never love the feel of the ocean again.”

13 Mendelbaum's Refuge

Mendelbaum entered the massive gym through his private door. The door was attached to his bathroom and allowed him to look into the gym through two-way glass. He only liked to watch Abigail work out, but seeing the shadows of the other crewmembers exercise whenever he was in his bathroom brought him a sense of calm. He closed the facility for his private workouts every evening from 10:00 p.m. to 12:00 a.m.

Exercising with others had always distracted him. He held his kelp shake in his right hand. He had already greedily sucked down half of it, more than he would normally allow himself before his vigorous routine. He shook the greenish brown sludge in the bottle and took a long drink before he set it down on the workout bench. Because he refused to work out with a partner, he never had anyone to spot him. He was forced to use free weights that he was sure he could handle and leave his real strength training to the safety of the machines.

After two hundred reps with fifty pounds in each hand, he headed toward the treadmill. His goal was to run ten miles each day. He turned the treadmill up to 6 but didn't step on. He needed to finish his meal first. He liked his shakes served room temperature, or the mixture started to stink. If the shake was too cold, he couldn't drink it fast enough, and he would sometimes throw-up the green goo. He sniffed the shake before drinking it, noting that the chef had aged it perfectly and the smell of the liquid from his private tank wasn't too overpowering.

It was right on the border of making him sick, but he kept it down. Something about the salinity of the bacteria really satisfied him. He thought he could feel the beginnings of a sore throat coming on, and he knew that he should take it easier in this workout. But that was never the way he did things. His latest logs indicated a sudden increase of crewmembers complaining of sore throats and flu-like symptoms. He would check into it again after his workout and see if he could isolate the pathogen.

He stepped onto the treadmill and began his run. His loping gate made a familiar rhythmic sound. He looked at his naked body in the mirrored wall and marveled at the slightly greenish hue his skin had taken on. This had been getting more noticeable over the last six months because of how much kelp he'd consumed. His Veganism was in no way inspired by a sense of moral outrage over eating animals. He simply knew that the research pointed toward a reduced calorie and animal fat-free diet as the surest path to longevity. The chef added large amounts of soy protein and acacia berry juice to his shakes to keep them nutritionally balanced, but Abigail produced the coveted fertilizer.

After an hour of running, his body was drenched in sweat. He glanced at the wall clock and reduced the speed of his treadmill to a brisk walk. She should be waiting for him by now. He headed to the stone slab that housed the spa and relaxation room and felt the breath of hot steam greet him as the massive granite door slid soundlessly back into its pocket. The lights were dim in the spa and he turned them up slightly, illuminating the room with high intensity lights hidden behind very thin slabs of marble. The room took on a purplish tint, and the water and steam clicked on automatically and began to gush from the walls and ceiling.

After bathing under a deluge of warm water that fell from twenty feet overhead, he dimmed the lights so that they did not reflect too harshly off the polished black granite walls. The steam slowly obscured the high ceiling and then the walls around him. He threw his jock strap into the laundry hamper with all the other soiled workout suits he required everyone to wear when they worked out. The uniform helped keep everyone on the same team. The thin, rip-stop nylon helped build a nice sweat quickly, and left nothing to the imagination physically. It clung to the fit and the fat alike, encouraging all to stay in proper shape.

He ducked beneath a blindingly cold five-foot-wide waterfall and sat down on the bench built into the wall. He leaned forward with his elbows on his knees and let the freezing water pound down on the back of his neck. He felt a familiar nervousness over his upcoming meeting.

Mendelbaum entered his private suite wearing only a towel. His quarters were not as large as his brother's, but they were by far the finest aboard. He had given himself a total of six thousand square feet. Mendelbaum's bathroom and sleeping quarters were of equal size. On the far side of his sleeping quarters was a recessed sun deck. In pleasant weather he could extend the deck fifteen feet out and retract the ceiling, leaving a nearly one hundred-foot private balcony. Built into the wall that separated the sleeping quarters from his lavish bathroom was a thousand-gallon fish tank visible from either side. He used it to grow his kelp, rather than house anything as common as fish. The bathroom contained his massive marble Jacuzzi tub that he could fill with either purified water or liquid ozone. The liquid ozone treatment did wonders for his skin and had probably saved his brother's life. He kept Guillermo's private pool filled with the expensive gas at all times. The cost was staggering, but ultimately irrelevant.

Abigail Valquist was on his private balcony, looking out at the clouds over the water. She was sipping the cocktail he had left for her, as she was supposed to. The automatic sliding door stood half open, letting the smell of the ocean waft into the room. The clouds on the horizon told of a coming storm. The captain had no doubt noticed them, but Mendelbaum hated rough seas. He would have to check to be sure the infernal little Irishman, Maguire, had corrected their course.

Mendelbaum would never tire of this view. He dropped his towel and pulled on a fresh robe, never taking his eyes from Abigail and the setting sun beyond. Sitting in the low light, working his platinum puzzle game, he could almost imagine that she wanted to be here with him. Abigail was the most beautiful woman he had ever known, but she was as cold to him today as she had been the day he first manipulated her into coming aboard—he convinced her that he would kill her husband and child if she didn't commit fully to his cause. Her blond hair stirred slightly in the ocean breeze, revealing the low-slung uniform he insisted she wear. He had considered taking her by force, but ruled out the idea. That was Guillermo's way, not his. Never his.

This was his time to reflect and work the puzzle box he wore around his neck. He could solve it easily, but he enjoyed the complexity of working through each possible solution. The smooth swastika was hinged in fifty places and could be manipulated like a Rubik's Cube. The six pieces of the device all rotated smoothly on their well-worn fittings. There were a thousand possible combinations to the puzzle, but only one would open it and provide access to the ship's override switch. He glanced away from the puzzle at Abigail. He made her stand on his balcony this way once a week. It was the only thing he forced her to do, stand on the balcony and let him look at her. His thoughts wandered to the remarkable set of circumstances that had brought her to him.

Abigail was one of the lead child psychiatrists in her field of memory repression. Mendelbaum did not recruit women as a rule, but her reputation dictated that he at least vet her. His plan had been to bring her aboard only for a very short period to socialize and reawaken the memories from the donors in the host children. When he found her in Sweden, she was married to an Olympic Nordic skier, Albert. Her son was a seven-year-old firebrand redhead. Mendelbaum had made his case eloquently, but she had refused the generous offer on the spot.

Mendelbaum had been forced to use more persuasive measures. He could just tell that she was vital to the success of the RYE Project. It was never ideal to take someone like her by force, but he had to have her. There were other research scientists that could have filled her role, but she brought something special.

The best way to recruit and retain new talent was through peaceful coercion such as blackmail, drugs, or sex addiction. Addicts could be controlled; they made useful members of the crew. Outright terror was to be avoided because it led to unpredictable results. He knew that she was plotting against him. How could she not? He could see it in the hatred etched around her eyes, the only flaw in her perfect face, and the way she grimaced when she moved her bowels in his private bathroom for him. He was a fool not to strangle her with his bare hands and throw her overboard this instant. Did he really want to or was it just that he dreamt of feeling her flawless pale skin quiver beneath him?

He had kidnapped her family and brought them here. He had shot Albert in the head on the deck of the ship. He couldn't stand having the man aboard. As long as he lived, she could never be his. He had spared Edvard the sight, but had forced Abigail to watch. The next day he brought Abigail back to the deck of the ship and placed the barrel of the gun to Edvard's head. She looked back at him, open contempt on her face.

If only she knew what he had spared her from. Guillermo had wanted her the first time he saw her. Mendelbaum knew the look in this brother's sunken eyes and it scared him. Guillermo had been allowed to roam the ship with limited supervision at first. The latest outbursts were unacceptable. He had increased the sedative dosage and restricted the amount of self-administered stimulants he could take. His survival suit was programmed to inject him with massive amounts of adrenaline if his heart stopped, even to shock him with a defibrillator if need be.

Mendelbaum had saved Guillermo and even improved his life. But the old ways had come back so easily. He could never be allowed around Abigail.

Guillermo's suit had been outfitted with offensive and defensive weapons in case of an attack. But Guillermo was too unpredictable to be allowed free rein of the ship. He had killed several women before Mendelbaum caught him. The ship's code of conduct required that he be thrown overboard, but that was out of the question. Mendelbaum destroyed the evidence of Guillermo's crimes and limited him to his quarters. He had the quarters expanded and outfitted with a gym and play area, and he did his best to ignore the fight club that he and Jacques ran.

Mendelbaum was startled from his reverie by Abigail gliding back through the open door. A lump stuck in his throat when she locked her ice-blue stare on him. She set the empty glass of prune juice on his large office table and didn't make eye contact with him as she walked into his toilet and shut the door.

He knew that she would gladly throw herself overboard if Edvard were not still in his control. Mendelbaum had made it clear that Edvard would be used in the RYE Project if she killed herself or attempted to escape. She knew he was serious.

He heard the toilet flush and watched the clear tube connected to his massive kelp tank take her prized fertilizer on its short journey. The delectable green leaves waved lazily in the current of sustenance she had just delivered. She walked back into his bedroom defiantly. “Anything else?” she asked.

14 AL-BARQ'S SOLACE

Fawwaz al-Barq awoke with a curse on his lips and raw feeling in his throat. He was drenched in sweat, his head pounded, and he felt like he had eaten glass. He was coming down with something, but that was not the cause of his real discomfort. There had been no way to know what his superiors were assigning him to—he might have killed himself if he'd known. He fumbled with the Dramamine tablets next to the bed. Today marked his six-hundredth day at sea, and still he was sickened by the constant motion. He climbed out of bed, looked at his compass, and prayed toward Mecca.

He hadn't seen his wife or son a single time, in person, since his assignment began. The place needed his constant attention and he could not risk leaving for even a day. He only saw his family through the devilish computer screen that he allowed himself to use once a week. He was used to dealing with difficult personalities, but working for Dr. Mendelbaum was a new low. Fawwaz was the head of security, and therefore, was kept abreast of all the experiments on the ship, a fact he would never be able to forget.

The torture chambers of Riyadh could learn a thing or two from the sterile rooms of the *Pura Vida*. *Quite a name*, he thought mirthlessly. Even after all this time aboard, after all the bizarre experiments he had not been able to look away from, the one last night was the most troubling. He had watched as Mendelbaum had thrown the switch with a smile to begin the "upload" process to an infant.

Almost immediately the child had gone into hysterics, thrashing in pain, scratching at his ears to stop the flow of raw data into the deeply implanted chips. The fighting amused Mendelbaum; Fawwaz had become ill. This only heightened Mendelbaum's enjoyment of the moment. The man reveled in the weakness of others. Fawwaz prayed for a day when he could have Mendelbaum alone for a few hours in Riyadh.

Fawwaz had spent most of his day in the gym. Even his extreme workouts couldn't put his mind at ease, and he had slept poorly. He knew the screaming baby would chase his dreams for months to come. He pressed his fist into his eye socket until it began to throb. He removed his fist and stared through the pulsating stars at the bag of opium his cousin had given him. He rarely allowed himself the indulgence, but it was the only comfort he enjoyed in this heathen hell-ship.

The filthy whores of the lower decks revolted him; the very smell of the place was enough to turn his stomach. Fawwaz longed for his wife's purity and chastity. Six hundred days were too many for a man to go without his woman.

He knew he could have the opium any time he wanted it, but he did his best to avoid it. Only one day per week, when the oversight of the ship's security was handed to Mendelbaum personally, would he even consider a true dose of relaxation. His hands shook as he loaded the ornate hookah Zakar had lent him. It was not his night off, but Zakar had been more than willing to cover for him. He took a deep breath and let it out slowly. Then he lit the small black ball and drew evenly on the mouthpiece. An image of a baby appeared in front of him and he sucked even harder.

Zakar swiped his cousin's ID card and entered the lavishly appointed suite. His luck was beyond good. Fawwaz had asked him to cover an easy shift so that he could turn in early. Technically, he was supposed to be on the bridge, but he had time for an unscheduled stop; Fawwaz was supposed to keep a close watch on the girls anyway. Only Fawwaz and a few other select crew members could visit the new arrivals before their unveiling. Zakar hoped to make a good impression on a few of the girls before they got a taste of the rest of the animals aboard. The suite was by far his favorite place on the boat. It smelled like stripper oil and sex. Zakar had gladly covered for Fawwaz when he asked; he owed him far more than he could repay. Besides, this was a great way to get more credits when he ran low and a surefire way to sneak into the suite after hours. The girls were all asleep but one, and she was the one he wanted to see.

"Do not be afraid," Zakar said. "I'm allowed in here."

"I'm Kayla," she said with false bravado.

"Nice to meet you, Kayla. What's your real name?" She looked away. He changed course. "I hate boats, you?"

"Never liked them much, either. What kind of boat is this, anyway?"

"I'm not allowed to say."

"This place must be huge; that pig Jacques parked the entire yacht inside it."

"All I can tell you is that as long as you do what you are told, no one will harm you."

"Even Jacques?"

Something about the question resonated with him. "Stay away from him if you can. Remember, you get to decide who you fuck aboard this ship."

"I want you," Kayla said, her face reddening.

"No, you don't," Zakar said easily. She was not like any prostitute he had ever met. She was not good at seduction at all. Yet he was fully aroused by her. He fought the urge to grab her. "Where are you from?"

"Do you always make small talk?"

"Usually."

"Cut it out. Are we going to do this or not?"

"Do what?"

"You know why I'm aboard."

"You're a slutty nurse, right?"

Kayla couldn't help but laugh. She seemed to be at ease for the first time since the ferret-faced Jacques brought her aboard the day before. "Can you sneak me out of here with you? I'd love to see the rest of this place," she said.

"They will throw you overboard if you are caught."

"That sounds better than Jacques getting his hands on me."

"Fair enough. I have to go on duty in a while; my cousin is taking the night off. I'll come back for you later."

15 BUCCANEERS

"The plan is straightforward enough," Jim said to the laptop image of his boss.

"This ship is making me nervous," Carmichael said from CIA headquarters in Virginia.

Jim leaned in close to the monitor, searching the assistant director's face. He had never seen the man this upset before. "Everything makes you nervous. We can't scrap the mission now; we are too close to the launch. I take full responsibility for overriding your objection."

"Overriding my objection?" Carmichael screamed. "I'm still *your* boss!"

"Look, this thing has to be done. I have a good feeling about the team here. What is it that you're nervous about? Is there some intel you're not sharing?"

"No, nothing like that. It's the info from the boy, Noah."

"What about it?" Jim asked, distractedly. Carmichael had a habit of overreacting. He was notoriously thin-skinned in the hours before a mission began. Somehow this seemed a little different, but Jim's mind was elsewhere.

"There was a lot of data that was damaged and unusable. You were briefed on the general layout of the ship, but we still don't know anything about its defensive capability."

Jim's team was briefed and ready, they were steaming north along the Somali coast toward the projected coordinates of the *Pura Vida* near Yemen. Jim's pulse pounded, thinking of the upcoming raid. His team appeared to be a group of Somali pirates. Their ship had been commandeered the week before from just such a group. An attack on the *Pura Vida* was a ruse to allow him and his team to access the ship, document the contents and make an escape.

"Jim! Are you listening to me?" Carmichael asked. "You can still scrap this thing."

"No, we're a go. I'll update you as I know more. Out." A dull sense of unease settled into his gut after he severed the connection. He shook his head and opened the rusted door of his cabin.

Fifteen minutes later his second in command banged at the door and signaled him to head topside. He looked out at the *Pura Vida* in the distance from the top deck of the "borrowed" pirate ship. He put his hand on the barrel of the .50-caliber machine gun mounted on the bow of the converted fishing boat. It was the perfect weapon to get their attention.

Jim made eye contact with his second, a man named Seymour. He hadn't worked with Seymour or his partner before, but the men's credentials were impeccable.

"Head straight for her. Don't stop until we have the ship in range of the jammer," Jim said.

"Got it. Charging pulse weapon now."

The ship had the appearance of a typical Somali pirate ship; rusted, barely afloat—but it had in fact been retrofitted with a complex electromagnetic pulse weapon designed to be powerful enough to disable the *Pura Vida's* electrical systems. Once they were within range, they would fire off a pulse that would leave the ship crippled and allow their entry. The pirate crew knew nothing about the weapon, nor would they be allowed to keep it. The weapon was secured to the underside of the vessel and would automatically drop free once used and never be seen again.

Three minutes until optimal range.

"Weapon charged. *Pura Vida* in range."

"Hold your fire until we are right under her," Jim said. His words were drowned out by a humming noise like millions of bees that carried over the water from the tanker. Jim recognized the sound of a Gatling gun. He knew they'd missed with their first volley because the rounds were traveling at nearly three times the speed of sound, if they had been on target he wouldn't have heard a thing. A split second later the second torrent of bullets cut through the water fifty feet in front of the small ship and sent a cascade of angry white foam into the air.

"Engage the EMP!" Jim yelled, too late. His final order was lost in the cacophony of gunfire that followed, not that it would have mattered. They were still out of the EMPs effective range. Jim struggled to the top deck and stared in awe at the destruction. The tanker had unleashed a hail of depleted uranium shells and cut the stern of his pirate craft into ribbons. Jim couldn't even sound the Abandon Ship warning with the rate at which the craft began taking water. The damage was clearly enough to sink her, but the unseen deck guns rained fire down on them anyway. Jim thrashed at the twisted rigging in front of him to clear a path to the water. He threw himself overboard with a life vest and swam hard. The guns were not trained on the men in the water; the attack was meant merely to destroy the pirate vessel. They wanted survivors.

He floated in the debris for several minutes before he saw the first small boat approaching at high speed. He watched as the men in the boat scanned the survivors and chose to leave them bobbing where they were. Moments later the boat stopped in front of him and an angry barrel-chested Arab man with blood shot eyes looked him over. "That one," was all he heard before he was hauled aboard at gunpoint. He was sat roughly in the corner of the boat and jabbed in the arm with a gas-powered syringe gun as the boat sped away. The last image he had was of the rear of the massive tanker looming closer and closer and a section of the ship sliding away to reveal an internal dock. The speedboat didn't slow as it hurled into the *Pura Vida's* dark cavern.

16 Pure Panic

Zakar walked into the main bridge ten minutes late. His stomach turned to water when he saw the main screen. A Somali pirate ship his cousin had warned him about was steaming directly toward them. It would be within range of the deck guns in only a few seconds. Zakar grabbed the com link and brought up the screen in Fawwaz's room. He screamed for his cousin to report to the bridge, but got no response. He had a decision to make. With a shaky hand he engaged the deck guns and yelled for Fawwaz to wake up. But his cousin was too high on his drugs to respond. Hands shaking, he brought up the screen in the reactor room next.

"Shut down the reactor?" Jacques said. "You had better have a good goddamn reason for this," he hissed.

"We are under pirate attack!" Zakar snapped back. "We have no choice, protocol dictates that we shut down the reactor and enter stealth mode if the ship is threatened."

"Pirates? This better be a serious fucking threat. Have you cleared this with al-Barq?"

"Y-yeah," Zakar said as he muted the connection to the reactor room and switched the com link back to Fawwaz's room. He howled for his cousin to respond.

But he had smoked too much, again. Zakar reopened the connection to the reactor. “Fawwaz left me to take care of the defense of the ship.”

Mendelbaum’s voice cut in over the screen. “Al-Rashid, why the hell is the active cloak engaged?”

“Fawwaz left me in charge and I engaged it,” Zakar said with mock confidence. “We were under attack by pirates.”

“You engaged the cloaking system over Somali pirates?” Mendelbaum snapped.

“The security of the ship was in jeopardy! I was just ordering Jacques to shut down the reactor!”

“Did you engage the deck guns?”

“Of course, the pirate vessel has been sunk. I’ve given orders to launch a rescue boat to collect survivors.”

“Belay the order to disengage the reactor, Jacques.”

“But-”

“In the fifteen years we have had the reactor operational it has never been taken offline,” Jacques said.

“You are relieved, Zakar,” Mendelbaum said as he closed the connection.

Jacques snickered.

"What?" Zakar yelled.

"Fucking sand-niggers," Jacques said, laughing and nodding his head. He severed his connection to the main bridge and left Zakar alone, shaking slightly.

The main debriefing room used aboard the *Pura Vida* was a small, brightly lit chamber next to the surgery center. Although rare, torture aboard the ship was done with thoroughness and vigor. Mendelbaum had seen to the precise design himself.

Standing in the middle of the water-boarding room, Mendelbaum inhaled deeply and held his breath. Fawwaz knew that the smell of fear was still present. Mendelbaum felt that water-boarding was a great starting-off point, but it never really got the message across. It was vital that the crew understand that the security of the ship would always take priority over anyone's life, even lead scientist Horst Mendelbaum's.

Fawwaz had trained the security forces in the Saudi tradition. The style was actually quite familiar to Mendelbaum because of his father. He had even offered pointers to Fawwaz to help facilitate the effective administration of terror. Symbolism was the key in

Mendelbaum's opinion. The Saudis had been trained in the Nazi style, and their thoroughness was astounding. Many of the most important Muslims of Jerusalem, Saudi Arabia, and Iran had spent World War II in Berlin, near Hitler. Sheik Abdul ibn Jabara, the *Pura Vida's* key financier, was one such man. The Muslim fascists in Gaza and Iran and throughout the Middle East today were direct descendants of the Reich, a deeply comforting fact to Mendelbaum.

Fawwaz was shaken from his reverie as his cousin was led in slowly, deliberately. He'd broken the cardinal rule of ship security: over-exposure. One pirate ship was hardly enough to justify using the ship's most sophisticated defensive technology within sight of the shore. It was close to nightfall when the cloak had been engaged, so the potential damage was fairly minimal. But the lapse was still inexcusable.

"Bring him in," Mendelbaum said over his shoulder. Fawwaz complied, the fog of his opium binge gone. He could only guess what was in store for his cousin.

It was his fault for being weak, but Mendelbaum would never publicly acknowledge a failing in the security chief. The chief was a necessary component of the ship. Discipline was vital. Plus, his reports to the sheik on the ship's progress kept a vital piece of funding in place. So far, Mendelbaum had succeeded in keeping Sheik Abdul bin Jabara's wife alive far longer than any other clinic in the world could have. A degenerative disease had ravaged her spinal cord. Constant injections of a custom-engineered stem cell treatment had saved her until the scans were complete and her cryonic chamber prepared.

Al-Barq watched as his cousin was marched in by a two-man security detail. They sat him roughly on a chair and left. The ship's security team was made up of twenty mercenaries he had personally selected. Most were military washouts that had been in the private security sphere working for American contractors in Saudi Arabia. Fawwaz would have preferred his own men, but Mendelbaum had refused, preferring instead to have men that he could easily control.

Fawwaz looked at his cousin. He was unhurt. Zakar had been kept in solitude since Mendelbaum discovered the depth of the mistake. The upcoming punishment was meant for him, but his importance to the continued funding of the ship clearly made any truly harsh penalty impossible. Mendelbaum seemed very calm as he looked from Zakar to Fawwaz and back again.

At long last Mendelbaum turned to Zakar and smiled. "You deployed a defensive system of last resort over a tiny speck of a craft. But it's not really your fault. You are only to assume control of the bridge if your cousin is incapacitated," he said, leveling his gaze on Fawwaz. He took a deep breath, and asked, "Why was he responsible for the response to the pirate ship?" It was his first acknowledgment of Fawwaz since the incident the day before.

"I was not well. I had medicated myself and placed him in charge—"

"Medicated?" Mendelbaum interrupted. "My pharmacy log indicates that you are not prescribed any medication. I do show a regular dose of recreational hashish. Have you begun a regimen of opium as well?"

"I was weak," Fawwaz said though gritted teeth. He would kill a less important man with his bare hands for insulting him so. He would be dangerous to be around tonight. There must be a way off this wretched ship.

"These are trying times for as us all," Mendelbaum said without a hint of malice. The tone disarmed Fawwaz, who was expecting to be publicly humiliated.

The reprieve was welcome, but the issue remained of what to do with his incompetent cousin. Zakar had always been a terrible disappointment. He was occasionally hardworking, but afraid of his own shadow. It was not surprising that he used every means at his disposal to throw off the attack; he probably soiled himself as well. The Gatling guns would have been more than enough to sink the ship and kill the boarding party. But Zakar had chosen to engage the active camouflage system.

"At least we got a proper test of the system," Mendelbaum said. "I have spent my morning contacting the VIP guests that were expected to join us for the quarterly award dinner and gala. I have decided to move into safer waters for the time being and will be making a ship-wide announcement of the postponement shortly. I know that there will be disappointment at the delay in meeting the new entertainment, but security must take priority."

The meaning was clear to Fawwaz. His cousin was on notice. Mendelbaum could not kill him, at least not without severe consequences. Anyone else aboard the ship would be walking the plank by now. He probably had something else in mind to make his point.

"Instruct Phineas to join us immediately," Mendelbaum said.

17 Sacrifice

Phineas felt better. At least the end was near. Knowing that he would be put to death helped calm him. He had thought that he would quiver and beg for mercy, but he stood his ground instead. "How long have you known?" he asked.

Mendelbaum ignored him. He glanced at Fawwaz and motioned for him to prepare the execution chamber. The security chief turned wordlessly and entered the small hatch that led to the final holding cell.

Phineas knew that they had put many men to death aboard the *Pura Vida*. Rarely would they televise the execution for the entire ship, but this was a special occasion.

"I have known that you were unhappy here for months but I didn't think that you would really betray me, not after the opportunity I gave you."

"You can't run the ship without me," Phineas said.

"You are wrong. Jacques is a nuclear scientist of the highest caliber. He has studied your computer systems and is fully competent to provide the routine maintenance they require. You've perfected the RYE Project and tried to hide it from me. I knew that you were planning to set six-oh-nine free, so Jacques and I manicured the data you were able to upload to him."

"His name is Noah."

"I could have let you live if you hadn't also released this Norovirus. Save me the hassle of synthesizing an antidote or you are going into the water."

It was Phineas's turn to ignore him. Abigail had not been implicated, so their plan was still a success. Phineas had allowed himself to be taped by the security cameras. It was the only way to protect Abby and the child. She would never have agreed to his plan. Phineas smiled in spite of himself. If she were able to get a hold of the override key, Mendelbaum would have a nasty surprise in store when he finally restored his reactor.

Mendelbaum motioned to al-Barq to seal Phineas in the chamber.

Abigail and the rest of the crew had been assembled in the Great Ballroom. The chandelier was dimmed and the spotlight focused only on the speaker at the podium. The roulette wheels, and extravagant bar were quiet. The church-like atmosphere was gone, as well. Mendelbaum waited for silence to fall, then waited a few more moments for dramatic effect. The tension in the room could be heard from all the stirring, coughing, and nose-blowing. The assembled doctors, nurses, and guest services staff looked back expectantly. In all, there were nearly two hundred people. The room moved slightly to the left as another ocean roller hit Pura Vida's prow.

"Welcome," Mendelbaum began. "As some of you know, we have had an internal breach of security aboard the *Pura Vida*. We are here today to level charges against the one responsible for the treason. As you are all aware, the punishment for treason on the high seas is, well, severe." He turned to al-Barq. "Sergeant-at-Arms, please read the charges. Then, in accordance with the *Pura Vida* charter, Article one point three, which states that video evidence shall suffice to pass final and binding judgment on the accused, we shall levy the mandated punishment. The penalty for treason according to Article one point six is the Sea March at Full Steam. Sergeant, if you please."

Al-Barq strode to the podium, cleared his throat. "The charges against Phineas Kostopoulos are as follows: One: That he did knowingly and with knowledge aforethought make known ship secrets to a foreign power. Two: That he did knowingly and with the intent to permanently deprive from the ship, certain valuable computer algorithms. Three: That he did knowingly aid in the escape of ship property. Four: That he did knowingly spread an infectious disease through the ship's water filtration system to cause permanent injury to the health of the ship's crew and patients. Five: As a result of said conduct, the *Pura Vida* and its investors have been permanently deprived of valuable and irreplaceable property and have lost incalculable productivity. In support of these charges we offer the following security surveillance tapes."

The room lights dimmed as the projection screen came down from behind the podium. The podium sank into the floor, allowing the entire hundred-foot screen to settle into place. The high-definition IMAX projector glowed to life from the ceiling two hundred feet above and played the damning tape of Phineas's exploits over the past year. Abigail's breath caught. She tried to look away from the screen but couldn't. Mendelbaum had the proof. How he'd known what to look for, remained a mystery.

Phineas was pounding silently at the door of the plank-enabled room. Everyone aboard the ship knew this space well, if not by actual knowledge, then by whisperings. It was the formal execution chamber, a small room at the bow of the tanker with an opening at the far end. A two-foot-wide mechanical plank extended out from the door over the open water a hundred feet below. The condemned were prodded onto the plank where they could either walk to their deaths of their own accord or be dropped once the plank was retracted into its housing in the ship. Abigail opened her mouth to speak, but found no words. Tears streamed down her face as she turned away from the monitor. The camera mounted high above the plank on the outside of the ship came into focus. Phineas was frog-marched onto the narrow platform and the hatch was shut behind him. He clung to the plank on his hands and knees. The microphones connected to the plank came to life and carried his pitiful wailing throughout the ship. Slowly the plank began to retract. She watched Phineas's last feeble efforts to hang on before he fell into the churning water far below.

18 Jim's Interview

Jim opened his eyes for the first time in several hours. He was in a perfectly clean room like the kind private hospitals use. Every surface gleamed and a dim light seemed to emanate from the walls themselves. He found himself dressed in some kind of silver tracksuit; his Somali pirate rags nowhere to be found. He closed his eyes and thought back. The attack had gone just as planned, at first. Then they realized the scope of the technology they were up against; the rusted hulk of the oil tanker was far from defenseless. They had suspected as much, but had not been able to put together a fair appraisal of the vessel's defenses from the info that Noah had provided.

The pulse should have knocked the oil tanker offline; electronics for a quarter mile should have been fried. Then the mission would have been a simple boarding and execution run. Something about the prospect of assassination work had been exciting to Jim for the first time. He had killed many men, but had never enjoyed it. This task had been the first thing he had looked forward to since losing Sharon. That was a disturbing fact.

Jim had been waiting for his interrogation. He knew that it was coming. He looked forward to it. As a master interrogator himself, he didn't think his captors realized he would be learning as much about them as they were of him. Judging from the dark bruises on his arms from the attack on the pirate ship, he hadn't been aboard more than a day or two. The door to Jim's cell slid open with a slight hiss and two figures stood just outside. Jim recognized Horst Mendelbaum from the CIA photo he'd seen back in Freddy's office. The man before him was tall, thin, and very pale. His skin seemed to have a vague greenish tint to it. He had a hawkish nose and deep-set brown eyes. There was a well-built guard next to him, an Arab. He held a rifle loosely in both hands, clearly familiar with its use. Jim recognized it as an FAMS G-2, a French-made weapon popular with NATO Special Forces. Its safety was off.

"Hello, James, my name is Horst Mendelbaum," he said as if they were meeting under normal circumstances. He walked into Jim's room a few paces and stopped. Jim remained seated on his bed. "I want you to know that no one is coming for you, so please try to be civil and make the most of this experience."

"I know who you are. But call me Jim."

"Thank you. You are aboard a state-of-the-art hospital. This ship can accommodate as many as two hundred critically ill patients at any given time. We are a completely self-sufficient mobile treatment and research facility. The craft runs on nuclear power," he said with a smirk. "Ironic for a converted oil tanker to bridge the green technology gap. We are completely emission-free."

Jim knew he was being given a lot of information at once. This was an interrogation technique he was familiar with but didn't trust. It overplayed your hand as often as it elicited relevant information. "Where is the rest of my team?" he asked.

Mendelbaum ignored Jim's question, which confirmed his fear. "Your mission was declared a failure and the CIA has announced that you were acting alone. Not even your father's influence is going to be enough now, if he wakes up. However, you are useful to me here. You possess certain talents that this ship could put to good use. My Sergeant-at-Arms needs a better second-in-command," he said, looking coldly at the man next to him. Jim realized that he was the red-eyed Arab that had pulled him out of the water. "You are perfect. I know all about what you did in Iraq. Your father told me all about the successful interrogations you ran and how you trained the bumbling local police into a hardened military unit. No small feat considering how worthless those Shia camel-humpers are."

"You want me to work for you?" Jim asked, bemused. This was clearly an attempt to win his confidence and keep him off balance. Mendelbaum would never give him free rein of the ship.

"Yes, on a trial basis, of course. If you disappoint me I'll kill someone you care about." He smiled broadly and his brilliantly white teeth caught the light. "It's really pretty simple."

"No, thank you," Jim said.

Mendelbaum was pleased with his politeness. "This ship is not going to be seized, Jim; you need to accept that. Our guest list is a who's who of the world's elite. Nearly half my patients in cryofreeze were once powerful Americans. My ship operates with the tacit approval of the world's important governments." He scratched at his pale chin for a moment. "You see, secularism has enlightened and informed the rich of the world's community. This life is all we have; there is no such thing as an afterlife. You must know that by now."

"You killed my team. There will be others looking for us. They are going to hunt you down."

“We will move into safer waters for the time being; a minor setback.”

He had admitted to this being a setback. Good. “Your little ship doesn’t stand a chance,” Jim said. He leaned back onto his bed and looked toward the wall behind Mendelbaum.

“You are so wrong!” Mendelbaum’s face reddened and for the first time he seemed passionate about his topic. “The *Pura Vida’s* mission is bigger than all of us. It will last far longer than you or me. Our nuclear reactor will power our systems forever. Societies will rise and fall and this ship will still be here, afloat somewhere in the vast ocean. We grow all our own food and desalinate all our own water. Even so, I make a point of bringing select members of every major government and every important family I can find aboard the ship. But discretion is the key. The highest standards of confidentiality are maintained. This ship adheres to a code of ethics, the violation of which can constitute the most severe penalties.”

“And you make people commit crimes to ensure their silence once they leave,” Jim said. He had learned that from the files Noah had provided. But those files were incomplete. There’d been no mention of the defensive capabilities the ship could employ.

Mendelbaum was either going to kill him soon, or he was seriously entertaining the idea of allowing Jim to work aboard the ship. Interesting.

"If necessary, of course. The *Pura Vida* is the blueprint for humanity's green future. We are emission-free. Did you know that international shipping creates as much greenhouse gas as all the cars on Earth?"

Jim knew that to be true, but he wanted to keep Mendelbaum talking. He stared at Mendelbaum a moment before rolling his eyes and gazing off into space. "Like a giant hybrid car? Now I know I hate it."

"Transoceanic ships burn barely processed oil sludge. They use and reuse their fuel until it is gone without any regard to the carbon they release. Shipping accounts for half of the world's greenhouse emissions, yet there is not a single enforceable emission standard."

"I know why you chose a ship for this place; it allows you to run any kind of hospital you want. If the busybodies in Washington and Copenhagen can't legislate emissions, they certainly can't meddle in your affairs."

"That's right," Mendelbaum said, smiling at him. "I started treating my brother in the ship infirmary while the *Pura Vida* was in dry dock twenty years ago. We flew the flag of Venezuela then. The family business had failed, and the ship was the only remaining asset. It was the only place I could bring my brother after the hospital refused to treat him. It occurred to me then that the ship was the perfect place to run a full-scale facility. I could treat anyone I wanted with any treatment I deemed necessary. The Saudis offered the most impressive registration options. But you knew that, that is why you intercepted us where you did."

"Your brother was accused of the rape of a senior government official's daughter. I don't think you were welcome in Venezuela anymore."

"Wrongly accused," Mendelbaum said.

So that was it. Guillermo was the chink in Mendelbaum's armor. The file was clear about Guillermo. He was wanted in connection with the rapes of at least ten women in three countries. But that wasn't the point. He was a man who could have anything, but was never satisfied. And Mendelbaum wouldn't admit it. Jim smiled at him.

Mendelbaum cut his smile off by saying, "He and the young lady had been dating for many months. When it became known that he had been infected with HIV, the blame didn't fall on her because of who her father was. She was a harlot, everyone knew it."

“Guillermo is still wanted in connection with several sex assaults.”

This seemed to hit a nerve. Mendelbaum’s lips were a thin line. “His file was manipulated. Women threw themselves at Guillermo. He could have had anyone he wanted, so why rape?”

“Because he got off on hurting them, right? He used them for sport. Does he still?”

“My brother is not your concern.”

“So this ship was created to save your brother. What do you do with the patients that you can’t save?”

“We either cure them or preserve them for a day when we can.”

“This is insane,” Jim said with a dry laugh.

“Hardly. We are here to save the species. There are members of humanity that must be preserved. I realized that after my brother got sick. I couldn’t risk letting him die. Socialism has entrenched itself in our governments and personal greed has outpaced our ability to evolve and survive. Our species is at the precipice; we are in a position to fail horribly or evolve into the most important iteration of life the universe has ever known. The great nations of the world will try to redistribute wealth to make everyone comfortable. We will end up with a society of paupers that can never provide for one another."

"How has your brother adjusted to life at sea?"

"My brother is none of your concern," Mendelbaum hissed. He took a deep breath and regained his composure. "However, this video of your father is." Mendelbaum turned on his heel and left the room.

The door sealed with a hiss and the screen in Jim's room glowed to life. After a moment he was treated to an overhead view of a sterile hospital room much like the one he was in now. There was an unconscious man lying on a gurney; tubes connected him to a wall of machines. The video contained a time stamp from two years earlier. Jim watched as another man entered. He instantly recognized his father's broad shoulders and purposeful gait.

Lawrence Lantana walked to the edge of the bed and looked down at the patient. "Now what?" he asked.

A voice that Jim recognized as Mendelbaum answered from off camera. "The machine in front of you has three dials controlling the flow of his medication. All you need to do is turn off the first two and increase the third to its maximum setting. The rest will happen very quickly."

“And if I do this, you guarantee that you can help her?”

There was an annoyed exhale from Mendelbaum. “There are no guarantees,” he said. “We will agree to undertake her treatment pro bono. You agree to continue to allow the ship to operate without interference from the U.S. Navy.”

“I don’t control the Navy, I’m retired. Killing this man won’t change that in any way.”

“That may be true, Admiral. But I think you understand the power this video gives me over you.”

“Give me your word that you can help her.”

“You have my word that I will try. And if I can’t, there are the other options we have discussed.”

“I’m not interested in that. Just do your best to save her,” Lawrence said. And with that he approached the machines attached to the comatose man and worked at the dials. A moment later the EKG machine began chirping loudly and then almost immediately went silent. The video screen went blank and Jim sank to his bed.

Two hours later Mendelbaum appeared on the screen, an armed guard behind him. Jim glanced up at him but said nothing for a moment. "Why did you have my father kill that man?" The video might help explain the suicide attempt, but it still raised more questions than it answered.

Mendelbaum ignored the question. He looked Jim him in the eye. "I would say that your father's decision to end his life was a wise one."

Jim knew he was being baited and fought the rising anger he felt.

"I would have thought that an Admiral would be been more successful, but my reports indicate that he will probably never wake up. That's why you're such a gift, Jim. With your experience in CIA operations we can keep this ship running the way it was meant to. Do you know why your father was here?" Mendelbaum asked.

Jim took a deep breath and played the video of his father in his head again. He knew the answer, but he refused to face it.

"I would like to introduce you to an important member of my crew, Dr. Abigail Valquist," Mendelbaum said. Jim could see a trim female form moving around behind him.

The door slid open and Abigail walked into the room. She met Jim's eyes as the door sealed behind her. She was striking up close. He had been around beautiful women his whole life, but there was something different about this one that he could not place.

When neither spoke, Mendelbaum said over the intercom, "Dr. Valquist will help you understand your father's motivation." Mendelbaum turned from the screen, but stopped before leaving. He looked over his shoulder and said absently, "Be sure to introduce Mr. Lantana to Katarina, my love."

Abigail paged someone after Mendelbaum left, and a moment later a thick-shouldered male assistant brought a young girl to Jim's room. The man glared at Abigail but she ignored him.

Katarina looked vaguely familiar to Jim. She had large, almond-shaped eyes and dark, wavy hair. Her fair skin was lightly freckled. She reminded him of Sharon. She could have been their daughter if he hadn't put his career before their lives together.

"Hello," Jim said.

The two year old smiled at him.

"Katarina is one of many children born aboard the *Pura Vida*," Abigail said. "She has never known anything but the ship."

"So?"

"So nothing," Abigail said. "I was told to introduce you to her." With that she picked up the toddler, kissed her on the top of the head, and handed her to the annoyed-looking man who shuffled off with her.

Her tone implied that she was not happy about being ordered around. "Do you always do what you're told?" he asked.

Her eyes flashed with repressed anger, and Jim felt his pulse quicken. She was tall, nearly six feet. But she couldn't weigh more than a hundred and thirty pounds. She was lithe and athletic-looking, even under her white coat. Her hair was so blond it was nearly colorless. Jim wondered if the carpet matched the drapes and blushed in spite of himself.

"What?" she demanded.

He cleared his throat and avoided her question. "How long have you been aboard the ship, Dr. Valquist?"

"Call me Abigail. Three years."

"Why?"

"I . . . I came aboard with my husband and my son," she said uncertainly.

"Where are they?" Jim asked. When she didn't respond he changed course. "Your accent, it's Dutch?" he asked, knowing that it wasn't.

"Swedish."

"What is your area of expertise?"

"Child psychiatry and neurobiology."

"How many children are aboard?"

"I'm not permitted to discuss that."

"Who's listening?"

"Dr. Mendelbaum. At all times, assume that he is listening."

"Why was I shown that video?"

"You were shown the video to help you understand your father's motivation and desire to help your wife," Abigail said. She clicked several buttons on the touch screen and the cell darkened. A new video recording loaded, showing a date ticker displaying his room nearly two years earlier, about six months before Sharon had passed.

This was not the same video he had seen of his father. In this recording his father was led into the small room where a patient was lying on a bed. The facts were being presented logically, but he still couldn't process the gravity of what he was seeing. The epiphany was in front of him, but he shied from it. It couldn't be. The video camera panned out and he recognized that the patient in the bed was his wife, Sharon. Pieces clicked into place.

"Jesus," he said. "What did you do, Dad?" he asked the recorded image.

"He brought her here for treatment, James," Abigail said.

He forgot to correct her. He sat down on his bed and looked away from her. Sharon had been aboard this ship with his father. The suicide attempt was beginning to make more sense. His father had lied to him about his own wife.

He was startled by Abigail's hand on his shoulder. "This ship has a good reputation among the world's power elite. Your father brought her here to try to save her, but it was too late. Unfortunately for your father, Dr. Mendelbaum only undertakes treatments after he has been paid. In your father's case, the first payment was to make the video."

"So that Mendelbaum could own him. Fool."

"No. He was not a fool. This ship was his last hope. We have had some success with gene therapies for patients in her condition. But her illness was too advanced when we got her. She could have gone into a cryonics tank but your father refused."

"Cryonics? You mean you freeze patients that you can't treat?"

"Yes, regularly. Once it was established that we couldn't save her here, your father took her back to the United States to pass on peacefully."

"But Mendelbaum still had the video. He wasn't done with my father," he said. Abigail said nothing, but her expression confirmed that he was right. Jim took a deep breath. "Thank you for telling me," he said. For the first time the words didn't feel forced. Jim hadn't spoken of his wife's death voluntarily to anyone, yet here he was talking to her, a complete stranger. Was she more than his captor's whore? There was something about her that implied a deep empathy but he couldn't pin it down. Mendelbaum was probably manipulating him through her.

She smiled at him.

"You seem to live a comfortable life here," he said with a bit more venom than he intended. His words found their mark.

Her demeanor changed, and she recoiled a few steps toward the door. "I'll report that you are feeling better," she said over her shoulder.

"I thought you were Mendelbaum's girl."

This stopped her. "If it would keep my son safe, I would do anything." She turned back toward Jim, defiant, luminous, her cheeks flushed in anger, "But it's not that way." She caught herself and lowered her voice to a throaty whisper, "He likes to watch me."

"Real Romeo."

"He murdered my husband." She said, tears forming. She stared at the camera in the corner of the room. She was no longer talking to him.

"And yet you could stand to be near him."

She stared at the camera. "I told you, if it keeps Edvard safe, I'll endure anything."

19 SWIM

Mendelbaum approached the pool area carefully, hoping not to distract Guillermo from his exercise. He could never understand why he had to force people to work out, even his own brother who needed the exercise as badly as any patient aboard. Mendelbaum's own exercise regimen was the only thing that kept him sane. This massive private pool had been the last addition to the set-up. He had put it in specifically for Guillermo because his condition didn't allow any other good exercise options.

Helping Guillermo may have been the motivation, the desperation even, to start a treatment facility on the ship, but the money quickly grew to be as important. He never dreamed of making so much money. He smiled at the thought. All he did now was manage a facility that he loved. In exchange, he lived the most extravagant lifestyle he could have imagined.

Guillermo had lost nearly all his muscle mass as a result of the rapidity with which his HIV progressed into full-blown AIDS. Mendelbaum had been forced to use an unorthodox combination of steroids and antibiotics to stabilize him. The steroids had worked. They had saved his brother's life. But he required massive daily doses and constant exercise just to stay alive.

Guillermo was down to nearly 130 pounds, a far cry from his original six foot three, 190-pound frame. He had been a lissome and enthusiastic athlete before getting sick. Now Mendelbaum had to force him to work out by threatening to withhold the only things that gave him pleasure any more: prostitutes and drugs.

The steroids had changed Guillermo's personality. He had always been a bit rough with women, that couldn't be denied, but they had still flocked to him. Once his body failed him and he became repulsive to the opposite sex, his steroid-fueled rage had become a major burden on ship security. Once the design was finalized by Phineas and Jacques, Mendelbaum had commissioned the Caulfield Corporation, known for their work with the U.S. military, to build the custom survival suit Guillermo had come to rely on. The suit had given him back the ability to walk and carry heavy loads, but his illness had robbed him of the only thing he really cared about, his libido. Jacques and Phineas had helped modify the suit and had inadvertently turned Guillermo into a killing machine, if left unsupervised.

The first incident had been only days after Guillermo had been outfitted with the new walking aid.

The suit was essentially a frame that fitted around his legs and arms, and fastened around his waist. The hydraulics allowed him to lift hundreds of pounds effortlessly. The suit was clumsy and awkward, but Guillermo learned to use it very quickly. A nurse named Erin had given him a strange look and he had slapped her. He intended only to teach her a lesson, but the blow crushed her skull. She died a day later. He knew at that moment that he couldn't let Guillermo have the use of the armored exoskeleton attachment that had been built at the same time as the primary survival suit.

Mendelbaum could hear the rhythmic splashing of his brother's stroke and felt a wave of relief. If he tired his brother out with a proper workout, he wasn't usually forced to drug him. He needed to be kept partially sedated anytime he was allowed around mixed groups. When he was in his private quarters, he could be left alone. He had never attacked Mendelbaum or Jacques, but anyone else was at risk when he was in the suit and lucid.

He watched his brother in silence as he sliced through the water. His movements were precise, but slow. The steroids, adrenaline shots, and methamphetamine gave him adequate energy, but his muscles would give out if he pushed too hard. Then even his walking suit wasn't enough to help him move about. He needed to spend more time conditioning his muscles, but he was easily frustrated.

Mendelbaum felt a familiar pang of anger wash over him at the memory of the way his brother had been ejected from the clinic all those years ago. Perhaps if Guillermo been allowed access to cutting-edge treatments when he was first diagnosed, he would be in as good a shape as the basketball player Mendelbaum had had his most success in treating. In those days, Mendelbaum had charged two million dollars for his HIV treatment. The price was now nearly twenty-five million. It was a proven commodity that had not been replicated in any other laboratory.

"Hello, brother," Guillermo said breathlessly.

"I am glad to see that you are using the pool again."

"I need to be strong for the new batch of girls."

Mendelbaum felt a spray of acid in his stomach. "We have discussed your access to female companions. After this latest incident, you are on indefinite suspension from female leisure time. We will reevaluate your behavior in one month in a controlled meet-and-greet. If you are able to handle yourself, we will talk about adding companionship time, also on a supervised basis."

A cloud passed over his brother's thin brow. There was no way that Guillermo was going to behave now. He would either have to drug him before the gala or let him blow off some steam somehow. Perhaps it was time to allow Guillermo to stage another fight night; that usually did the trick. He might even let him use Jim Lantana in a fight if the man didn't accept the opportunity he was being given soon. And besides, he didn't like Abigail being around Lantana any longer than necessary. She'd been far too willing to share the private details of her life with him.

He tried to soften his tone as he said, "Why don't you prep the Beast for a fight?"

20 Fight Club

Jim woke up in the small room and wondered how long he had been asleep. There were no clocks for reference, no windows to track the movement of the days. He estimated he had been alone for nearly a week. He received regular meals and his room had its own treadmill built into the far corner. The machine had no clock, only a speedometer. Jim had run until he was exhausted and then slept. He estimated that he was being fed three meals a day, but the meals seemed to come at precise intervals. It could be more like four or five meals per day. And if the food were laced with something to alter his mind, he would have no way to know how long he had been a prisoner.

His only human contact since his meeting Mendelbaum and Abigail Valquist had been with the guards that came and went. The man assigned to guard him was not the same one that he had seen with Mendelbaum the first day. The new guard that had appeared with Mendelbaum's Sergeant at Arms had been introduced to Jim as Zakar al-Rashid. "Please don't screw this up," the big man had said to the new guy in Arabic. Then he'd made eye contact with Jim and said in English, "Be good."

That was it. He had been left in the charge of the skinny Arab who brought him his meals and made sure that he wasn't acting up. This assignment was some kind of punishment, judging from the way he held his shoulders during the long shifts.

Zakar approached the door with a fresh set of linens and asked Jim to sit on the bed at the far end of the room. "Sure thing," Jim said easily. "What did you do to draw this crappy assignment?" he asked in Arabic.

Al-Rashid was clearly surprised to hear his native tongue. "I overreacted to you and your pirate game," he said in English.

Jim smiled. He liked this guy. He was out of place on the ship. He looked like a disc jockey, not a hired gun. He was clearly no researcher. And the gold Rolex on his wrist suggested wealth and vanity. Perfect.

"Mendelbaum has approved limited TV time for you."

"Wonderful," Jim replied without making eye contact.

"It's better than nothing. Besides, if you're getting to watch TV, it means that you are probably not going to be thrown overboard."

“Fair enough,” Jim said with a chuckle. He was right. “How long have I been here?”

“Three days.”

“That’s it? Felt like longer. What’s worth watching on this boat?”

Zakar clicked several buttons on the LCD display and the screen slowly glowed to life. “The fight club, when it’s on. Mendelbaum doesn’t approve of it publicly but he does nothing to stop it either. He needs a way to let the crew release some pressure, you know? Otherwise all Dr. Mean n’ Green lets us watch is the in-house surgery channel.”

“What’s his deal, anyway?”

“You didn’t hear it from me, but rumor is the guy’s a turd-taster.”

“Huh?”

“That hot doctor he keeps around. The cooks say *she’s* the fertilizer for his kelp shakes.”

“Scrumptious.”

Zakar laughed but Jim knew he’d gained a valuable insight.

21 JACQUES' GAMBLE

Jacques moved around his control booth easily. It had been over a week since the pirate attack, and things were back to normal finally. He was most at home in this room. He had access to all the video feeds of the critical areas aboard ship—and to the Hooker Suite. He loved to visit the rest of the ship as well, but he was fully aware of how most of the crew viewed him. But they didn't matter a bit because only the Mendelbaum brothers really appreciated the ship the same way he did, and they allowed him free rein.

He had felt a deep affinity for the ship from the first day he arrived. Its well ordered procedures and intuitively laid out decks, treatment areas, and crew quarters were clearly the work of a superior mind. At least he had felt that way when he had first come aboard. Today, for the first time in his many years here, he was uncomfortable with the ship's direction. Horst needed to take control of his brother. Jacques had been summoned to Guillermo's quarters an hour earlier, but he had seemed to find an unending stream of mundane tasks that needed his attention. When the second summons came, it was less than friendly. It was, in fact, a demand for his presence, the first he had ever received from Guillermo.

He didn't dare ignore the second summons any longer. He left his control booth with a halting gait and began the long walk to Guillermo's private quarters. The first of two giant sealed doors loomed out of the well-lit corridor ahead and he found that he was breathing hard. He slowed his pace and tried to calm himself. His fear of Guillermo was misplaced, he knew that. They had become friends quickly after he had come aboard. But Mendelbaum had decided after the last incident that Guillermo had to be kept quarantined, so Jacques was his only guest now, and that was a bit nerve-wracking.

Jacques stopped in front of the final door to Guillermo's quarters. It was designed to stay sealed if Guillermo were standing too close to the other side of it; that way he could not rush the door when guests entered. The door remained sealed, indicating that Guillermo was thinking of charging it. Jacques entered his access code on the touch screen next to the door and the massive chamber within glowed to life on the small screen. It was very dark and Guillermo was out of sight. Jacques cleared his throat and said, "You know the door won't open if you stand too close to it."

A moment later, Guillermo said, "I know that my own brother is keeping me caged like an animal." His voice was a menacing whisper, and Jacques could not see where it came from. Still, the door did not open.

"Only your brother can override the door. What do you want me to do here?" Jacques asked with more confidence than he felt. He knew why Guillermo had summoned him: He wanted access to something special.

"You know my brother first used the ship as a hospital after I was refused treatment at the hospital in Caracas. The chief doctor believed that I had infected his daughter with AIDS. Horst knew that without treatment I would die. He took me to the *Pura Vida's* infirmary for what he thought would be a temporary stay. A week turned into a month, and then a month turned into a year. Horst outfitted the ship with everything he needed to treat me, and then realized the possibilities. That was twenty years ago. But now he keeps me locked in my cage like a fucking dog!"

"Yes, Guillermo, I know the story by heart. But what you are asking me to do could get me thrown overboard," Jacques said. It was an exaggeration, he knew. But he couldn't stand the idea of what Guillermo wanted. Not this time.

"I am kept here like a freak. My brother has all but cured my sickness, and in the process created the most cutting-edge medical facility in the world. But now I think he has forgotten why he built it in the first place. I think that he has forgotten that I am his brother."

Jacques took a deep breath. He could hear the fear and anger in Guillermo's voice. He was genuinely distraught. Jacques was honored to be an integral part of the ship, and that made the sick feeling in his stomach even harder to bear. Guillermo had summoned him with a brief message. He replayed it now, and it made his skin crawl. Guillermo told him that he found the new batch of girls disappointing. Except for one. Only Kayla would do for him.

Jacques had thought about her non-stop since picking her up ten days before. The girls had only been cleared for administrative visitors since their arrival. Jacques hadn't even had a taste, and he was the whoremaster. Before Guillermo stomped that stupid Angela's head, he had always been given first pick. It was the unwritten rule. If Jacques helped him violate Mendelbaum's ruling, the penalty would be severe. Even he could be replaced if the situation demanded it.

It wasn't his fault that Guillermo had been banned this quarter; it was Horst's decision, but Guillermo had himself convinced that Jacques could help him find a way around the edict. He had never defied Guillermo before. Jacques was flattered that he was the only one he trusted on the whole ship, but as the door finally slid open and the familiar sickly sweet stench of body odor wafted over to him, he felt the blood drain from his face.

"Where will she be tonight?" Guillermo asked finally. He had moved to the far side of his chamber and was standing in his large bathroom, the door half open. Jacques could only see his pale, skinny leg, and he shuddered slightly. Guillermo was looking at his reflection in the massive mirror over his shoulder. Periodically, he glanced at a small hand mirror clenched in his pallid hand. He had seen the photos of the new girls early. The big reveal was not until the quarterly award gala, still ten days off. But Guillermo had full access to Jacques' computer drive and always whetted his appetite well before the girls were cleared.

"You know that Horst gave explicit orders. I can't do anything about it openly." Beads of sweat formed on his brow as Guillermo turned his whitish body toward him. "But when the crew is done with them, I'm sure I can arrange some kind of accidental meeting for you."

Guillermo turned back toward his mirror, ignoring Jacques.

“So, are we on for a fight tonight? Did Horst give the okay?” Jacques regretted his choice of words immediately.

Guillermo turned away from the mirror again. “He did, yes. My own brother gave me permission to live my life the way I choose.”

“Well, I think Brian the Beast is ready for another fight. He needs to earn more credits in a bad way. Dr. Valquist had him removed from her team and placed on orderly duties.”

Guillermo’s body tensed at the mention of Abigail’s name. He turned toward Jacques too quickly and smashed the hand mirror against the edge of his sink. The glass cut the palm of his hand, and a thin line of anemic-looking pink blood flowed freely from the wound. He did nothing to stop it. Instead, he strode out of the bathroom, naked and bleeding, and stepped into his massive suit. The suit’s automated systems secured him in place with heavy straps and connected to his permanently implanted IV hook-up with a sickening hiss. The automated controls hummed to life and he stepped out of the suit’s charging station.

Jacques knew better than to provoke him now. Guillermo’s penis had stiffened slightly, as much as it did anymore, and it looked massive attached to his emaciated body.

Guillermo sucked the wound on his hand, seeming to enjoy the taste. He walked powerfully up to Jacques and leaned into the shorter man's face, his mouth near his ear. "Never mention her name," he whispered. The sound was picked up by the microphone near his mouth and amplified into a horrible wheeze.

Jacques winced as his sore testicles withdrew into his abdomen. "P-perhaps we can have some fun with fight club tonight," Jacques said. "That filthy al-Rashid has been guarding a big man, some American that was captured last week by your brother."

"Is he fit?" Guillermo asked. The wheels were working again. Violence would sate his need for sex for the time being.

"He's a huge man, over six and a half feet tall. And I think your brother wants him for something. He would be most displeased if he were used in a fight, I should imagine," he said, smiling. Jacques felt like he might vomit. He didn't know why he had suggested the prisoner be used in a fight, but he had been panicked. He needed to keep Guillermo's mind off the new girls, at least until after Jacques had tasted the cream. But he didn't want to upset Horst, either.

If Horst found out that he had suggested the fight with the new prisoner, it would be terrible. But what was he going to do to protect Kayla? He couldn't expose Guillermo to Horst. Guillermo would know he had told on him and he would not let Jacques come around anymore. And he knew that Guillermo would love nothing more than to anger his brother, so all in all, this was the best he could hope for.

After Jacques had taken his time with Kayla, Guillermo could do what he pleased with her. But not before. Never before.

"Tell the Beast we need him tonight," Guillermo said. Jacques felt his nerves calm slightly. "And tell that fucking Arab that you'll give him a thousand credits to bring his prisoner to the club tonight."

22 Jim's Beast

Zakar al-Rashid awakened Jim from a deep sleep by massaging the barrel of a Smith and Wesson revolver into his ear. Jim rolled over and stared at his jailor with open confusion. "Yes?"

"How would you like to earn some ship credits?" Zakar whispered.

"Well, considering I am a prisoner and can't use them, I think I'm all set," Jim said, rolling back to the wall.

"Look, you're not gonna to be a prisoner here forever. Mendelbaum is just trying to wear you down a bit before he makes his big pitch."

"You think he really wants me to work for him?"

"Of course. No one else stays alive as long as you have unless he needs them for something. You're gonna want ship credit, believe me. Guillermo made Jacques give me a thousand credits to bring you to the fight club tonight. If you beat the Beast I'll split the credits with you."

"Fight club?" He pretended to be too groggy to understand, but this was good. His jailor was offering him an unauthorized tour of the ship and a chance at escape. It was probably a trap, but he would have to see it through. He feigned a yawn, stretched and said, "Lead the way."

Jim stepped out of his cell behind Zakar and considered breaking his neck on the spot. It would have been easy; Zakar looked thin-boned and sinewy. But Jim had no idea where he was on the ship or where the ship was in the ocean or how to contact help. Best to take this free tour and think things through. Fight club? This was unexpected. He followed him down the brightly lit hallway past rows of rooms just like the one he had been in. He was not in a special prison; he was just being kept in one of the secure hospital suites.

Zakar stopped in front of the bulkhead that led from the hospital center and waited. He removed his radio and clicked it on near his mouth. "We're at the hospital exit."

"Processing," came a grainy, French-accented reply. Zakar glanced at Jim. He had security clearance to move where he pleased, but Jim did not. "Stand a few feet away from the door, the Worm is loading your RF chip data into the door controls." Jim did as he was told. A second later the bulkhead slid open noiselessly and revealed a long, dark corridor with a low, rounded ceiling. Zakar stepped in and the lights clicked on automatically, lighting the corridor ten feet at a time.

God, this place was massive. Jim could see nearly five hundred feet down the corridor and closed his eyes against the feeling of vertigo that crept in. The corridor was bisected every thirty feet or so by bulkheads that led off into the rest of the ship.

"Coming?" Zakar asked over his shoulder.

Jim ducked under the bulkhead and fell into step with him. "Where're we headed?"

"Reactor, but don't talk, okay?"

Jim nodded and stayed silent. He began to commit their route to memory by quickly recalling each step they had taken so far. His mental map was just about complete as they stopped in front of a well-marked bulkhead and Zakar clicked on his radio once again. "We're at the main reactor hatch, over." Jim recognized the three-bladed yellow-and-black radiation-warning symbol pasted on either side of the entrance. The door slid silently away and Jim entered. When he turned toward Zakar, he realized that he had not followed him into the chamber. He was smiling at Jim as the door sealed.

Jim turned back into the dim room just in time to see a massive man charging toward him. He recognized the angry assistant that Abigail had summoned with Katarina. So this must be "the Beast." He sidestepped the onslaught by ducking behind a rusted steel beam, forcing his pursuer to come to a halt and grope for him, looking first one way and then the other as Jim played possum. He used the confusion to drop into a crouch near a deep shadow at the base of the beam and wait for The Beast to step around.

The second he saw him, Jim popped to his feet and landed an uppercut squarely on the Beast's jaw. He followed with a short jab to the Beast's eye and ducked out of sight. After watching the video of his father's crime, hitting someone sent a surge of relief through him that made him want to do it again. They were quick shots, intended to stun his opponent while he took in more of his surroundings. The fight had begun the moment he had been led into the large room; he had barely had time to take in the yellow-and-black radiation hazard signs posted on every wall but one. That must be the actual reactor. It looked innocent enough; it was a sealed black dome the size of a typical single family home. It was secured to the deck with one-inch bolts at regular intervals.

When he glanced back toward his adversary, he truly appreciated his name. He wore a loose-fitting

Patriots sweatshirt that had been cut off at the shoulders, exposing his steroid-enhanced biceps and triceps. He reminded Jim of the men he had seen in strong-man competitions who liked to roll boulders up hills and carry car axels on their shoulders for fun.

Jim had been trained in hand-to-hand combat at the CIA school in Langley. His real skill had always been with firearms and interrogation, but live action was nothing new to him. He had never needed to fight an opponent hand-to-hand; he had never lost control of his weapon and was among the CIA's deadliest shots.

But here he was, face-to-face with Brian the Beast. The man circled him carefully, measuring his steps. He had not thrown any punches yet, and his left eye showed an angry red mark where Jim had hit him. He seemed to be waiting for Jim to make another move. Jim obliged him by feigning a groin kick and instead lurching in with his elbow. He caught the Beast in the bridge of the nose and he crumpled. This was going to be easy.

Jim stepped in for a closer look at his downed opponent and realized his mistake. The Beast had lured him over a loop of rope. Before Jim could pick up his foot the Beast rolled to his side and jerked the end, firmly lassoing Jim's ankle. With a firm yank the Beast pulled Jim's right leg into the air and moved in for a gut punch. The force of the punch was amazing. Even seeing it coming did nothing to help him weather the blow. He sucked hard for a breath, but was knocked back with a second blow to his chin.

Jim fell to the floor, dazed. The Beast tossed his end of the rope over an exposed blue pipe that ran the length of the chamber and pulled Jim up into the air. He tied the loose end off and left Jim dangling three feet above the rusted steel deck.

Jim recovered his senses long enough to know that he was spinning in the air when he came face-to-face, albeit upside down, with the horrible, bloodied visage of his opponent. The Beast smiled at him before winding up for another brutal left hook to Jim's head. Another like that and he would lose consciousness.

The Beast seemed well aware of this fact as he chose another straight right to Jim's kidneys. The pain spread through him from the impact point on his left all the way to his right flank and left him swinging like a side of beef. Through the quickly descending veil of a blackout, he saw the door handle of the black-domed reactor looming toward him. He reached feebly for it and missed by several inches. The Beast met him at the end of the arc with another glancing blow to his head.

This one was meant to inflict pain, not to knock him out. The Beast was playing.

Jim could see the handle of the door growing closer again though his swollen eye. He reached again and this time grabbed on. He hung in mid-air, horizontal to the floor, and kicked as hard as he could at the rope tied around his foot. The force of the movement was not enough to free him, but it did loosen the knot the Beast had tied to the far wall. Unfortunately, it also made him lose his grip on the door handle.

The Beast had changed tactics when he saw that Jim was hanging onto the door. He was stepping forward when Jim lost his grip and didn't react in time to the wildly spinning man flying toward him. Jim hoped for a lucky shot as he swung his fists together in a sledgehammer arc and was greeted by a satisfying blow to the Beast's genitals. The Beast crumpled in pain and the knot he had tied gave way. Both men lay motionless for a moment.

Jim recovered first, but he was ten feet away from the Beast, who rose to his feet as Jim circled him. The two men locked arms in a tight grapple, jockeying for position. Jim twisted his shoulders, released his right hand, and brought his elbow down on the Beast's exposed ulna, snapping the smaller of his wrist bones like dry kindling. The Beast yelped in pain and stumbled back. Jim pushed his advantage, punching him in the face with short jabs in rapid succession. The Beast tried to jump back, but tripped over the rope and went down hard. The back of his head landed on one of the floor bolts securing the reactor with a sound like a ripe cantaloupe. He convulsed violently at first, and then slowly began shaking.

The twitching stopped a moment later.

23 Hospital Room 31G

"I am freezing your credits completely for this quarter," Mendelbaum said.

Zakar blanched. Only the creature comforts made this monstrous ship remotely bearable. He knew that getting Lantana to the fight the night before was out of line, but this freak was going too far. His uncle couldn't keep him here any longer. He would speak to him as soon as the sun was up in Riyadh and plead with him, again, to let him leave.

"But Mr. Mendelbaum, I was only doing what your brother told me to do. He gave me a thousand credits for bringing Lantana to him for the match. No one has ever gotten this badly hurt. How was I supposed to know he would kill the Beast?"

"Brian was a valuable team member," Mendelbaum said. He glanced at Jim Lantana lying on his gurney, through the thick glass, and took a deep breath. "And call me *Doc*tor or *S*ir." He turned back to Zakar. "This man was your prisoner, your charge. All you had to do was make sure he was eating and wasn't going to try to hurt himself. That was it. Instead, you snuck him out of his quarters and allowed him to participate in an illegal fight in which he beat Brian to death. How do you expect me to react, Zakar?"

"I understand, but taking all my credits—"

"It's already done. You are removed from any active duty. You will confine yourself to your quarters and to the dining areas during meal times. And don't worry, I have personally requested that your uncle remove you when we are in contact range."

Zakar couldn't repress his smile. He was getting off the fucking boat! He had a little of his own money socked away, so he wouldn't let his uncle dictate his life to him again. Maybe one day he could track down Kayla and spend some time with her. He wiped the smile from his face as Mendelbaum looked at him and only shook his head as he moved back into the secure hospital room.

Abigail stood next to Jim and looked up when Mendelbaum entered. His breath caught in his throat when she made eye contact with him. Her icy stare still did that to him, even after all this time. "How is he?" he asked.

"He'll live. They've implanted a permanent IV hook-up to his spinal cord so that he can be medicated properly whether he wants to be or not."

"Looks like you won't be working with Brian any longer," Mendelbaum said.

"Thank God."

"A little respect for the departed, if you please," he said.

"His nickname was the Beast, but they should have just called him the monster."

"Brian was a talented researcher. I know you didn't agree with his methods, but his results were beyond question." Mendelbaum said. "Someday we may be able to bring him back, but for now, the results he achieved will rest with him in the cryo-tanks."

"You'll let this crew do anything if it brings results," she said, glancing back at Jim. "The monster lacerated this man's liver slightly; he's going to need to stay under for a while."

"Does the surgeon think he'll recover?" Mendelbaum asked, ignoring her impertinence.

"Ask him yourself."

"Page me when he wakes up," Mendelbaum said as he left without another word.

Jim opened his eyes slowly and blinked several times. He seemed to be dreaming but he felt awake. An angelic form hovered over him, adjusting dials behind his head. The fog cleared slowly from his vision and he thought he recognized the beautiful woman he had seen with Mendelbaum. He struggled to recall her name until he felt her soft hand on his forehead. Abigail.

"How long have I been out?" he asked.

She seemed startled that he was awake. "Less than twelve hours." Her voice was kind but firm.

He tried to sit up and felt a searing pain in his gut like a hot knife.

"Try not to move," she said.

He stared into her face, trying to gauge her. She didn't look away. Odd. The normal reaction would have been to avert her eyes. He needed a more visceral reaction to gauge her.

"So you're the one that tortures the kids, like the boy called Noah?" Jim asked.

Her look could have cut through steel. It quickly clouded behind tears, and she turned away from him. Interesting. She had given a genuine emotional response. She was so goddamn pretty it was hard not to stare at her. He fought it and held her gaze. Her lips twisted around something she wanted to say, but nothing came out. She didn't want to lie. Why?

24 Abigail's Gambit

Jim had never eaten this well, ever. At first he had refused the food, but soon found it impossible to resist. Eating was his only distraction, and once he tasted the offerings, he couldn't help but look forward to each new dish. The guards brought his food at the same time every day. He was relatively sure that they were not poisoning him. Each morning started with the delivery of a handwritten parchment describing in detail what was on the menu for the day. A nice but unnecessary touch; he would have eaten his own socks, he was so bored.

The menu was surprising. Roast quail with red wine reduction sauce, braised beef with sweet Lingonberry glaze and truffle-infused new potatoes. Extravagance at every meal appeared to be the standard for the ship. Breakfast was poached eggs topped with hollandaise sauce and caviar.

He was allowed out of his cell every two days for an hour while it was cleaned. Like clockwork, a member of ship security came onto his screen and explained that he was to stick his hands into the opening in the door to be cuffed. He complied. Fawwaz al-Barq was personally checking in on him, but several other security team members had control of his daily oversight.

When al-Barq looked at Jim, there was unconcealed scorn. It was the only reminder he was a prisoner. Al-Barq would answer no questions and rarely appeared after the first day. But he clearly wanted to kill Jim. Only al-Barq would lead him into the other cell. He would only be left in the support cell for an hour at a time. When he was taken back to his own, much larger cell, it was always spotless. Perfumed silk sheets, fresh and new every time. He had begun ripping small holes in the sheets to see if the same ones were ever used. Never. Always brand new silk linens. Every surface of the room was wiped clean. It was actually rather nice, and it reminded him of a time when and Sharon had first lived together.

At last count, he had been served thirty-seven meals. He divided the meals by three and guessed he had been on the ship for about twelve days. He had not seen Abigail since his last terse words to her, and he was beginning to miss her terribly. There was no reason for her to visit him, but he desperately hoped that she would. He would have to make a move to escape soon. He might have to kill a guard and take his weapon to do it. He hoped that wouldn't be al-Barq. That might not be possible.

The waiting was unbearable.

He was awakened from a brief nap by the familiar ping from his LCD screen indicating a visitor. His mouth watered in anticipation of the upcoming meal. He rolled away from the wall and wiped his lips. Instead of the usual bored-looking guard, though, he was staring at Abigail. There was no sound. Just Dr. Abigail Valquist standing alone, staring back at him. She looked terrified. She held a finger to her lips, and then held up a dry erase board like those used by teachers. Jim didn't speak. She wrote the word SILENCE and underlined it. Under it she wrote STORM APPROACHING, BE READY. Then she pushed a button on the large console next to her and the screen faded.

Jim spent the next day waiting for night. He ate his food but didn't notice how delectable it was. This was surely some kind of trap. If she were foolish enough to open his cell, he would capture her and use her to make his escape. The image of Dr. Mendelbaum came on the screen in front of him and cut his thoughts short. He hadn't seen his green-tinted captor in days. His cold appeared to have worsened. His nose was red and angry-looking, and he wiped it gently before saying anything.

“Good morning,” Mendelbaum said thickly as he tucked his silk handkerchief into his pocket. It sounded like anything but a good morning for him. When Jim didn’t reply, he continued, “An unauthorized communication was made to you last night.”

“Oh?” Jim said.

“Ship security has access to the audio but not the video. Nothing was said, but nonetheless someone on my staff is communicating with you without authorization. This is your chance to tell me who it was, or at least what he looked like. I will uncover the breach, and when I do I will have several options open to me. I can confine the offender to quarters until a suitable port is found, or I can throw him overboard. The choice is yours. Now, who was it?”

“Zakar al-Rashid,” Jim said without hesitation. “Go easy on the guy; I think it was an accident.” Jim’s gamble paid off. Mendelbaum’s face went white, and then flushed. He removed his handkerchief and scrubbed at his nose.

“I would like you to meet your wife,” Mendelbaum said. He lifted the three year-old Jim had met weeks before, Katarina, onto his shoulder. When Jim didn't respond he said, "We took samples from Sharon while she was aboard. This girl is genetically identical to her. Although we have not completely perfected the technique for uploading her memories, we have them all stored aboard the ship's mainframe. Would you like to chat with her?"

"With who?" Jim asked, finally.

"With Sharon, of course."

"That's impossible, she's dead."

"Not nearly so dead as you might think. Don't give up hope, Jim. You're aboard the *Pura Vida*," he said with a smile. "We give hope to the hopeless. We step in where society inevitably fails. We are proof that science cannot be regulated; people can only delay its progress for awhile."

Jim stared at the child Mendelbaum held in his arms, and knew that he was telling the truth. He was looking at a clone of his poor dead wife. The thought of escape vaporized.

25 SHARON/KATARINA

Jim's screen came slowly to life, and he saw with a horror that he was looking at a clean hospital room like the one he had watched his father in. Katarina stared back at him from the monitor as a researcher hooked electrodes to her small head. It was the upload program.

"Don't do it!" There was no response. "I know you can hear me," he yelled. "I will do whatever you want. Don't hurt this child!"

The scene in the examination room continued unchanged. The researcher was finished hooking the nodes to Katarina and moved out of the room. There was a pause. Then, suddenly, Katarina grasped at her head and screamed. Her voice was not carried to Jim, but he could see that she was howling in pain. Hatred like he had never known rose in his stomach as he drove his fist into the LCD screen, destroying it.

"No, not that one," Abigail said.

Mendelbaum had been watching her on his balcony for the last hour as clouds gathered far out to sea. A storm was approaching, but they would steam south and avoid the worst of it. If they hadn't been forced to push back the quarterly gala and VIP tour because of the attack, they would have been well out of its path by now.

He was glad that he had never taken her by force. She looked at him with a mix of rage and horror most of the time, but she was beginning to soften. When he let her have more time with Edvard, she could see how he felt. She knew that he hated picking his clothing for the gala. He had told her that he was going to get dressed when she had appeared behind him. She would only help him pick his clothes when she was in an especially generous mood.

"This?" he asked, donning a brown-and-yellow cape over his usual silver tracksuit.

"You can't wear brown and yellow with a silver tracksuit," she said matter-of-factly.

His heartbeat increased with the exchange. He was clueless when it came to color coordinating and she knew it. She would almost never speak to him unless he spoke to her first. She entered his walk-in closet, brushing past him. The contact sent a tingle up his leg. She stopped in front of his long rack of similar tracksuits, one hand on her chin.

She stood still and tilted her head to the side. He reached out to stroke her hair, expecting her to move. She didn't. It was so soft. He leaned in and she did not pull away. He pressed his body to her gently and inhaled deeply from her hair. It smelled of sandalwood. She had never let him get this close to her voluntarily.

"This one," she whispered as she selected a dark blue tracksuit with a low-cut neck that displayed the tops of his pectoral muscles. He realized that it captured the colors in the cape he had selected perfectly. This was going to be an extra-special gala.

He pulled on the tracksuit and looked at himself in the mirror. His swastika charm was clearly visible, a fact he did not care for. It was not that he minded if the crew knew who he was or what he believed, it was that he didn't want to draw attention to this particular charm. He took it off and reached for the pocket of the pants. They didn't have one. He turned and looked in the mirror at his reflection and Abigail standing behind him admiring the ensemble. He wouldn't change this outfit for the world. He crossed the room to his bed and punched in the code to the drawer. It slid open noiselessly and he placed the charm carefully inside.

He turned back to Abigail and smiled at her. "Let's pay a visit to Mr. Lantana," he said, extending his hand.

She took it willingly, and he blushed a deep purple. This would be a fine gala, indeed.

It was Jacques' favorite night of the quarter, but he couldn't seem to get in the mood. The Award Gala was starting in ten minutes. After their mandatory waiting period, most of the girls were cleared for duty and it was his honor to introduce them one by one to the crew before casino night started. But that fucking Zakar had caused a huge delay with this screw-up. The whole crew had been waiting for weeks for a taste because ship tradition dictated that the new girls be unveiled at the conclusion of the award ceremony, not a second sooner.

All but two of the girls had passed the health exam. Both were infected with HIV. He entered the Hooker Suite proudly, like a feudal lord come to check on his stables.

"You two," he said pointing at a bored-looking blonde and her brunette friend. "You're going to wait in a special area. The rest of you, please get ready for your stage performances." Jacques had explained the process to them earlier in the afternoon. Each girl would be shown via closed circuit camera to the assembled guests in the Great Ballroom between dinner and desert. "You have been given the order of appearances, so be sure to stick to them," he said.

The test results on the two girls meant there were only eight women to be put into service. The bidding for all would be more intense than usual; the men had waited for pussy for way too long.

He sealed the room where the infected women were to be kept in isolation for the duration of their stay. They were fed and allowed to exercise, but they were not allowed near the crew—a pity.

A smile spread across his pale face as a brilliant thought occurred to him. He wondered if there wasn't some way to send one of the infected girls to al-Rashid. God, would that be a sweet turn of events. But Horst would probably have him thrown overboard if he found out. The nasty little Arab was the sheik's flesh and blood; there was just no killing him.

He didn't know why he had chosen to come back to the Hooker Suite before tonight's gala. He had already prepped the girls; they were perfectly ready to go. After each one was introduced at the gala tonight, the silent auction would begin, and by midnight, the first crewmembers would be enjoying the girls while the others gambled. There was nothing new about the system; he and Guillermo had devised it and it worked perfectly. Horst approved, it kept commerce alive on the ship, and kept the nearly all-male crew happy and entertained without causing a riot.

Bringing ten hookers aboard to service a crew of two hundred men took careful planning and constant vigilance. Yet the little Arab creep managed to get access to the girls early every time. They didn't even expect payment from him. Jacques had watched the security footage of the last time he had snuck in with his cousin's security pass card. He had probably even gotten his camel-fucking cousin's permission to do it. And yet all he had done was chat with the girls. He hadn't even gotten off while he was there, and he hadn't been the least bit scared when Jacques had confronted him in the suite. He had sniggered and left to cover his cousin's security shift. Jacques smiled, thinking back on how terrible that had gone for him, with the botched response to the pirate attack.

Jacques had witnessed al-Rashid's impressive sexual prowess many times, that was not what bothered him. It was that the little turd seemed to enjoy the girls' company and they enjoyed his. This last episode had been just him and Kayla. They didn't do anything but talk and laugh. She had seemed relaxed for the first time since getting to the ship.

That was why he was here, he realized. He needed to see Kayla, to explain to the little bitch that she had no business talking to men aboard the ship until she had been cleared to do so by him and Horst. He wanted desperately to beat her, but he hadn't decided how to do it yet. He couldn't bruise her before the bidding started, but after he won the bidding for her tonight, he would put his mark on her, of that much he was certain.

"Where's Kayla?" he barked. One of the girls motioned to the sleeping area. "All of you out. Tell her I want to see her now." The girls exited nervously to the sleeping quarters to await their turn on the stripper stage.

Kayla entered the grand sitting room and stopped when she saw him. She turned around to leave the way she had come, but he yelled at her, "Stop! I want a word with you."

"I don't have to talk to you," she said.

"Is that what that miserable little Arab fucker told you?" he said, spittle flying from his mouth. He was angrier than he had imagined.

"Yes, that's what Zakar told me."

The way she said his name made his stomach burn. She seemed to realize what he was thinking and she smiled. “Zakar says that you are not in charge. You’re more like the janitor.”

Something about the sound of his name coming from her lips made him want to scream. He picked up the bottle of Vueve Clicquot vintage champagne from the ice bucket and ripped at the cork. It shot off in a carbonated spray that he staunched with his lips, oblivious to the bubbly liquid that spilled from the corners of his mouth.

Kayla laughed at him and walked out of the room. Jacques gulped at the bottle and then slammed it down on the soft cherry table. He sat down for a moment and stared after her into the area that housed the stripper stage. His hands were shaking as he stood up to follow her. He needed to hurt her without leaving a mark, and something he had heard from that bastard Jean-Pierre came to mind. He turned and picked up the bottle of champagne.

26 Second Quarter Gala and Award Banquet

The quarterly dinner and award ceremony in the Great Ballroom was supposed to be a joyous night aboard the ship. But with half the crew sick from the unknown virus, spirits were subdued. Zakar was usually bored to tears by the gala, but since Mendelbaum had confined him to his quarters, this was the only public event he could attend. He would usually have tried to sneak out after Mendelbaum introduced the crew to the newest batch of girls, but before he started to hand out extra ship credits and awards to individuals. He had never personally been given special recognition for anything and couldn't stand the extra hour of talk from Mendelbaum.

He would usually sneak back into the gala around the time the casino night began, but since he didn't have any credits, there was no point tonight. He was stuck aboard for at least another week. So he sat in the corner of the massive room picking at the last patch of dry skin on his chin. He hadn't shaved in three days because there was nothing more Mendelbaum could take from him. At least the dry skin was finally going away. He scanned the room for Jacques again. The creepy little man was still absent. He never missed these stupid dinners. That wanker Jacques liked to sit in the front row and clap vigorously for each ship award. Zakar would never forgive his uncle for making him live aboard the ship for this long, but at least it was nearly over. What would he do once he was off? He smiled, knowing that this was the last gala he would have to attend.

It was time to go back to the family. He took a deep breath. The money he had saved up was not nearly enough to live the life he was accustomed to. Only his uncle could untie the purse strings to make that happen. He would have to go back to Saudi Arabia and see the old man. And undoubtedly he would have to listen to a lecture for the meddling family mufti who had been whispering in his uncle's ear about Zakar's love of the West since his college days. But this ship was a worse punishment than his uncle could have imagined for him.

Mendelbaum droned on about an especially tedious genetic test that a researcher had perfected and a thought occurred to Zakar. Once it had taken root in his mind he couldn't ignore it. It was something about the way Jacques had looked at Kayla that afternoon. He rose from his seat and did his usual disappearing act.

Jacques fumbled with the condom for a moment before discarding it. He had waited too long for her. It was worth the risk of bare-backing a whore. She smelled so clean and she was so vulnerable. He took another long drink from the half empty bottle and stared down at her.

She was not like any girl he had ever had. She was still crying a little from the punishment he had inflicted on the soles of her feet.

Her whimpering only heightened his need to feel her around his shaft. He held his erection with one hand and forced her legs apart with the other. He nearly ejaculated on her stomach as he massaged the tip of his penis on her pubic hair. She screamed as he touched the lips of her vagina. She was his. He closed his eyes as he pressed into her wall of resistance. His second stroke was harder and he felt the first moist embrace of her.

A dull click resonated in his left ear. He glanced over but only saw the flash of a muzzle before his world darkened forever.

"The award this quarter belongs to the cryogenics team for their perfection of the super-cooled gel used in the tanks," Mendelbaum said from the podium. "They have developed a mechanism to prevent the loss of energy associated with deep cooling of fluids that has all but eliminated the need for constant monitoring of the cryonics tanks. Temperature fluctuation within the electro-statically charged gel has been reduced to nearly zero." Even he didn't seem that excited by the news. It was a well-known, but little talked about, fact that the cryonics project was his least favorite aboard. Morale was at an all-time low for the ship to have produced no other worthwhile results.

Mendelbaum looked at the reactor table again. "As Jacques is not here to unveil the newest entertainment, I will do my best to fill in for him. Mr. al-Barq, please begin the live feed from the suite."

There was a moment of calm expectation in the Great Room as the IMAX screen descended from the ceiling. It clicked into place and the projector glowed slowly to life as the light from the grand chandelier slowly faded. Mendelbaum picked up the remote used to control the video feeds. "Forgive me for not being able to refer to the newest ladies by name; as you know, this job is usually performed by our zealous friend, Jacques."

He clicked the feed labeled “Hooker Suite” and dropped the controller as the image materialized. Jacques lay slumped onto the camera, half his head missing. Through the gore smeared onto the fixed camera lens, the assembly could see a lanky, bearded man helping a woman to her feet.

27 Abigail's Fire

Abigail looked at her watch a final time before setting out. The barometric pressure gauge indicated that the storm they were steering around was a large one. It was now or never. The gala had been horrific, but she couldn't say that she was sorry for what had happened to Jacques. After the scene in the Hooker Suite, Mendelbaum had assembled his security team and ordered the doctors and support staff back to their rooms until further notice.

She focused on the task at hand. Mendelbaum's suite was still a five-minute jog from the galley. She stopped running and took a breath to try to steel her nerves for what she must do. If she failed, Edvard would die. She exhaled deeply and took another long breath to fight her rising panic. It wasn't helping much.

This part of the plan had never been the strongest. She and Phineas knew that. *Had* known that, she reminded herself. She still couldn't believe that he was gone. The items Phineas had left her were still right where he told her they would be. A can of kerosene, a Bic lighter, and a hatchet were all she would need.

Phineas had injected the water supply with the Norovirus they had developed, and everyone aboard was infected even though they hadn't all become violently sick yet. Only a few aboard would have any natural immunity. She and Phineas had taken the antidote, and she had given it to Edvard and as many of the other children as she could. They had gotten through half the kids and, fortunately, Katarina was one of them. She should have known what Phineas was planning to do. He had let himself be recorded to keep Mendelbaum's attention off her. She would not let his sacrifice be for nothing. She took a deep breath as she approached Mendelbaum's quarters. The door sensor recognized her and slid open with a hiss.

She walked into his room without permission for the first time. She resisted the urge to spit on something, anything. What she had in store for him was far better. Hefting the small ax in one hand, she moved to the wooden bedside table. The drawer was locked, but Phineas had designed it. He knew that the only thing protecting Mendelbaum's coveted override key was an inch of varnished cherry wood. The trick had been getting him to leave it there at the right time. She swung the ax in a clean arc and felt it bite deeply into the highly polished wood with a satisfying thunk. Six blows later, and a hole as large as her hand was visible. She removed the hideous swastika and stared at it for a moment. She had watched Mendelbaum work the puzzle hundreds of times over the last two years. She knew the combination as well as he did.

She realized that she still held the small hatchet in her right hand. She wondered what to do with it as her gaze found the long kelp tank that divided the bedroom from the bathroom. She cocked her arm back and threw the small hatchet as hard as she could. The corner of the blade made contact with the middle of the twenty-foot glass panel and ricocheted back toward her. A hole no larger than a dime was left where it hit and a thin stream of green water sprayed out onto the fine carpet. She watched as a crack danced its way from the hole to the edge of the glass, and then in one mass of water and glass shards, the tank shattered, grimy water and kelp streaming out in all directions. She jumped back from the approaching filth and got on top of the massive bed in the center of the room.

Abigail used the entire can of kerosene to douse the silk sheets. When she finished, she stepped off the bed to the piano bench stuck in front of the baby grand Mendelbaum liked to play while he stared at her. She took the lighter out of her pocket. She balanced on the bench and reached carefully across the bed, the flame shook in her hand as she held it to the corner of the exposed silk sheet. This was a tricky part: If the fire worked, it would create a perfect distraction. The problem was that it was equally possible that the fire would not burn hot enough and would be put out too quickly, leaving her insufficient time for the rest of the plan. Of course, the worst possible outcome would be a fire that could not be controlled. One that gutted the ship and didn't give her enough time to put her new plan into place: spring James Lantana from his cell and rescue the children.

Abigail jumped back from the flames onto the top of the piano, realizing her blunder in staying distracted for those few precious seconds. The fire had spread quickly into the down of the soaked bed and as the horrible stench of burning feathers and foul water filled her nostrils, she choked and nearly became ill. She held her sleeve over her mouth and jumped down to the soggy carpet. As she ran toward the door in a half crouch, she reached out and grabbed the small hatchet. She felt light-headed as she stumbled toward the hatch that led back through the kitchen galley and into the holding cells. The general fire alarm began to wail, and she forced herself to run.

Zakar held onto the railing of the platform that connected the giant internal dock to the *Eir*. He was feeling less than steady. A stiff gale had blown in and was driving ten-foot waves into the prow of the tanker. The big boat was rocking back and forth in the waves. He knew that there was no turning back now. When he left the gala he hadn't thought through what he would do if he caught Jacques. And then when he saw what the bastard was doing…

He had never killed anyone before. The scene was painted on the insides of his eyelids. Vomit rose in his throat without warning. He retched over the deck rail and stared at the water.

"Thank you," Kayla said, the first words she'd spoken since he had saved her.

"For what?" Zakar replied. "They will come for us both. We can't outrun them in the yacht. They will fire on us as soon as we embark."

In a moment of clarity, Zakar had taken the key card that operated the *Eir* off Jacques' lifeless body. He had planned to send Kayla off alone and face his punishment. She hadn't told him who she really was, but he didn't care. His cousin would not allow Mendelbaum to murder him, but Fawwaz could not protect him forever. His palm was slick on the rail.

She leaned into him and kissed him on the cheek before boarding the yacht. The look of relief on her face was unmistakable. She was no hooker. “My name is Christiana Facchinetti.”

It was then that he heard the general fire alarm, and he made the decision to try to escape with her. “I’m coming with you,” he said.

She reached out and took his hand. “Do you know how to pilot this thing?”

“No clue. But we have to get out of here. Mendelbaum will have you thrown overboard, or else he will give you to his brother. Jacques was his favorite, you know.”

“I grew up around boats. Nothing this big, but the principles are the same.”

“My cousin will try to protect us, but Mendelbaum can do anything when he’s angry.”

“We better get out of here now,” she said, boarding the yacht.

She moved into the main pilothouse and began pressing the controls that activated the engine. An LED computer screen came slowly to life and asked for a pass code. Zakar read the message and removed Jacques’ ID card from his pocket. A moment later the engine came to life and a command prompt appeared on the screen. It read ACTIVATE OUTER HATCH? Christiana pressed the YES button on the touch screen and watched in amazement as the entire rear panel of the tanker began to slide back into itself. A moment later, ten-foot wind-driven waves rolled in at them and rocked the yacht violently.

The gaping hole in the rear of the tanker allowed tens of thousands of gallons of seawater to flood into the chamber. Far more water than the pumps could handle was quickly filling the internal dock. A second alarm, this one much louder than the general fire alarm began to wail. They had triggered the ship's scuttle alert.

Christiana engaged the *Eir's* massive twin engines and began to move slowly backward in a right hand arc. A moment later she had the vessel aimed toward the exit fifty feet ahead. The boat pitched and rolled inside the dock and she corrected hard to the left to avoid smashing into an internal wall. It was then that they heard the first guards.

Zakar looked back at the main entry door where five armed men stood staring in bewilderment at the scene. "Move it woman!" he yelled.

The first volley of gunfire from the guards broke out several windows in the pilothouse. Christiana and Zakar crouched down and she steered from her memory of where the exit should have been. The boat pitched forward hard as a giant wave surged into the flooded dock. The gunfire stopped as the guards were overcome by the wave and sucked into the deep water of the dock. The wave rolled all the way to the back of the chamber with a huge splash and began its return trip, carrying the yacht on its back. Suddenly they were in the open ocean in the middle of a terrible storm.

28 The Escape

Jim listened to the fire alarm wail for several minutes before his newly assigned guard finally appeared on his smashed LCD screen. "There is nothing to worry about," the disjointed image called over the wailing of several alarms. "A small fire has been detected in Dr. Mendelbaum's quarters; we are locking down the ship as a precaution and dispatching all security personnel to fire-mitigation posts. I'm going to join them, so I'll need to cuff you to your bunk."

"Whatever you say, Chief," Jim said. Then he saw that Abigail Valquist was standing just out of the guard's sight, holding what appeared to be a small hand weapon. "Just a second," Jim yelled as the guard was turning to grab a pair of restraints off a hook on the wall. "What about my lunch?"

"Oh, right," the guard said, turning away from the restraints and back toward Jim's tray of food.

Abigail saw her opportunity and rushed the guard with the hatchet held high over her head. She brought it down backward, using the dull side of the tool as a hammer. The blow was vicious but not deadly.

"Nice," Jim said. "But how are you going to open my door?"

Abigail removed a large silver swastika from around her neck and began bending the arms first one way, then another, as if working a Rubik's Cube. A moment later the swastika slid apart on hidden hinges to reveal a large red button. Abigail hesitated a moment. She looked up at Jim, smiled, and pressed the button.

Nothing happened for a few seconds. Then the annoying scuttle alarm stopped, followed a second later by the general fire alarm. Then the lights darkened completely and his fractured LCD screen went black. Jim felt a surge of adrenaline at being alone in the dark. As the background noise of the ship's systems faded away, a deep, loaded silence fell. It seemed like minutes passed.

"Abigail," he called. Nothing. He could hear the fear in his voice. His room was completely black. He found the wall with his hands and steadied himself. For the first time he was acutely aware of the rocking of the ocean. It was as if he had been insulated from the movement of the water for the last month and was suddenly in a violent storm. He used the wall in front of him for balance and tried to regain his composure.

Another eternity passed, and he felt like he might throw up. Then he saw it. At first he thought his eyes were playing tricks on him as a crack of red light appeared along a length of the wall in front of him. It took him several eye blinks to realize that he was leaning on the door, which was being opened manually. He realized that he was free as the door swung inward on well-oiled hinges and the red emergency lights flooded into his room.

"We must hurry," Abigail said as they stepped carefully around Jim's delectable lunch salad and the unconscious guard on the floor.

"How do we get off the ship?" Jim asked.

"It's not that simple," Abigail said as she punched a code into the thick, stainless steel door.

"What's not that simple?" Jim asked.

"We have to get my son and Katarina first."

Jim couldn't speak. His guts felt like water and his mouth went dry. Katarina. They had uploaded Sharon's memories into her.

"We have to get below decks. I know where we can hide," Abigail said.

Jim followed her without a word, moving as if in a trance.

29 REINHART

Mendelbaum entered his fire-damaged quarters and stared around in disbelief. He had been told that the devastation was complete, but he was still shaken by the actual sight of it. Everything had gone so wrong so quickly. Was it only yesterday that he and Abigail had stood in his closet and she had picked out his gala outfit? He realized that tears were streaming down his face and wiped at them with the sleeve of his dark blue tracksuit. He glanced around, noting the smashed kelp tank that housed his prized juice; it smelled somewhat sweet to him, even over the burned feathers. Then he stopped cold when he saw his bedside table. It was hacked open, the medallion clearly missing from inside. It was at that second that his ship went completely dark around him.

In the pitch darkness he felt the first waves rock the ship, side to side, as she drifted off course; then the dull glow of the emergency lights engaged in the corners of his room. They were on reserve power now. He removed the radio clipped to his belt and whispered, "XO, go to my brother's chambers and manually unlock them," An acknowledgment came a second later. "Alert him that he will be leading a search team.

Be sure to tell him which frequency we are using," He said. "And tell him that the code to unlock the exoskeleton attachment for his survival suit is our father's name."

He sloshed though the remains of his bedroom toward the small spiral staircase in the far corner that he had never been forced to use. The sealed hatch above led directly to the main control bridge overhead. A moment later he stood on the bridge of the command deck, bathed in red light. "How long until the reactor comes back online?" he asked the helmsman.

"It will take about half an hour to restart once the team reaches the reactor. We should have full operation within twelve hours," the helmsman said.

Mendelbaum clicked on his handheld radio. "Al-Barq? Come in." Without waiting for a response, he said, "Can you stop the flooding from the outer hatch?"

"Negative," Al-Barq shouted to be heard over the noise around him. "The *Eir* damaged several of the actuators that close the hatch on her way out. The most we can do is get it about three-quarters closed. I've slowed the rate of fill to a point that the pumps are balancing things out, but we need to bring in additional pumps to get ahead of the flood. We've sealed off the entire chamber from the rest of the ship, but we cannot divert any more power from the hospital. The emergency generators are at full capacity and reserve batteries will not sustain this for more than another hour. We cannot achieve full speed until the hatch can be repaired and the pumps are allowed to catch up."

"Understood." Mendelbaum released the button on his radio and exited the control bridge to the main deck and the gathering storm. He watched the plumes of steam billow from the mouths of the guards as they braced themselves against the freezing night air. The black ocean stretched out beneath the thick clouds before them, only lit occasionally by a lightning bolt from the massive storm. He ignored the fine rain that fell intermittently.

She must have considered the timing of her treachery very carefully. A nasty gale was blowing toward them, and they were struggling to get out of its path on reserve power. He couldn't devote his entire crew to the search for her; he needed them at their posts while they cleared the storm. His justice would have to be swift, and merciless. Did she think that he would spare her or the children? She had to know that he would not. She had to know that he would kill them as effortlessly as he had killed her foolish husband.

Yet she had done this anyway.

Mendelbaum scratched at a patch of dry skin on his hand and thought about rubbing more lotion into it. He knew not to scratch, but he ignored his own admonishment.

Scratching felt good, like killing did sometimes. Killing Albert Valquist had been such a moment, nearly orgasmic for him in its intensity. He had been hoping for an excuse to kill the man from the day he'd first met him. When the deed was done, he knew that she was his. She would always hate him, she would always want to kill or undermine him, but she would know that she could not. He had made sure of that the morning after he killed Albert, when he'd stuck the muzzle of his father's SS issue Mauser pistol to Edvard's head. It hadn't been necessary to say a word to Abigail that morning.

She had done all the talking. "Whatever you want, please don't." She had not raised her voice.

He had lowered the gun and let the little blond brat scamper back to her. She had been his every day since then, until today. Today she had betrayed him.

He radioed Al-Barq again. "She timed her deceit well. Disabling the ship this way was far cleverer than I gave her credit for. And Phineas must have known. He had some spine after all. Our ability to catch her has been thwarted for a time. Where is she now?"

"We still don't know. The video surveillance will have all of her movements up until she activated the override, but after that we may as well be hunting in a sandstorm," he said.

"My guess is that she went to the children. She wouldn't escape without them. But where does she think she'll go? Perhaps her plan was to use the *Eir*; she doesn't know what has happened to it yet."

"The repair team has reached the reactor. What of my cousin?"

"We're searching for him. You find the children. We'll have power back to the database to determine their location through their RFID tags within the hour. I'm ordering power be diverted from the hospital to the master database. Their capture is your only priority."

30 Pure Storm

The ocean pitched the Eir violently, but Christiana was able to keep a steady course away from the *Pura Vida.* The twin MTU engines roared beneath them, sending the knife hull of the yacht crashing into the waves, throwing thousands of gallons of water over them. "I have no idea which way to go," she yelled over the gale that poured through the broken windows.

"Away from the *'Vida* as fast as you can," Zakar yelled back. The sound of bees carried over the storm and he knew that his cousin had failed them. "Get down!" he screamed, but his cry was too late.

The first volley of depleted uranium shells was on its mark. It ripped through the entire fore section of the yacht, splinters of high-quality fiberglass and cherry wood flew apart and the ship began taking water immediately. The second spray of fire was upon them just as the splinters stopped flying, but the rounds missed them as their crippled vessel plunged down the trough of a large wave.

"Are you hit?" Zakar screamed.

There was no answer and the pilothouse was completely dark. The ship had lost all power and was spinning toward another huge wave, defenseless. Zakar crawled to Christiana and rolled her over. She had blood on her face, but she was breathing. He knew that they would certainly die here if he didn't think of something to save them very quickly. A bolt of lightning streaked into the water close by and illuminated the still intact aft of the yacht: Perched like a wonderful bird was the Eurocopter EC135 helicopter.

Mendelbaum surveyed the damage to his prized yacht. His first ten-second volley had cut the front section of the ship completely off. Nearly six thousand rounds per minute of heavy metal had pumped out of the barrels. Every tenth round was a magnesium tracer that drew a red line toward the target like a laser. His eyes still burned and his ears rang even though he had covered them. The second ten-second volley had missed its mark, but it was unnecessary. The *Eir* had gone dark and was taking water fast. She would be overcome by the waves within moments. The sheik would be livid that his nephew was killed, but he surely would understand the necessity of the act when he was shown the footage of Jacques' cold-blooded murder.

"Continue firing, sir?" his gunner asked excitedly over the driving wind.

"Negative. Let the sea take them," he said. For a moment he thought he spotted a dim light on the bow of the *Eir*. "Binoculars!" he ordered. As he raised them to his eyes he realized his mistake: al-Rashid was a decent pilot and he was trying to take off in the helicopter. "Fire, fire, fire!" he howled. The M134D Gatling Guns screamed to life once again, the tracers lancing out into the dark waves before them. But it looked like al-Rashid had the split second lead he needed. The helicopter was one hundred yards away, taking off from the crippled boat. The deck gunner could have swatted him from the sky easily in calm seas, but this was anything but. His gunner tried to compensate for the pitch of the *Pura Vida* in the storm but missed low, shredding the rest of the *Eir* from under the rising chopper. He adjusted his height, but was still a second too late as al-Rashid banked left. The gunner tried to predict where the chopper would go, swinging the twin barrels up and to the right. The tracers streaked by the helicopter by mere feet, but were then again off their mark as the ocean pitched the tanker. The helicopter rocked violently in the high wind and nearly struck the water, but al-Rashid compensated, dipped the rotor forward and rocketed off over the dark water and out of range.

31 TREACHEROUS DEPTH

Jim followed Abigail through the winding passageways off the main galley, moving deeper and deeper into the lower decks of the ship. Their shadows loomed out ahead of them in the dim red light and pitched back and forth as the growing storm enveloped the ship with violent waves. Neither had spoken in several minutes when Jim finally motioned for her to stop.

"How are you planning to get off the ship?"

"I'm not. But we need to take certain precautions." Her expression was tight. "You will need this," she said, holding a syringe at arm's length.

"What is it?"

"An antidote to the virus that is spreading through the ship."

"How can I be sure of that?"

"There is not time for this," she hissed.

The look in her eyes was pleading, but this could still be a trap. He swallowed his misgivings, "You do it." And rolled up his sleeve. He wanted to see her eyes as she injected him. The eyes never lied, and he would know whether or not he had to kill her on the spot—if he could bring himself to.

She moved to his side and took hold of his outstretched arm. Her touch sent a tingle up to his armpit that was immediately displaced by the prick of the needle and the burning liquid with which she filled his vein. Abigail snapped the cap onto the syringe and replaced it in a leather case.

"We must hurry," she said.

Fawwaz stood in the sterile room with a blank expression. The computer printout indicated that the children were supposed to be here. But these were not the children. This room contained an aged white man attached to a respirator. The printout was wrong. Fawwaz mulled this for a moment before clicking the intercom button attached to his collar. He cleared his throat. "Mendelbaum, we have a problem."

Nothing.

"Mendelbaum!" he yelled into his com-link.

"What?"

"They are not here. There's just an old white infidel in this room."

"Double check the manifest."

"I already did," Fawwaz said, anger building in his gut.

"Check it again!" Mendelbaum shrieked.

“I have, you dog. The entire manifest is wrong. Not one person listed on the master manifest is in the right room.” There was no response. Fawwaz said, “It might have been advisable to hold off on executing the fat man until the depth of his treachery was known.”

32 PLAY PEN

Edvard Valquist was scared and he didn't know why. His mom had told him that things were going to be fine, but she had seemed scared when she said it. She had taken them from their rooms and down to the storage chambers and led them inside. The doors opened automatically for her. She said that Dr. Mendelbaum liked to take her here sometimes to show off. When she left them, she had sealed the room and told him she would be back as soon as she could.

She had left plenty of food, and there was a small porta-potty, but the whole thing was not nearly as much fun as his mom had led him to believe. This was barely anything like the camping trips they used to take with dad.

"Do you want to play a game?" Edvard asked. The two year-old was pretty smart, but she couldn't play Monopoly with him the way his mom or Dr. Mendelbaum did. She really only liked to play with her blocks. So far things had been fine. Boring, but fine. Katarina hadn't answered him. She was busy making a really tall stack out of the pretty coins that his mom said they could play with. She had told Edvard as she dumped the bag out onto the floor that they could play with the coins, but that he was in charge of making sure Katarina didn't try to eat any.

Edvard had made his own huge stack of coins in the corner and then karate-chopped it. He was really bored with the coins. And Katarina was not paying any attention to him. Edvard picked up a coin, took careful aim, and threw it at the middle of her two-foot tower. His aim was perfect. The middle of the stack collapsed, followed a split second later by a cascade of coins. She howled with laughter at his trick. This kid was all right, Edvard thought, smiling. He turned to the stack of heavy bars that he had been sitting on. They were not as pretty as the coins; they didn't sparkle the same way at all. They had funny symbols pressed into them and he couldn't even move the ones that reminded him of loaves of bread.

He decided to build Katarina a fort out of the smaller bricks in the far corner, the ones that he could lift. She would like that.

33 SYSTEM REBOOT

Mendelbaum paced back and forth on the main control bridge. The lights had been restored and power was again flowing to the mainframe computer. The *Pura Vida* could not come close to meeting its power needs without the reactor. He had to pick and choose which areas of his ship to animate. "Divert thirty-percent more power to the mainframe from the hospital grid," he ordered.

"You will lose critical patients," al-Barq said. He coughed into a dirty handkerchief and replaced it in his pocket.

"I understand that. But if we don't figure out what she has done to my computer system, we'll lose the whole ship. What I need is Phineas or Jacques here to debug this thing. Instead, what I have is you and a bunch of IT support staff that can't fix a fucking laptop."

"My guess is that fat *Shatah*, Phineas, uploaded a malignant program that kicked in when she used your master reset key."

"That may be the case. But no matter what Phineas loaded into the system, he wouldn't have created a problem she couldn't solve. If he'd wanted to sink the ship, he would have tried to overload the reactor. His goal was to save her, and that meant he couldn't have risked sinking the ship."

"Camera's are back up. The RF chip data is still scrambled, so I can't tell who is where. But I'm sure she'll seek a remote area of the ship. We'll start the visual search with the lower decks near where she started the fire. My guess is that—"

"What?" Mendelbaum demanded.

"Lantana. Has anyone checked on him? His cell is on the other side of the ship from yours. The fire was meant to keep our attention away from her true destination."

34 GUILLERMO'S EPOCH

It was finally time. Guillermo whistled a happy little tune as he stepped into the armored exoskeleton attachment to his survival walker. He had overseen its creation by Jacques and the fat queer, but had never been given unfettered access to it. He was sorry to hear that Jacques had been killed—there was no one left to bring him girls now. He brought up his main command screen and tried to type his father's name. He was too excited, though; his hands were shaking like a Parkinson's patient. He took a deep breath and focused on typing out the letters R-E-I-N-H-A-R-T, and with a whirring hiss, the huge suit came to life around him and clamped firmly to his familiar survival walker. He had always viewed the silly little walker as nothing more than the pedestal for the large armored attachment that now enveloped him with an extra six-hundred pounds of killing potential. He clicked the Titanium and Kevlar-mesh face mask into place and admired himself in his mirror. This suit was unbreakable.

His brother had just given him the joyous news of his search and destroy mission. He cycled through the weapons that he might use to kill Abigail and Lantana, if his brother was right that they were together, as he strode out of his chamber to the waiting guards. His orders were to capture them, if possible. The guards took off at a trot before him and he checked his projection screen for available medication. He selected another dose of cocaine, the last he would be allowed for the next hour, and felt his heart rate surge. Objects around him came into sharp focus, and his penis hardened against the inside of his suit. He smiled at the sensation. It was his first natural erection in a very long time.

He clicked the spring release in his palm and watched a three-foot blade attached to his forearm launch out of its sheath and lock into position. The curved blade was affixed to a pivot just outside of his knuckle. If he turned his hand, the blade would switch directions to allow the thick scimitar to cut on the fore and back swing. He wielded it clumsily back and forth and the guard next to him dove out of the way with a curse. Guillermo had nearly taken the man's head off.

"Think you could be a bit careful with that?" the man asked.

Guillermo looked at him for a moment through the drug fog. He didn't know this man's name and he didn't care to. He turned away from the guard without a word and engaged another hidden mechanism.

The blade swung back into its Kevlar sheath with a dull *whoosh*, and Guillermo began scrolling through his armaments again as they set off toward their quarry. He was excited to the point of euphoria at the prospect of getting to destroy Jim Lantana. He had watched the way he picked apart the Beast; that wouldn't happen this time. He would make Abigail watch. Then what? Was his brother really going to let him *have* her? The prospect of the upcoming carnage was sweeter than anything he could have imagined.

The first list of weapons was defensive in nature—smoke screens to hide him, tear gas to disperse enemy fighters, mustard gas to kill indiscriminately. It was really a shame his brother had never let him play in his suit before. He walked heavily down the corridor in the thickly armored suit and marveled at how much louder his foot falls were in the augmented walker. It weighed nearly three times as much as the standard suit to which he'd been confined.

The second list of weapons was offensive, and he couldn't focus on the names of each, as his excitement grew. His brother had allowed him to shoot off the deck of the *'Vida* with a ten-gauge shotgun attachment on his survival suit, but that had grown boring quickly. His eyes jumped around on the list and stopped on a fully automatic shotgun loaded with titanium buckshot. He selected it, but then second-guessed his decision.

The weapon was too powerful. Lantana would be blown to pulp by a direct hit; there was no fun in that. He scrolled back to the familiar ten-gauge shotgun ammo he used to shoot skeet. He was a terrific shot with the weapon and would aim only to wing Lantana with the birdshot. Only a close shot would tear him apart. Guillermo whipped out the scimitar again and the guards scrambled away from him as he swung it in a vicious arc. This was how he would finish Lantana. Close, personal.

35 CRYONIC CLOT

Jim stood open-mouthed before the rows of glass tanks that stretched into the dark cavern and out of sight. An oily, bluish fluid flowed through the clear pipes that connected the tanks to one another. There were hundreds of tanks, each holding thousands of gallons of the liquid. And deep inside the hazy fluid, the vague outlines of people.

Jim realized as they walked deeper into the chamber that the tanks were arranged in a massive circle around a fifty-foot diameter central tank filled with the same viscous fluid. The antiseptic smell nearly covered the decay that hung in the room, but not quite. Jim tried to avoid looking too deeply into the tanks, but found his eyes drawn into them everywhere he turned. Each container held a pale, naked body floating in the gel. A huge set of pumps chugged away in the corner of the room, but some of the tanks had gone dark. That might explain the smell. Jim realized that nearly half the tanks in the room were in fact dark, the fluid steaming slightly as it sat in the still air. Jim looked up to the ceiling sixty feet overhead and saw ventilation fans that had been idled.

The farther into the room they moved, the more the smell permeated them. It grew stronger as they approached the central tank. Jim looked down an aisle of neatly arranged tanks and estimated that the line was one hundred yards long. There must have been thousands of people stored in these containers; one of the *Pura Vida's* central oil storage chambers had been dedicated to this cryonics lab.

"So this is the final clearinghouse for Mendelbaum's sales pitch," Jim said.

"When he can't help patients with available cutting-edge scientific procedures, he closes his clients with this: cryonics," Abigail said. She didn't seem offended by the smell.

Jim noticed that one large tank was connected directly to the massive central tank like a hood ornament. He looked at the data display set in the tank that listed the client's name: "Rafiqua Benzeria al Jabara," he read aloud. The display indicated that advanced peripheral artery disease had required that she be interred in the cryonics chamber two years earlier. Under the diagnosis, a counter ticked off the estimated time until the cure was expected. It was currently counting backward from eight years, ten months, sixteen days.

"She is the wife of a key investor, so Mendelbaum had a specially-designed tank added for her," Abigail said.

Jim realized that all the tanks had a similar display panel with the patient's diagnosis and a backward-counting clock ticking away the days until a cure was likely to arrive. "So these people all believe the same thing? That someday they are going to be thawed and saved?"

"It's usually family members who can't let go, actually. Each tank has a webcam that allows families to visit their frozen loved ones."

"Webcam, that makes sense. I wouldn't let anyone into this stink-hole, either."

Abigail laughed for a moment and then cut herself short.

"What's the matter?"

"That's the first time I can remember laughing at anything in years."

Jim approached the massive communal tank and held his nose. There was a small stepladder that led to a viewing platform. He didn't know why, but he felt the need to get a closer look. Abigail said nothing as he mounted the steps and walked to the edge of the platform. What he saw made vomit rise in his throat.

The tank was filled to capacity with corpses. Some looked partially decomposed.

"There was an incident last year when the coolant system failed and the less-rich guests were allowed to warm up. The very rich bodies were kept coolest, the rest were allowed to thaw partially. The smell was horrific."

"Does Mendelbaum really believe that the cryogenic freeze system is promising?"

"No, but it's a major money-maker. Family members like to visit their dead relatives and avoid dealing with death. Mendelbaum told me that the degradation in cell tissue caused by the freezing process is irreversible. Only bodies frozen in a very specific way have any real chance of recovering. That's why they need to come here before they die, so that Mendelbaum can inter them properly. Their families want a place to store them until the proper technology was developed to reanimate them." Jim could tell that Abigail felt profoundly saddened by their inability to accept their loss. "Death is part of life. Without death our lives have no meaning," she said.

"I would do anything to have my wife back," Jim said. He realized that his father knew that, too. That's why he had brought her here . . . but he couldn't have known what this place really was.

"Longevity and the maximum number of healthy years are noble goals, but not when they are a distraction from trying to lead a normal happy life," Abigail said, looking at the massive communal freeze tank. "This is where Mendelbaum is dumping the bodies that can't afford private chambers."

"Lovely. I've seen Iraqi torture chambers and Somali mass graves, but something about this is much worse. This must have been what the allies felt when they liberated places like Auschwitz." Jim turned around and looked into the clear plastic tank that housed a child. She was perfectly preserved, angelic-looking, even. Still, his guts turned to water and he ran down the ladder to a sink in the corner of the room.

He wretched twice, and when he looked up the guards were there, staring across the large room at their escaped prisoner and Mendelbaum's prized researcher.

Guillermo smiled at them from in front of the guards. "He'll kill your son for this," he called out.

"He'll have to find him first," Abigail yelled back.

"Surrender yourselves, there is nowhere to go," Guillermo said, taking a heavy step forward in his armored suit. He raised his arm and pointed the barrel of his shotgun at them. “You’re mine now,” he said, smiling thinly.

“You don’t know what to do with a woman anymore,” Abigail said.

“Bitch!” he wailed. The sound of his horrible voice carried to them across the room. For a moment he seemed to contemplate what to do. Then he smiled again, and said, “If I kill you now, my brother will be angry. But once he is through with you, he will give you to me, finally.”

Before she could respond, Jim jumped to his left and crouched behind the ten-thousand-gallon liquid nitrogen tank used to cool the circulating cryo-freeze gel.

“Grab him, he’s unarmed!” Guillermo yelled at the three guards next to him. None of them moved. Guillermo turned his massive shoulders toward them and cocked his helmeted head to one side like a confused dog. He raised his left arm and pointed it at the man closest to him. There was a distinct click before the shotgun blast erupted from next to his hand, blowing the top of the man’s head apart. As he slumped to the ground, the other guards snapped into action. They moved in a slow crouch across the room toward Abigail, scanning their flanks for signs of Jim.

“I have located them, brother,” Guillermo said into the intercom on his shoulder. There was a long, pregnant pause. “Understood, capture only.”

Abigail didn’t move as the men approached her. When they were within five feet of her, Jim yelled, “Get down!” He sprang from behind the canister, a hose held tightly in his hands. As he flipped the nozzle, Abigail leapt out of the way as a stream of smoking liquid nitrogen soaked the faces and arms of the two men approaching her. Only one was able to scream; the other was instantly frozen to death.

Abigail stared in horror at the scene from around the corner of a cryo-tank but said nothing.

Guillermo howled in anger and leveled his weaponized arm on Jim. There was no way Jim could get out of his way and the blast from the ten-gauge shotgun rang out with horrifying intent from fifty feet. The gun was loaded with birdshot, but a few pellets embedded in Jim’s upper arm before he dove back behind the central canister. Blood flowed freely from the small wounds, but Jim ignored it.

Guillermo screamed with triumph. “I was ordered to capture you, Lantana, but now that you’ve killed my men, I am justified in killing you.” He began walking forward, each heavy footfall echoing around the dark chamber. "I know that I wounded you, Lantana. Come out, surrender yourself!"

Guillermo looked down at the whimpering guard that Jim had sprayed and knew that he was of no further use. As he clomped toward the man, he could see that his arms and lower body had been soaked in the liquid nitrogen used to cool the cryo-gel, and they were frozen solid. With a sick grin he raised his foot and brought it down on the man's right arm. Abigail looked around the corner of the tank just as Guillermo's foot came down. She couldn't hold back her scream at the crackling sound the limb made beneath Guillermo's oversized boot. The man shrieked in horror and then passed out from the shock.

"Come out, Lantana!" Guillermo bellowed through his amplifier. His thin, sick voice seemed to fill the dark cryo-chamber and echoed eerily back and forth. Jim had taken the dead guard's 9-millimeter pistol and wasted no time finding the high ground to attack from. Guillermo's heavy-duty suit looked impenetrable with such a small caliber weapon, but the super-cooled gel might get to him. The hose he had used before was far out of reach now, but there was a six-inch feeder pipe connected to the top of the communal tank. He gauged the distance to be about ten yards.

Jim popped up from his hiding place and found a clear sight line to Guillermo. He didn't expect to be able to kill him, but hopefully he could anger him into making a mistake. He leveled his pistol, exhaled slowly, and fired three precise shots into the side of Guillermo's helmet. As expected, they didn't penetrate, but Guillermo nonetheless howled in pain. The carbon fiber stopped the bullets, but it was still like being hit in the head with a hammer. Jim was already on the move when the next volley of shotgun fire blanketed his last position.

"You can't hurt me with that, Lantana. But I can sure hurt you. I'm gonna rape this bitch to death for you!"

His plan had worked. Guillermo was not thinking clearly; he was reckless and angry. That was what Jim needed from him, naked aggression. Jim stopped before a cryo-tank and removed the bolts that connected the heavy nameplate to the tank. He placed the quarter-inch-thick steel under his shirt and tucked it into the top of his pants. As long as he didn't have to run, it would hold. There would only be one good shot at making this work.

He stepped out from the cover of the massive communal tank and methodically fired round after round into Guillermo's back.

The shots peppered Guillermo's armored head and neck as he spun around and saw Jim standing in front of the tank. Jim pulled the trigger again, and the gun was empty. Guillermo laughed and charged like a wild bull, holding his gun arm in front. He fired from ten feet, the pellets slamming into Jim's chest, blowing him back into the tank. He sagged to his knees in real pain, waiting for Guillermo to get in close enough to gloat.

Guillermo stopped short of Jim and looked down at him, weighing his next options. Jim stayed completely still. He wanted Guillermo to look away for a second to try to find Abigail.

"Do you see what I've done, Abby?" Guillermo called out into the dark. "Lantana's dead and you're mine!"

Jim heard the small motors engage that must have meant that his head was turning. Jim swiveled out to his left and grabbed the release valve of the feeder pipe with his right hand. He yanked as hard as he could and the plug gave way. Super-cooled gel spewed from the communal tank in a six-inch-wide stream, soaking Guillermo's face and torso.

He fired his shotgun reflexively, barely missing Jim's feet. As Jim scrambled backward, Guillermo tried to raise his arm. It moved slightly, still a bit shy of Jim's legs and he fired again. There was a horrible scream from inside the suit that cut off suddenly, and then the only sound was the hissing stream of blue gel that continued to pour over him and harden into a widening mass.

36 Frozen Foam

Jim knew that they didn't have much time left. Guillermo had called in their position. From the schematics he had accessed with the key card he had taken off the dead guard, he knew that there were only two ways into the cryonics lab. One was through the main door they'd used. The other was through the water purification chamber located behind the cryonics lab. But that would take them toward the wrong end of the ship, away from the main control room where they might be able to call for help.

An idea occurred to Jim as he looked at the massive pipes high overhead. The water purification system must use the same plumbing system the rest of the ship did. So the pipes carrying fresh water to the ship would run through the cryonics chamber. And water mixed with super-cooled gel equaled ice, he assumed. Moving to the far side of the room he located the industrial sink he had gotten sick in earlier. He filled a glass beaker with a few cups of water and walked back to the mass of spilled gel that covered Guillermo.

With a brisk motion he threw the water onto the gel and regretted it immediately: A sizzle like pork fat poured on a bonfire was followed a moment later by a grayish mass of ice that expanded to an ugly lump the size of a garbage can and stopped inches from his feet. The reaction was so quick that he hadn't even had time to consider jumping away. He was lucky he hadn't used more water.

"Abigail," Jim said sharply. His breath froze in the super-cooled air rising from the gel.

"You scared me," she said from the other side of the spilled gel. She stood staring at Guillermo and his guards' frozen bodies. She held one hand out toward the gel and pulled it back as it began to get too cold. Even from several feet away the blue mass radiated cold, as if a miniature ice age had dawned at their feet. "What are we going to do?"

"We need to block the door. Once they deal with the fire you set, the entire security force is sure to be headed this way."

"What do you suggest?"

Jim looked up at the pipes running the length of the cold room. "Any idea which of these carries water?"

Abigail smiled at him. "The blue one, of course."

Jim gave her a cross look that he didn't feel and picked up a dead guard's Fabrique Nationale tactical 12-gauge shotgun. "Stand at the far end of the chamber;

this is going to get messy in a hurry."

The central holding tank had emptied nearly half of its gel onto Guillermo; a trickle still flowed from the hole Jim had left when he pulled the plug. Jim walked behind the communal tank and followed the central feeder pipe to its source, a fifty-foot-tall stainless-steel holding tank at the far end of the chamber marked with pressure warnings. It took Jim two rounds of buckshot to determine that he was never going to punch the necessary holes in the canister of super-cooled gel. He would have to open the hatch manually and control the flow himself.

Jim eyed the thick blue plastic pipe and felt a flicker of fear as he realized how dangerous his plan was. To shoot the pipe would cause a massive flow of water. He knew that the gel and water mixture could be highly volatile, and from his rude experiment, he knew the chemical reaction would create an ice wall that could trap them in the chamber. Abigail walked up behind him and tapped him on the shoulder.

"Would this help?"

She was almost too pretty to look at in that moment. She was holding a hand grenade recovered from the dead guard.

“That should work,” he answered dryly. “Now this time, do what I tell you. Go wait in the water purification chamber and be ready to seal the door in a hurry.”

Jim cocked the shotgun, aimed at a spot on the twenty-inch plastic pipe where it met the frame of the main hatch and fired. The buckshot knocked a twelve-inch hole through which a geyser of water erupted from the ruined plastic. As soon as it made contact with Guillermo’s gel-soaked body, the reaction that Jim had watched earlier hissed and burned to life. Half of Guillermo’s body was quickly encased in expanding foam and lost from view. Jim methodically emptied all but the last three rounds in the shotgun at several more blue pipes around the room.

He had another problem as he attempted to pin the grenade between the stainless steel cylinder and the main valve assembly. The water purification entrance was ten feet away, protected by a thick hatch left over from the tanker’s original design. If the grenade went off before he was in the hatch, he’d take shrapnel in his back. And he only had one grenade to make this work; he couldn’t risk wasting it. In a moment of inspiration, he tore a strip of cloth from a dead guard’s clothing and attached it to the rusted hatch. He carefully tied the other end to the grenade pin and admired his handiwork.

Jim entered the tube that connected the chamber to the water purification chamber behind the hatch. As he pulled the door closed, he heard a sound he didn't like. The hinges the door sat upon were horribly corroded. The door barely shut at all and there was light visible around its edges. As he spun the handle to seal the door, he felt the concussion from the explosion in the next room, followed a split second later by the crushing force of the door as it ripped cleanly off its hinges and pinned him to the floor. The last thing he could hear was the hiss of the frozen foam.

Abigail jumped when she heard the explosion from the next room. Then she waited. Jim should have been coming around the corner by now. She walked to the hatch and opened it a crack. What she saw made her call out. Jim was pinned beneath the steel hatch and a monstrous shape was growing in the ruined cyro-freeze chamber. It looked like a cancer cluster on steroids, and it was slithering toward the hatch where Jim lay pinned.

She ran into the narrow tube and felt the freezing embrace of the rapidly cooling air. Her face burned the closer she got to it. She knelt down next to Jim's right ear and called out. Nothing. She called again, this time prodding him with her hand. He stirred. She tried to lift the hatch and knew instantly that she would never be able to.

"James!" she howled. The ice snake was nearly to the edge of the tube. "You have to help me!"

Jim seemed to know what she was saying. "Just – just go," he stuttered.

"Push, damn you! What are those muscles for, anyway?"

Jim smiled in spite of the fact that he was pinned under a door and maneuvered his arms into a bench press position. Abigail moved to the side of the door and grabbed with both hands. She squatted down and put everything she had into moving the rusted door. The sharp sides bit into her palms, but she ignored the pain. The door moved slightly and then fell back; she feared that Jim had given up. The ice foam reached the outer lip of the hatch and bubbled up, a menacing snakehead that fell back on itself and then rose higher as more fuel was added to it.

"Push!" she screamed, but she didn't need to. Jim had maneuvered his legs under the hatch into fetal position and had placed both feet against the door.

“Move,” he bellowed as he kicked the hatch toward the approaching ice. They scrambled back together as the three-foot-wide cylinder of ice foam overcame the rusty hatch and chased them toward the water purification room.

“Keep running!” Jim shouted as they scrambled clear of the hatch and into the treatment facility. “What’s on the other side of this room?” Jim asked.

“The garden,” Abigail said.

He gave her a quizzical look, but said nothing as he approached the valve on the enormous central water tank. It took another three shots of buckshot, the last the weapon contained, to punch a hole in the plastic and send a twelve-inch geyser toward the approaching ice snake.

37 RAGE

Mendelbaum sat in the reactor control room that used to belong to Jacques, Fawwaz al-Barq sitting behind him. The reactor was back online, finally. But it wouldn't be at full power for quite some time. Waiting for the reactor had given Mendelbaum time to think about Phineas. It was clear that Phineas had been helping Abigail plan her escape all along.

But why? As the monitor attached to the main frame glowed back to life, Mendelbaum had a stroke of inspiration. In the months before he had put Phineas to death, he had downloaded his memories. Phineas had been one of the lucky crewmembers to earn his shot at immortality through his valuable service. The final session had been completed just prior to his pathetic death march. Mendelbaum was by no means as adept at mining the data as Phineas had been, but that wouldn't matter. He didn't care if he destroyed the data he didn't need. He could charge through Phineas's memories like a bull in a china shop, crashing through the details that made up the queer's life, in search of the delicate fragments that would lay bare the rest of Abigail's plan.

Mendelbaum typed a query into the mainframe and the file that contained all of Phineas's memories appeared. It was massive, far bigger than the Library of Congress. He could never search it line-by-line, but he only needed the last few months' worth. Mendelbaum opened the compressed file and typed his deletion parameters. He clicked the Enter command and smiled as forty-three years of Phineas's memories vanished from the rest of the data. A much smaller, more manageable file was left in its place.

"Why would you do it?" Mendelbaum asked the remaining memories by typing into a search file. There was no response. He continued typing, "After all I gave you aboard this ship, why would you betray me?"

The remaining code that comprised Phineas' memory offered nothing for several seconds; then finally a line of text appeared. "You can't stop her now." Mendelbaum smiled. Everything he had come to suspect over the last hour was confirmed.

"Where will she go?" Mendelbaum typed. He hit the Enter key with his middle finger much harder than he needed to.

The screen gave no response.

"We are on a ship in the middle of the ocean. They cannot escape. When I find her son I will kill him on closed circuit camera for the whole ship to see. Then I will hunt her and Lantana down and kill them as well. All they have done is delay me a bit." Mendelbaum stopped typing and dabbed at his nose instead.

The blinking cursor that was now Phineas said nothing.

He knew that Phineas could hear him in there, he was caught in the RYE, but he was ignoring him. "She was clever," he typed. "Infecting the ship would slow down the search." Still no response.

He queried the data file for the make and model of Phineas's watch. It was the same barometric pressure gauge that Abigail had worn. She had been far cleverer than he could have imagined. And Phineas knew all of it. He knew that he would be captured, and he had gone to his death anyway. They had waited until a storm blew in before she put her plan into motion.

His head swam with the realization that she was hitting him from multiple fronts. Brilliant, really. He should declare a general state of emergency and quarantine the ship immediately, but that was exactly what she would expect. No. That would not do at all. He had to stop playing into her hand. Mendelbaum blew his nose like a farmer, uncaring at the moment about the vile germs with which he covered the pristine floor. Where would she have hidden the children?

“Is the RF chip data back online?” he asked the tech assistant.

The small man looked back at him with a terrified expression. Clearly the data was still scrambled. “I think that we will have to manually re-load the signals from each RF chip by rescanning them,” the man said meekly.

“Yes, but Phineas doesn’t know that,” Mendelbaum said. He began typing again. “Jacques has repaired the RF chip data. We have located Edvard Valquist.”

“Impossible,” popped up on the screen.

Mendelbaum stared at it. The essence of Phineas really was still alive in this mainframe. For now. And he was off balance. He couldn’t know that Jacques was dead; the murder had occurred after Phineas’s execution.

“You were not as clever as you thought. Al-Barq,” he called hoarsely. “Open the outer yacht hatch.” He typed the instruction for Phineas to see as well.

“You will never take them,” Phineas replied. So they were still on the ship.

Fawwaz looked at him for a moment without understanding. “But that will flood the ship,” he said. Mendelbaum glanced up from the screen for the first time and locked eyes with Al-Barq. Realization spread across his security chief's face. Flooding the ship was exactly what Mendelbaum had in mind.

It was then that the call Mendelbaum had waited for came over his radio. Guillermo's thin voice reported that he had pinned down Abigail and Jim in the cryonics chamber.

38 Succor

Mendelbaum pounded down the stairs behind the guards and cocked the pistol he had taken from the main armory. His men were not moving as fast as they should be. This angered him almost as much as Abigail's betrayal. His cold was momentarily forgotten as he thought about killing James Lantana in front of her. She honestly thought that she could just spring him from his cell, start a little fire, and escape? Abigail would not be so lucky as Lantana. She would have to watch her son die first, and then he might kill her. Perhaps he would just let Guillermo have her. But Lantana would die at his hands very soon.

The team of security guards reached the outer hatch of the cryonics chamber and stopped. They knew that they were not allowed to enter without a proper decontamination scan, and they stared back at Mendelbaum expectantly.

"Just open the hatch," he said.

"Sir?" a stupid-looking man called Jones said.

Mendelbaum pointed his pistol at the man's head and repeated, "Open the hatch."

His order was obeyed.

Mendelbaum scrambled into the room and slipped on the ice that coated the floor. He landed on his back and lay still, barely able to comprehend the sight before him. His cryonics chamber was filling with a nasty gray-and-white foam, the byproduct of water and gel. The whole room was freezing cold; his breath billowed out of his lungs in great white gasps. Super-cooled gel continued to spew from the smashed tank at the far end of the room, and fresh water gushed out of several broken pipes overhead. The gel hissed and cracked as it added to a wall of ice that covered the entire back of the chamber.

What he saw next made him scream, but the noise caught painfully in his throat. Guillermo was stuck into the growing mass of foam like a turd on a frozen pond. The half-submerged suit exposed only his face and upper torso. The rest of his body was hidden in the foam. A horrible expression of anger and pain was fixed on Guillermo's bone-white face.

"No!" Mendelbaum howled.

The guard named Jones muttered, "At least he's in the cryo-freeze room; we can just add him to the main tank like the sheik's wife and cure him later."

Mendelbaum did not say a word as he carefully stood up and turned toward Jones, pistol outstretched.

Jones opened his mouth in protest and Mendelbaum shot him. The bullet entered Jones' mouth and exited the back of his head; a spray of red carpeted the ice behind him and froze quickly.

The sight of the blood sobered Mendelbaum. He looked back at his brother and felt a fresh wave of anger. He was not sure if it was the virus or the fact that his brother was lying dead in front of him. Abigail and Jim had presumably sealed themselves on the other side of the ice. This room had been the perfect place to pick. It was the highest security spot on the ship. There were only two ways into it, the door he had just come through—and the one that was now blanketed in fifty feet of ice.

They would need cutting torches to melt the super-cooled ice quickly, and the maintenance and storage area was on the other side of the ice wall. With a torch, he could have cut into the water purification room from above and been on them in minutes. Instead, they would have to do this the old-fashioned way.

"Bring pick axes from every fire control box on the ship that we can still access," Mendelbaum said. "Instruct all laboratory personnel to begin synthesizing as much magnesium chloride as they can. I want teams of six men chipping around the clock until the ice-melt solution is ready, then we'll begin spraying our way through."

"Do you want us to free your brother first?" a guard asked.

"No. Leave him where he is. I want Abigail first," he said as the ship pitched violently in the storm. "I will be in my quarters. Keep me apprised of your penetration."

39 Strange Garden

Jim flipped a large red switch in the corner of the darkened chamber to override the automatic lighting system. The room smelled of clean dirt and ozone. The lights buzzed far overhead and came to life very slowly, one row after the next, illuminating the massive space ten feet at a time. The room was at least a hundred yards long and just as wide. Sturdy tables bolted to the floor stood in neat rows across the entire room, sectioned off every ten feet by small signs indicating the plant being grown.

Ripe tomatoes hung innocently in front of Jim, their cracked skin betraying their heirloom heritage. Behind them were rows of peppers, squash, cucumbers, and lettuces in every color—a massive bounty floating somewhere in the Atlantic Ocean aboard a rusted oil tanker. Jim felt his stomach grumble but fought the urge to eat.

"The place is a fucking city," he said over his shoulder.

"I've never been allowed inside this room. Mendelbaum limits the access to every part of the ship to the personnel needed to run it. This room is his garden and seed bank. He feeds the entire ship from produce grown here. The meat he brings in with the hookers. He thinks that the world as we know it will end very soon. If it's not climate change, it'll be massive terror attacks. Once the world ends he has plans to repopulate it with the pure genetic stock he has been collecting . . . from humans to carrots."

"Horst's twisted Ark," Jim said.

Jim thought back to the weeks he'd spent in captivity eating delectable food at every meal and gave in to his hunger. He reached out and plucked a ripe yellow heirloom tomato as large as a softball. His mouth watered as he bit into it messily; juice and seeds squirted in all directions.

"Gross," Abigail said, playfully flicking a tomato seed from her shirt. "I have to wear this in public, you know."

Jim smiled, already eyeing the next tomato on the vine. Neither had eaten in at least twenty-four hours—Jim because his meal had been interrupted by Abigail; Abigail because she'd had no appetite since the day before. He ate a second tomato and then moved toward the carrots. Abigail followed him, picking among the smaller fruits and making far less of a mess. Jim stopped before another tomato plant and began picking handfuls of the small, ripe fruit. He retracted his hand as a pang of guilt washed over him. His expression went flat and he stopped chewing.

“Don’t worry about the kids,” Abigail said around a mouthful of cucumber.

Jim looked at her without speaking. Sharon was the only person who’d ever been able to read him like that.

When he didn’t speak, Abigail said, “I made sure that enough canned food to last them a month went into the vault with them. Edvard knows what to do—”

Jim couldn’t stand it any longer. He moved forward slowly and grabbed her waist, pulling her toward him. She didn’t resist. He picked her up with one arm and set her on the table, knocking tomato plants out of the way with his free hand, spilling dirt onto the pristine floor with their movements. He wiped juice from his chin and he kissed her roughly. She kissed him back, twisting onto her back, the soft dirt molding to her body.

They kissed like that for several minutes, feeling each other’s bodies. The longer they lay together the more intense their mutual arousal became. Jim hadn’t felt like this since before Sharon took ill. She entered his mind, and he stopped what he was doing.

Abigail sensed the change in his mood and stopped moving as well. She looked up into his eyes, and they lay there, staring at one another for what seemed an eternity to them both. Jim realized that she understood the deep pool of loss that he was swimming in. They were in it together and they had found one another, lost and adrift on the open ocean of misery and heartbreak. The spell between them broke, and in unison, they tore at one another's clothes, desperate to be naked. She slowed him down with a soft hand on his cheek and unbuttoned her pants for him. Moments later he was inside her, lost to the strange garden around him.

40 Rapture

"Mendelbaum, come in," al-Barq said over the radio. "We have all the cameras working properly again. We are scanning the chambers beyond the ice wall now and—"

"What?" Mendelbaum demanded. "What have you found?"

"The cryonics lab, it's destroyed. What of the patients?" al-Barq asked. He hadn't been with the wave of first responders.

"They are fine," Mendelbaum lied. "The reserve tank of coolant gel is undamaged. Once we clear the ice we will be able to restart the tanks. The VIP patients remain in stasis." He hoped this was the case, but ultimately there was no way to be sure without significant testing.

"I am sorry for the loss of your brother." Mendelbaum made no reply. "I will patch the camera feed into your quarters."

Mendelbaum had walked back to his quarters slowly, working at controlling his breathing to contain his rage. The large LCD monitor was smudged and blackened from the fire. He used his ruined sleeve to wipe it and watched as it glowed to life with the feed from the cameras in the cryonics chamber. He avoided looking at Guillermo and waited for the next chamber. Slowly, the first camera in the water purification room came online and showed that the ice had flowed through the hatch and found another ruined water pipe to feed it. The hatch was completely filled with the gray-and-white foam and would take hours to clear.

Mendelbaum went back to his closet and disrobed. He selected his favorite silver tracksuit and pulled it over his head. It reeked from the fire, and he nearly became ill as the rank smell of burned feathers and carpet filled his nostrils again. With the garment still over his head, he heard a sound like an adult film coming from his bedchamber.

“What channel have you selected, al-Barq?” he asked into his com link. There was no reply. Mendelbaum knew what he was hearing but he refused to accept it. It was too much. He must be mistaken, she couldn’t be—! He ran back into the bedroom and tripped over the ruined bedside table that had once housed his prized medallion. From his hands and knees, he looked up, and there, on the screen before him, was the most hideous scene he had ever witnessed.

Abigail was naked, her long legs astride a heaving Jim Lantana. She pressed her hands into Lantana's chest and arched her back. They were making love feverishly in his prized garden, defiling it, and themselves. The scream came to his lips and he forgot to disconnect his com link. His howl was broadcast to all the security crewmembers aboard, and he thought he heard laughter carry back over the radio. Abigail's eyes closed and she appeared to be in pain. Mendelbaum realized that she was climaxing atop Lantana's substantial body.

He looked away from the screen and back toward the floor. He recognized the familiar odor of his kelp shakes. The giant tank had been smashed and the kelp water had spilled everywhere. The carpet was thoroughly soaked with it. He hadn't eaten in hours and his stomach grumbled. He lowered his face to the carpet and sucked at the familiar juice. He was hardly able to get even enough to swallow. Then the nausea swept over him like a tidal wave. His head swam with the horror of what she had done, and he vomited.

It took him a few moments to crawl onto the soggy remains of his burnt bed. He lay there motionless for several minutes. He had watched his brother bed hookers for years, but never before had he seen Abigail compromised. He usually liked watching. But this was so different. They needed to be taught a lesson. Killing them was not nearly enough.

At long last, he rose and crossed the chamber to the monitor. He switched from the security camera to the mainframe login screen with shaking hands. He had control of the ship again, and he would not need help from anyone for his next tactic. Besides, if anyone knew what he intended to do, they would try to stop him. He was well aware of the fact that flooding any more of the ship was dangerous, but he needed to flush them out like the filthy rats that they were.

He punched his access code into the soot-stained keypad on the screen and brought up the master schematic of the ship. He selected the control hatch on the docking chamber where the Eir had once been. The pumps were still laboring to remove the seawater. He disabled them and reopened the hatch. A smile spread across his pale face as a rush of ocean poured into the docking chamber again. The lower decks of the ship were already flooded, which prevented Abigail from moving anywhere but farther back into the ship. It was time to bring home to her the depth of the betrayal.

He returned to the main ship schematic and selected the flood control hatches beneath the galley that protected the ship's middle decks and heard the screams of protest from the crew echo over the com link. Many would die, perhaps all if he didn't close the hatches soon. That was okay. It was almost worth sinking the ship now to punish her.

Al-Barq screamed in his ear, begging for an explanation.

With a sigh, he turned the com link back on. "I will stop the flooding once I am sure they are contained. We have at least another million gallons of water we can take on before maximum scuttle parameters are violated. You worry too much, 'Wazzie, trust me." Mendelbaum turned off his radio to silence the string of obscenities that poured over the airwaves.

Al-Barq raced into Mendelbaum's ruined chamber moments later. "I can't believe you flooded more of the ship. You could kill us all."

"It was a risk worth taking. I would rather die than suffer the indignity of a defeat at the hands of a treasonous whore and her mongrel lover."

"I'm sorry that she betrayed you, but you have probably drowned half your crew. Those left alive want an explanation of how this flood could have occurred. What would you have me tell them?"

“Say nothing.” This was tiresome. “Flooding the mid-decks was the only way to hem them in. The flood control hatches I opened are accessible from the internal dock now. We can use scuba equipment to swim through the flooded lower deck and flank them amidships. They will be trapped between the ice foam and the gold storage—!”

“What is it?”

“The gold!” Mendelbaum howled. “That’s where she’s put the children, by god.”

“How is that possible?”

“I gave her access.”

“You what?! How could you be so reckless? Even my foolish cousin wouldn’t have allowed a woman access to a gold vault.”

“Don’t bet on it,” Mendelbaum said.

Al-Barq raised an eyebrow but Mendelbaum didn’t see it. He was too caught up in the realization that he had located the children. He had control of the ship again, but all the failsafe systems had been activated. He couldn’t eject the gold chambers without manually re-keying them first. But at least he knew where the brats were.

"Prepare a diving team at once," he said. "Send them to the dock and tell them to kill anyone they meet on sight."

Fawwaz entered the internal dock and took stock of the gear available for the mission. There was only proper equipment for two divers. The rest of the equipment had been aboard the *Eir*. All that was kept in the docking area was diving equipment to perform routine maintenance on the Eir's hull and the docking doors' mechanics. The internal storage chamber, currently blocked by the ice foam, held enough diving equipment for fifty men.

The assembly in the internal dock was less than confidence-inspiring. Several of his more competent guards were present, but none had any diving experience. Of those that could dive, one had done significant safety and salvage work but seemed undersized and frail—hardly a man to take on Lantana. The other was a decent physical specimen, but was as stupid as a camel turd. Fawwaz had demoted him and docked all his credits earlier in the month for sneaking pork rations to Zakar in exchange for extra time with a whore.

“You two will have to do,” Fawwaz said. “The mid-decks have been flooded and we now have access to the bowels of the ship. I need you to swim up behind Lantana while the ice-melt crew continues its work. They estimate that they need another two hours to penetrate the rest of the ice. You two can be on Lantana in less than ten minutes. If you encounter him and Dr. Valquist in the flooded chambers, use the spear guns. If they’ve made it to a dry area, be prepared to hunt them with pistols. Remember, Lantana is very dangerous. Shoot him on sight.”

The men nodded. The smaller of the two was visibly nervous. His larger companion seemed too stupid to know how risky this plan was. The swim through the submerged decks alone was extremely unsafe. If a diver became entangled in the floating debris, there would be no rescue attempt. He would simply drown. And if they found Lantana, they had to deal with Lantana. Fawwaz took a deep breath. This hardly seemed worth the risk that Mendelbaum had taken. The ship was compromised and could scuttle at any time. The pumps were working overtime again, and the storm was still sending large waves crashing against the hull.

Fawwaz removed two spear guns from their storage bins. The only bolts left in the bins were intended for whale-tagging. They were designed to penetrate whale blubber and hold on with large barbs. They were quite nasty-looking. Fawwaz removed the heavy transmitter and battery packs from the back of the bolts. They would be far more accurate without the added weight. It took nearly all of Fawwaz's strength to draw back the super heavy-duty rubber cords on the spear guns. He handed each man a weapon and a spare bolt. "Well, then, into the hole with you," he said.

41 THE FLOOD

Jim stared at Abigail's back while she sat at a console in the far corner of the terrafarm chamber. She had found some gardening clothes in a locker by the door and taken some for them; then she'd gone to work on the controls. Their tryst had lasted no more than an hour, but it seemed to have gone on for days. Jim sensed no awkwardness between them, only a deepening sense of dread and an unspoken desire to escape together.

"I'm checking to see if I still have access to the whole ship. Mendelbaum will be able to re-boot the ship's mainframe, but he'll need to manually re-key the access codes. Phineas built a failsafe into the system without his knowledge."

"So we need to get to a working radio."

She looked at the screen with deep concern. "He's flooded the lower decks of the ship. He's trapped us here, but . . ."

"What is it?"

They heard a groaning from below them, followed by the strong smell of seawater.

“Holy God,” Abigail said. “He’s flooding the ship’s mid-decks. He’s opened the control hatches below the galley. He intends to drown us!”

“Will the children be safe?”

“Yes, for now.”

“Then let’s get moving toward the equipment storage chambers. It’s a natural place to store broadcasting equipment.” Before the words were out of his mouth, seawater had begun gurgling up from the floor grate next to his feet. The spilt soil turned to mud and drifted innocently across the room with the pitch of the ship.

They sprinted for the far end of the chamber toward the door that led deeper into the belly of the tanker. The water was already at their ankles when Abigail pulled open the hatch and scrambled into the passageway that connected one chamber to another. She couldn’t open the hatch that sealed the next chamber; something was pressing against it. Jim put his back into turning the screw the final few revolutions it required, and the hatch flew backward beneath a rush of oil-tainted water. They waded into the murky chamber and held onto the wall for support as the ship pitched violently in the storm.

Jim strained his eyes to see across the hundred-foot chamber, and saw the next hatch emerge from under the dark water—and just as quickly submerge again with the shifting of the ship. An oily, ten-foot wave rocked from one side of the filthy room to the other; then it rolled toward them and broke short of their feet with a splash. The water was rising before their eyes. The hatch at the end of the chamber was submerged again and was lost. Jim was a strong enough swimmer to make it across, but Abigail might not be. She could drown here. The look of terror in her eyes convinced him that she needed to stay. She was a civilian doctor; she was not trained for anything remotely like this. Anyone would be scared.

The look of panic on her face confirmed her words. "You go, uh . . . get to the children."

"I won't leave you here for long. I have to get breathing equipment. This chamber has about another three minutes before it will be underwater. Hold on for me, I'll be back."

She smiled despite the freezing water that lapped against their legs and looked at him for a moment. "I forgive you," she said.

Jim said nothing. She didn't think he could make it back for her. She didn't know him very well. He winked at her and began hyperventilating his lungs for the long swim ahead. If he could make it to the fire control room attached to the maintenance and tool storage chamber, he should find emergency breathing equipment. Lantanas always found a way.

As another great wave rocked the ship, Jim launched himself beneath the oil slick. He let his mind empty and focused only on his powerful stroke. He cut neatly through the water and opened his eyes just before he swam headfirst into a pile of floating debris. This room appeared to be used for outdated medical equipment. In the dim light he could make out old gurneys and mattresses. He swam around the obstacles and approached the far end of the chamber. He surfaced and took another long breath. The water was already fifteen feet deep at this end. He dove down and within seconds had the submerged hatch in his hands. The hatch swung open under his brute yank and he moved through it without looking up. He swam to the next bulkhead and ripped it open as well.

As he had hoped, there was a pocket of air trapped at the top. He stuck his mouth into the air and greedily sucked out the stagnant gas pocket. Then he dove back down, swimming hard, not caring about the oxygen he burned. The room was nearly seventy feet long, and was littered with floating debris. The ghostly shapes of floating chairs, tables, and silverware brushed against him. Apparently the galley had been flushed into this chamber. Bodies of those drowned here bobbed serenely in the current. He only dimly noted the final panic frozen on their faces as he pushed them aside.

He reached the fire control room at the far end with the last of his air. He pulled on the door handle and couldn't move it at all. It was locked. His lungs felt sticky and a viscous fluid bubbled in the back of his mouth. He had only a few moments of clarity left. He looked through the three-foot-square glass window into the small room and saw what he was looking for: Breathing equipment. He pounded on the glass with his fist, but was unable to break it; this wasn't plate glass that could be smashed with an elbow. Jim slowly remembered the body of a cook that he had pushed aside: the man had been armed.

He swam slowly back toward the area where he imagined he had seen the drowned man, but couldn't find him. He must have floated off in the current and was invisible in the weak emergency lights. A curtain of red spots began to fall over Jim's world as he searched. It was no use. He gave up on the search and drifted to the bottom of the chamber, a deep sense of calm settling over him.

Then he saw it: the cook's gun had come loose when Jim brushed him out of the way. He picked up the revolver and dragged himself lethargically across the floor toward the window. He squeezed the trigger. Nothing. The rounds were water logged. He squeezed again, and then again—and nearly dropped the gun from the powerful shock wave the exploding cartridge created. The round did its job, smashing the window to the fire safety room. Jim hauled himself though the window, and, oblivious to the deep gashes it caused, forced himself through the small space.

The first life-giving breath of air from the mask nearly made him sick. The red spots cleared from his vision and he felt a moment of giddiness. The moment was torn from him instantly as his mind re-focused on Abigail waiting in a flooded room hundreds of feet away.

How much time had passed? He had no idea. He grabbed two gas masks and a weatherproof radio and tried to avoid the broken glass as he swam back through the opening. He still managed to cut his knee badly and when he looked down at it, he realized how cut up his hands and stomach were, as well. He ignored the burning saltwater and kicked hard, thinking only of the beautiful woman he had left to die in the other chamber.

The trip back was like a swim through Jell-O. He swam as hard as he could, but seemed not to move. By the time he was back at the main bulkhead to the chamber, he was exhausted. He realized in horror that the room was completely flooded. How long had it been submerged? He searched for Abigail, but she was not where he had left her. He swam the length of the chamber and then doubled back. She had to be here.

Then he saw her. She was floating motionlessly at the top of the room. He pushed off hard from the bottom and stroked toward her. He feared the worst as he grabbed her leg, but she simply took her mouth off a bubbling pipe and smiled her wonderful smile back at him. He nearly forgot to breathe.

He handed her the other emergency breathing mask and started the flow of air on the small tank. He reached out for her and they joined hands, happy for a brief moment at this tiny victory. As Jim led the way back into the dark, he could feel her small hand shaking in his. She was freezing, and he was afraid she would go hypothermic any moment. He needed to get her out of the water. They moved through the same chamber he had just swum, this time moving at barely more than a crawl. She was like a dead weight behind him. He stopped and pulled her in close, facemask to facemask. She was still conscious, but her eyes were glazed. She was shivering slightly. That was when Jim saw the air bubbles.

Divers were coming for them. As Abigail had feared, they were no longer protected by the ice barrier. Mendelbaum's gamble had paid off. The divers would be on them any moment from the submerged internal dock. The chamber they needed to cross was fifty feet long. He would never make it with her trailing behind him. He still had the pistol he had used to break the glass, but it was probably completely water-logged by now. The men Mendelbaum sent were likely to be armed with underwater weapons.

Jim stopped swimming and motioned for Abigail to keep moving. She obeyed. Jim turned back toward the air bubbles in time to see a diver pull the trigger on his spear gun. The barb moved in slow motion toward him, but he couldn't move from its path. It struck him in the abdomen with a horrible, slow-motion *thwump*. He screamed inside his mask. The wound wasn't mortal, but the pain was nearly unbearable.

He could see the guard struggling to load a second barb; the man wasn't strong enough to pull the heavy rubber cord into place. Jim grabbed the shaft of the bolt in his abdomen and pulled. It was barbed. He gritted his teeth and ripped it free. The pain was replaced by a momentary coldness as seawater entered the wound.

He swam slowly toward the man who'd shot him with one goal in mind. The man saw his approach and panicked. He dropped his spear gun and turned to swim away, but Jim was already on him. He grabbed the small man's flipper and pulled him backward into a bear hug. He squeezed the air out of the terrified man and slowly massaged the tip of the large barb into the soft spot just under his rib cage. It took several seconds and nearly all his strength to force the large barb all the way through his organs and into his heart. Jim released his hold and let him drift away in the current, their blood mixing together in a pink cloud.

More bubbles erupted from the open hatch. Jim saw the fallen spear gun and swam for it. Each stroke felt like searing death in this stomach. He had the spear gun in his hands seconds later, but felt like he might throw up from the pain. There was no bolt in the gun. It lay discarded on the floor where the terrified guard had dropped it. The bubbles wafted past him, and he realized that the second guard was not swimming for him: He was pursuing Abigail. Jim grabbed the thick, surgical rubber band with his right hand and drew it back halfway before the pain from his exertion halted him. It was too much.

Abigail was only twenty feet ahead of her pursuer. The man stopped and brought up his spear gun. Jim's heart froze. The man fired at her back and the bolt streaked out of the weapon. But his aim was poor and he merely grazed Abigail's shoulder.

Jim had seen enough. Without regard for the misery in his guts, he yanked the rubber band on the spear gun back into position and locked it. He grabbed the bolt and loaded it. The guard was closing on Abigail with powerful strokes when Jim fired. His skill as a marksman translated from weapon to weapon: The bolt caught the guard in the back of the neck and killed him instantly.

"You don't look good, Jim," Abigail said.

He wouldn't let her see the wound. He had taken her through the flooded decks, but he was clearly hurt. "Call me James. And that's not what you said earlier," he said through a pale smile.

The flooding of the mid-decks stopped near the bow of the ship. They had entered a pressurized chamber connection tube, sealed the door, and activated the small pump to clear the water. They were within minutes of the gold storage chambers when Jim had finally collapsed.

"I'm not going to hurt you," Abigail lied.

Jim lifted his shirt and exposed his abdomen's torn flesh. The barb had taken a great deal of meat with it when he ripped it free, but it had also probably saved him from an instant death. "The barb kept the bolt from completely skewering me," he said.

Abigail could say nothing.

"I don't think I've got anything more than a nick on any organs," he said. "Just let me rest a moment and we'll get moving again."

She couldn't believe what she was hearing. "A nick? If by that you mean you may have a lacerated organ, then yes, it's just a nick. It's a nick that will kill you if you don't let me treat it."

"I thought you were a child psychiatrist, not an internist," Jim said playfully. She didn't smile. "You need to get to the storage chambers and out of the ship for this radio to broadcast a signal that anyone will be able to pick up," he said seriously.

"If you're bleeding internally and we don't stop it, you'll die. Lie down and let me have a look."

He obeyed again. The bleeding had not stopped. That was what really concerned her. If an organ were really damaged, he probably didn't have more than a few hours to live, and there was nothing she could do. But if all that was damaged was a vein, he might survive if she could locate it.

"I need to feel around in there for a minute, okay?" she asked.

Jim just smiled at her.

She waited until he had taken a few deep breaths and trained his gaze on the dark ceiling far overhead. Then she inserted her pointer and middle finger into the wound. Jim gave a reflexive shudder but otherwise stayed perfectly still. She thought the pain had to be excruciating, but he didn't make a sound. She felt the inside of the wound for depth first. Her fingers slid in two inches and stopped. That was plenty to have hit something vital. She probed to the right and found the outer wall of an organ. It felt smooth to the touch, no jagged edges.

Blood continued to flow around her hand. He must have lost a few pints at least by now. He was a big man, but no one could lose this much and not feel the effects. Still, she detected nothing resembling a damaged vein. She moved her fingers around to the left and touched the outside of another organ, probably the liver. What she felt made her hand freeze in place.

"Wh-what is it?" Jim asked.

She couldn't respond at first. "Your liver is damaged," she said as evenly as she could. "I have to get you to the hospital ward—"

"No time for that. Get to the kids and use the radio."

"I can't leave you like this. They'll kill you if they find you."

He reached up and wiped the tears off of her cheek. "You need to get moving."

“What are you going to do?” Abigail asked. But she knew the answer. She could tell by the set of his jaw that he had no intention of making it out alive. He was heading back into the fray so that she would have enough time to locate the children. “At least let me cauterize the wound.”

“There is nothing here that we can use to heat a tool. I have an idea of where I can find something that will work, though.”

“You’re going to use the liquid nitrogen,” she stated.

He nodded. That could work, but it was going to be gruesomely painful, and she doubted he would make it back to the cryo chamber with the amount of blood loss he had sustained. She made up her mind and looked deep into his eyes. Her stare stopped him. He looked back at her slowly and met her eyes.

“Katarina is like my own child now and I’ll protect her with my life.”

“Somehow I knew that from the first moment I met you. G-go now. Save Sharon… ” He caught himself but couldn’t, *wouldn’t* correct the words.

“Save yourself,” he said as he pulled himself up.

He pressed his hand into his wound and glanced back toward the hatch. He leaned in and kissed her on the forehead, then stepped back into the dark and disappeared.

"I love you," Abigail whispered. But he was already gone. She was alone for the first time since helping him escape, and she felt a chill pass over her.

"I love you, too," he called back from the dark. She smiled in spite of herself.

She had basically lived alone on the ship for the last two years. She had relied on no one but herself and Phineas until James came into her life. The memory of their lovemaking sent a tingle up her spine, and she felt a wave of crushing loss and guilt that nearly made her lose her balance. So much lost, so much left to lose. She held onto the wall and tried to banish the weakness in favor of the children. She had lived through so many horrors since Albert was murdered that it seemed like her time with him was another life, a dream experienced by someone else. Only this ship was real anymore, and it was sinking. She had to get through the last few hundred yards of abandoned oil storage chambers to reach Edvard and Katarina. They were safe in the gold storage chambers, the one place that Mendelbaum would never destroy. She had planned to use the override key to jettison the chambers, but she'd decided that it was more important to use the key to free James. She'd made the right decision: She never would have made it this far without him.

The way that Mendelbaum had immediately unleashed Guillermo against her was a misjudgment on her part. She believed that he was far too in love with her to let Guillermo have her. Perhaps she had underestimated how in love with her he really was. He'd gone straight for the worst punishment he could think of. Rather than try to recapture her, he had sent his brother to butcher her. He had also reset the reactor more quickly than she had anticipated. Her override switch was useless. She took the necklaces off and looked at the swastika. With a wry smile she realized that it might still be useful. He had loved this thing, treated it like a coveted symbol of everything that his ship stood for. Destroying it now didn't make sense.

She tucked it back into her shirt, turned on her flashlight, and waded through greasy ankle-deep water toward the hatch at the far end of the pitch-black chamber. She stayed close to the wall for balance because the ship was pitched thirty degrees to starboard now. Mendelbaum had allowed a vast amount of water aboard, attempting to flush them out; his pumps would need days to clean up, and the ship wouldn't be moving anywhere in a hurry. The storm still raged outside; she felt the deck beneath her feet shifting again as the tanker rocked back to port.

She had waited for this storm for weeks and now it was almost too big. She hadn't counted on Mendelbaum flooding the lower decks. That was bold. She imagined that Mendelbaum's entire deck crew was on the bridge, scrambling to keep the ship pointed into the huge waves. She hoped they were successful; a single mistake could scuttle them.

She reached the far end of the last oil storage chamber and pulled hard at the hatch. It gave way slowly, its oil-slicked hinges swinging silently inward. The chamber beyond was as black as the other she had moved through, but much smaller. The ceiling was only inches above her head, and the walls nearly touched her shoulders. A grown man would have had to move sideways. The noxious odor of old oil died away as she moved away from the chamber and she breathed more easily.

Her flashlight cut a beam of yellow before her, and a single sign was illuminated: OFF LIMITS. She had reached the outer shell of the gold vaults. She grasped the handle and turned it easily. It snapped open and gave way to the rooms beyond. Before her stood the doors to ten self-contained chambers. Each could be ejected in the event the ship sank and used as an escape pod. The chambers were each attached to sets of three self-inflating Kevlar balloons the size of dirigibles. They were so large that even one would be sufficient to support the weight of the cargo stored inside each chamber. She selected the fourth door from the left and entered.

"Mom!" Edvard screamed. He charged her and they embraced tightly. "We thought you'd never get here. Katarina's been crying for like an hour." Edvard scrubbed away the tears from his own red cheeks.

"Katarina," Abigail called across the rows of oddly stacked gold. "Come here and give me a hug."

Katarina ignored her at first and pouted in the corner. She quickly relented and charged toward her, knocking over the piles of gold coins as she came. She didn't say a word, and she didn't have to. She clung to Abigail's waist next to Edvard and refused to budge.

"When are we getting outta here?" Edvard asked.

"Soon," Abigail said, although she had no idea. This was where the plan ended. She could unlock the outer egress system, but she had no way to know if help was close enough to hear the SOS. Her plan had always been to use the override key now, take control of the SOS system and radio for help. She could eject the storage chambers, but as long as the storm outside raged, they would drown within a few hours if help did not come. In calm waters she could risk it, but then Mendelbaum would be able to attack her easily. The only hope was for Jim to give them enough time. The guards would be back this way as soon as they cleared the ice. As with the rest of the ship, the only way to reset the manual locks after a reactor shut-down was to manually reset each one. But if the guards came too quickly, she would have to eject the storage chambers whether she had made contact with help or not.

She removed the small portable radio Jim had recovered from the maintenance and storage chamber and extended its antenna. She hadn't gotten any outside signals when she'd tried it before, but there was far less steel around her now to block incoming transmissions. She pressed the handheld receiver to her ear and hit the auto scan button. The radio tracked through all bandwidths, and she picked up on something very weak. Before she could stop on the weak signal, though, the radio had locked onto something else. It was the familiar inter-ship radio system Mendelbaum was using to manage the catastrophe she had created.

His voice was emotionless as he barked orders to the crews overseeing the pumps and the search effort. She listened for a moment and realized that there was no way he had captured Jim yet. There would be triumph in his voice. She smiled and kept scanning for the weak signal.

43 Pure Life

Jim knew that his wound was mortal. There was no escaping the look on Abigail's perfect face. The knowledge that he would die sharpened his anger to a diamond point. It was okay to die. He had lived a lifetime in the last ten hours. His death would not be in vain. He needed to give Abigail at least an hour's head start. If she could get to the storage chambers and eject all the bins, Mendelbaum would have a hard time finding her. He wouldn't just sink a billion dollars worth of gold. He would try to investigate each pod to find her and the children. That would have to be enough time for help to arrive.

Jim moved into the chamber where they'd left their diving equipment only a few minutes earlier and checked the air supply. His hands looked very pale. His tank was half full, plenty of air to swim back to the ice wall they had created—if he weren't wounded. It would have to do. He looked at his wound and clamped his hand back onto it. The bleeding had mostly stopped.

He sealed the door to the back of the chamber and opened the hatch to the flooded chambers. The water poured in around him. As it splashed over his feet he braced himself for the sting of the salt water, but there was no way to prepare for the shock. The freezing water felt like hot acid poured onto his raw guts. The pain cleared his vision. He realized that he was holding his breath and tried to take a few normal inhalations from the regulator. The air helped. He found it strange that he felt fine as he swam through the chamber, one even stroke after another. He dimly realized that he was in shock from the trauma he had sustained.

He couldn't tell how long it took to cross the chamber, but suddenly he was at the far end. The hatch hung open as they had left it and Jim lost his bearings as soon as he swam into the terra-farming chamber. The fertile topsoil that had once blanketed the precisely-laid planters was mixed with seawater, and the room was a cloud of black and brown. Unperturbed, Jim swam for the floor of the chamber and located the central walkway that had separated the tables from one another. The grate had a distinct feel to it that the smooth floor did not. He hooked his fingers into the steel openings in the grates and pulled himself steadily on.

He was at the end of the chamber when his air ran out. He realized with a kind of sinking horror that he hadn't even considered how hard he was breathing. Under normal circumstances, when one was forced to free dive a half-sunken oil tanker, oxygen conservation would have been the first priority. Jim realized he was smiling, and knew he didn't have much time left. Delirium was setting in. He discarded the useless emergency breathing tank and fought the tendrils of panic that wrapped around his pounding heart.

He wanted desperately to draw a breath: His body demanded it. His brain fought his body as he pulled along the floor of the once-wonderful garden. He was at the door to the far end of the chamber when his body overpowered his brain, and he sucked in what his body insisted was a life-giving breath of air only to have the misery of the soil-laden water pulled into his lungs. He coughed hard and involuntarily sucked in another breath of ocean and dirt. He couldn't see his hands through the mist of red that closed over him but he could feel something in front of him. It was the door. He twisted the screw once, then twice, then three times before he felt as if a huge unseen force was pulling him out of this life toward something else.

Voices. He coughed and sputtered and vomited seawater. But he was sure that he could hear muffled voices close by. He blinked several times and then held his eyes closed. His vision cleared slightly, and he realized where he was and what must have happened.

The water purification chamber had been sealed behind the terrafarm room in which Mendelbaum had started his flood. It had stayed dry until he opened the hatch. When he opened the hatch, he had been sucked into the dry chamber along with thousands of gallons of seawater. Fortunately, this chamber was nearly ten times the size of the terra farm and easily absorbed the flood.

He had no idea how long ago that had been or why he was alive now. But he was alive, and there was work to do. He tried to stand up, but was only able to flop his arm out from underneath his body. His limbs were not responding to him. His vision was still very hazy, and he was aware that he was still coughing in long, ragged hacks every time he tried to take a breath.

He tried to survey the room and found that his head was spinning. He felt horribly drunk. He could tell that the far end of the water purification chamber was still encased in grayish icy foam, but his eyes seemed to be playing tricks. There seemed to be lights flashing inside of the dirty foam. That was where the voices were coming from. As he stared at the grayish mass, the points of light inside it seemed to grow brighter and the voices come closer. He realized that his eyes were not playing tricks; he was looking at the front lines of the battle. He was watching the final push to break through the ice barrier that he'd created.

He'd made it back to the enemy in no shape to fight. They would be on him in moments and he couldn't get off the floor. The same metal grate that had lined the floor in the terrafarm room was beneath him in the ship's water purification chamber. He rolled to his stomach and began pulling himself forward again. An idea was forming. He wanted to make it into the cryo-freeze chamber to cauterize his wound. But then he remembered something else about the room. He needed to get out of sight. Frantically, he looked around the chamber. The only suitable hiding place he saw was high above on the scaffolding or on top of the central water tank. But there was no way he could climb that far in his condition. He looked back at the ice foam barrier at the far end and made a decision.

He began dragging himself toward the ice blockade and the men behind it. It was slow, grueling work, and he didn't remember to keep his wounded abdomen off the ground until he scraped it painfully over the metal beneath him. He let out an involuntary cry, and the lights behind the foam stopped moving. A second later they began moving again at a frantic pace.

Jim crawled to the entrance of the tube that connected the water purification chamber to the cryonics lab where he had detonated the grenade and released the flood of super-cooled gel. The passageway was blocked with the foam, but the tube had not been constructed to be flush with the ground. As with most ships, there was a ten-inch gap between the floor and the opening of the hatch to help prevent water from flowing easily from one section of the ship to another. This had allowed a large air pocket to form in the overhang between the ice foam and the floor. It was just big enough for a woman to fit in comfortably. Jim realized he was far too big to get into the hole easily and getting back out might be impossible. The realization was no more than a fleeting thought as he rolled onto his back and wedged himself into the space. He held perfectly still.

The frozen foam around him vibrated and shook under the men's rhythmic efforts above. He could make out changes in the light as it filtered down to him through the dark mass of corrupted foam. The men were working just above him. They were nearly through. Then a sound like concrete being broken up with a sledgehammer echoed into the ruined water treatment and purification room, and the first of Mendelbaum's men climbed through the hole. Jim heard the crisp feedback of a radio.

"We're in, over," the man said.

"Very good," came Mendelbaum's metallic reply. "Begin draining the terrafarm and the rest of the chambers. Swim to the gold, if you have to."

"It sounded like there was someone in here before we broke through. Over," the man said.

"Well, do you see anyone now?"

"Uh, no, but the flood control hatch to the terrafarm has been breached—"

"I suggest you begin your search of the ship and stop wasting time on things you may have heard." Mendelbaum made no attempt to hide the contempt in his voice.

"Yes, sir," the guard said as he severed the connection. "You heard the green bastard. You three get moving on draining the chamber. You two get the water system back on line. I'm due for a smoke."

There were grunts of disapproval and then the sound of men moving across the chamber.

Jim pulled himself forward inch-by-inch, his chest pressed against the filthy ice foam above him until he was completely stuck. He couldn't draw a deep breath, and a wave a claustrophobic panic swept over him. His arms felt like lead, and the harder he pulled, the more he wanted to take a deep breath. His wound rubbed against the rough ice and blood began to drip from it again. The pain was nearly unbearable, and he bit the inside of his lip to avoid crying out. After nearly a minute of pulling, but not moving, the blood from his wound had soaked him from his groin to his neck, but a strange thing began to happen. The blood was beginning to lubricate the ice and he began slithering forward. A moment later, he poked his head around the side of the ice and looked at the men in the chamber.

They were more than fifty feet away from him when he began hauling himself up and into the newly cleared tube. The ice stung his hands as he dragged himself along the coarse, frozen ground. The men had used a combination of pick axes and some kind of foul-smelling liquid they were spraying to penetrate the twenty-foot blockade. He saw the rusted hatch beneath his hands, stuck in the ice where he had kicked it off after blowing the hatch open. The exertion was too much, and he had to stop for a moment.

He looked over his shoulder and could see the guards with their backs to him. If they turned now, they would see him. He realized another problem. He was leaving a smeared trail of bright red blood six inches wide behind him. It wouldn't take long to be discovered. He had one final shot at helping himself. He pulled as hard as he could and made it through the tube.

He was too injured to marvel at the destruction he'd caused in the cryonics chamber. From a glance he could see that the super-cooled gel had mixed with the water and an ice-foam blob had risen nearly eighty feet into the air and fallen in on several tanks. The ruin was superficial but the odor was overwhelming. It didn't appear that the bodies in the private tanks had been damaged, but unless repairs were made soon, they couldn't stay cold much longer. Many tanks appeared to be in working order, though, but no new bodies could be added.

"What the fuck is that?" a guard yelled.

He must have seen the blood. But Jim's target was in sight. He pulled himself toward Guillermo's body with the last of his strength and leaned against it, wheezing. The suit had been freed from its ice barriers, but Mendelbaum had not dealt with his brother's corpse yet. It appeared that he had unlocked the suit to view the body, but it had probably still been buried in the ice, unmovable. Jim unhooked the straps that held the long, pale body in place and rolled it out unceremoniously. Guillermo was stiff; his blood was still frozen. He banged onto the steel floor and seemed to leer at Jim.

As the first pistol shot rang out, Jim pulled himself behind the suit and used it as a shield. He rolled onto his back and stuck his legs into the suit first, then his arms. Pistol shots peppered the back of the suit that was exposed to the men. They were running to get clear shots at him as he felt a horrible stinging sensation in the back of his neck. He was worried for a moment that he had been hit, and then he realized that the suit had connected itself to the IV tube still implanted in his spinal cord from his fight with the Beast.

The suit came to life and enveloped him, small motors tightening straps in a mechanical whir of poking and prodding. A small screen was projected before him with a list of commands. Jim raised his hand and selected from the virtual list. He chose the command that said ARM. The helmet slid over his face and the breastplate snapped into position. Another prompt on the screen alerted him to the fact that he was scheduled for a dose of both morphine and adrenaline. Jim accepted both.

44 Too Much, Too Fast

"I don't know what you want me to do, sir," the helmsman yelled over the din in the main control room. "There's just no way to divert more power to the pumps. Cryonics needs everything it's getting and we have to be able to navigate the ship. The pumps have enough power to stay ahead of the flood you, ah, created," he said as carefully as he could.

Mendelbaum gave him a dismissive shrug and pulled the outer window hatch back into place.

The helmsman didn't get the point; he continued yelling even though the storm was locked outside once again. "When we're clear of the storm, we can divert full power to the pumps to get the ship cleared." He realized he didn't need to shout any longer and continued, "But right now we only need the pumps going at half capacity to stay afloat. If anything, we need more power diverted to the engines to steer into these waves. If we misjudge one, we could scuttle the whole mess."

Mendelbaum turned on him. "I am well aware of where we stand. My chief concern is capturing that whore." He took a deep breath. "The ocean will have her one way or the other."

The helmsman looked back at him as if he didn't understand. "We shouldn't need to evacuate the ship. If we can steer into the waves we shouldn't lose her."

Mendelbaum ignored him and kept speaking. "Not that an evacuation would save any lives in this storm. Divert power away from the cryo-freeze generators to the pumps," Mendelbaum said. The helmsman shrugged, but did as he was told. Seconds later, al-Barq came on the radio.

"It appears that we are losing power to the cryonics chamber. What do you want me to do?"

Mendelbaum thought about the question and realized his potential blunder. "The tanks will be fine without power for the next few hours," he said carefully.

"But that's not what you told the sheik when he toured the ship. You said that Rafiqua would be safe so long as the ship's nuclear power held out. You said that reserve power was a last resort and that the tanks would never be allowed to warm."

"Goddamn it, al-Barq," Mendelbaum yelled. "The ship will sink if we don't divert additional power to the pumps!"

“Dr. Mendelbaum, I respectfully disagree,” the helmsman said.

Mendelbaum turned on him and considered shooting him on the spot.

“We have enough power to run the pumps, the navigation system, and the cryonics chamber at minimum power—”

The helmsman bit off the end of his sentence as he made eye contact with Mendelbaum. Mendelbaum was holding a pistol outstretched in his hands. He gripped the gun so tightly his fingers appeared white instead of slightly green. “Divert power to the pumps! I want them found!” he howled.

Al-Barq said nothing.

45 Bloody Flower

Jim looked serenely around the chamber at the chaos he had wrought. He blinked several times as the heavy dose of drugs began to subside and, even then, it seemed like a dream—or a nightmare. The three guards that had come in firing had been tough to dispatch at first. It had been hard to balance in the suit, and he had fallen over several times before finally getting the hang of it. All the while he was being peppered with pistol fire. The bullets were harmless but noisy inside the suit; they seemed to tap out a kind of musical beat to which he swayed uncertainly as he learned to balance.

Once Jim found his footing, however, he wasn't able to deploy any of the firearms; instead, all he could engage was some kind of nasty-looking blade by squeezing a release in the palm of his right hand. This was fine, except that the men firing on him were twenty yards away. He charged at them awkwardly, but only one was too slow to avoid him. He rammed into the guard like a bull and sent him flailing into the rear wall of the chamber. The man slumped to the floor and appeared either dead or unconscious. It had taken more dexterity to catch up with the other two, and Jim quickly realized how nimble the suit was if he didn't fight the movements.

He had missed cleanly with his first stroke at the guards, but he used the momentum of the swing to bring the blade around in a second spinning chop behind him that caught a man in the midsection and cleaved him in two. The other guard had screamed in horror and tried to run, but Jim had been able to catch him easily. He had brought the curved blade straight down on the guard's head and split it neatly.

Standing still now, soaked in blood, Jim looked back at the hole in the ice foam where the rest of the security team waited. He hoped that they would abandon their search for Abigail and the gold and come back to check on their comrades. Seconds later, his hopes were confirmed. The remaining guards entered the chamber and fanned out. There was shocked disbelief at the carnage, and then a palpable fear as they looked at him.

Jim squeezed the palm of his right hand reflexively, and on the second squeeze, a powerful spring released and the curved blade spun away in a vicious arc. He missed the guards, but he made a note of where the blade landed. It took a few moments of searching the

LCD screen to locate the primary offensive weapons display.

Abigail finished the last of the canned tuna she had spread out for the kids. They had been left with plenty of food, but neither had eaten much until she sat them down and got them to relax. The simple task of feeding them had nearly made her cry with relief. If they died here, at least it would be on her terms and not Mendelbaum's.

"Are you ready to do what we practiced?" she asked Edvard. He nodded happily, and the three exited the storage chamber and sealed the hatch behind them. They were in the main control room; from here they had access to each of the ten gold vaults that held Mendelbaum's accumulated wealth. It was time for a test.

"Okay. We have to turn these handles at the same time," she said, pointing to the large red handles on either side of the room. Edvard nodded and grabbed the handle located just to the right of the door to the chamber they had just left. Abigail sat at the main control panel; her hand around the main release valve.

"On the count of three," she said, locking eyes with her son. She felt a surge of *schadenfruede* for the pain she and Edvard were about to cause Mendelbaum.

There wasn't enough gold in the world to quell the horror Mendelbaum had wrought upon her family, but this was a nice start. "One, two, three," she said as she and Edvard turned the levers to the right as far as they would go.

There was a nearly instantaneous hiss as the outer pressure hatches released, and storage chamber number four jettisoned into the Atlantic.

Abigail looked back at the external camera and followed the erratic course of the chamber as three seventy-foot balloons inflated in seconds and bobbed away in the giant swells. Each chamber was attached to massive support balloons that were designed to self-inflate the moment they came in contact with water. The storm raged, but the balloons held chamber four above the water easily. They appeared to be working. The other nine chambers could now be manually released from either inside the chamber or from her control booth. Mendelbaum designed them as his escape pods of last resort. She would know soon how Mendelbaum would react. Would he just let the gold float away, or would he try to intercept it? Or would he do the unthinkable?

Her heart missed a beat as her worst fear materialized. A thin red line streaked off the deck high above toward the dark waves in front of her. The uranium shells hit the water fifty feet from the first balloon and sent a column of water up into the night as the gunner quickly corrected, dragging the maelstrom back to the nearest balloon. It exploded on her screen noiselessly. The storage chamber, now supported by two balloons, bobbed precipitously beneath the black waves. The gunner made quick work of the other two support balloons and the chamber disappeared into the abyss.

"I bet that hurt," Abigail said.

Edvard gave her a quizzical look and moved to the lever for hatch number three. She smiled and gave him a thumbs-up. It all depended on Jim now.

47 WISHING WELL

"What is the status of the search team? Over." Mendelbaum asked. There was no response from al-Barq. Mendelbaum sat down opposite the helmsman and wiped his face. It was over. She had forced him to sink a fortune of his own gold, but she had gone down with it. Lantana was still at large, but it didn't matter now.

"We've lost contact," al-Barq replied at last. Mendelbaum detected a note of disdain in his security chief's voice. "I've dispatched fifteen men to their last location. That leaves you a skeleton crew of trained guards to protect the rest of the ship's vital systems. Unless you want me to pull the maintenance men, support staff, and doctors off their duties to aid in the hunt."

"That shouldn't be necessary, but I'll keep it in mind."

"Sir," the helmsman asked, "what are your orders to the deck gunner?"

"What?" Mendelbaum asked. He was perplexed as he rose from his chair and looked back into the storm. He blinked several times and refused to accept what he was seeing.

“Sir?” the helmsman asked again.

Mendelbaum swallowed hard. “Fire at will, destroy them all.”

Flashing before him were the strobes atop twelve massive yellow balloons. She probably wasn’t aboard any of those chambers, either, but he couldn’t take the risk that she might escape in one of them.

Al-Barq came back on the radio. “What’s the status of the cryonics lab?”

Mendelbaum could not answer him for several seconds. When he finally did answer, he chose another lie. “The lab is fine.”

48 Die Well

Jim left the dead behind and moved farther into the ship, the way he and Abigail had come hours earlier. His wound no longer hurt. He fought a wave of painkiller-induced nausea by closing his eyes, but it only made the world seem to swim and slosh around him. The insides of his eyelids flashed surreal images of the carnage he had wrought. He opened his eyes and looked down at his suit: He was soaked in the gore of the encounter. He shook himself like a wet Labrador to clear the images. They didn't matter. He conjured an image of Abigail and felt his stomach relax. He had done what was necessary against armed attackers and bought her more time.

He hoped to avoid killing the support staff, but if Mendelbaum chose to arm the non-military personnel, he would not hold back. Abigail and the children were safe as long as he was between them and the rest of the crew. But a ship this size probably had a considerable security apparatus that had not been brought to bear on him yet. They would be coming, that much was certain. He scrolled through the available medications and offensive weapons and stumbled onto something else: He had access to the ship's camera systems and detailed schematics. He tapped into the feed. They were presently trained on the dark waves outside and the massive yellow balloons that were being systematically destroyed by the deck gunner. That was not a good sign. If Mendelbaum was willing to destroy his own fortune, he was clearly willing to sink the ship before he allowed Abigail to escape. The only way to protect her was to disable the deck guns, or disable Mendelbaum.

Jim stared at the ship schematic and turned over tactical solutions. He decided that facing the guards here was not his best option; he needed to move on Mendelbaum or the deck guns directly. He had to prevent Mendelbaum from firing on any more support balloons. He took off at a heavy trot toward the end of the chamber. Any guards who came toward Abigail now would have to drain the ship or bring breathing equipment. He doubted that they had any other diving gear, or they would have sent more than two men to intercept them earlier. No, they were going to have to drain the chambers to get to Abigail and the kids, and that would take time.

As he rounded a corner, he realized that he was back at his original holding cell. His stay here seemed like another lifetime. He moved past the holding cell, and climbed a long flight of stairs to a gray outer hatch. He threw open the door and inhaled fresh air. The deck was soaked in rain and the bright spotlights hardly illuminated more than a few feet. It wasn't until a bolt of lightning streaked overhead that Jim could see the entire massive ship lit up. The waves rocked violently and Jim grabbed the doorframe for support. Referencing the schematic on his small screen, he located the deck guns. They were mounted on fifteen-foot bases to give them easy clearance over the sides of the ship.

Jim didn't need his map to pinpoint the forward gun battery: He could hear it even over the storm, firing intermittently at something in the water, probably Abigail. He took off across the deck as fast as he could toward the sound, heedless of the danger. If he were spotted and a Gatling gun turned on him, it was over. Another bolt of lightning arced into the water and backlit the far deck gun. The waves seemed to be less intense, but the rain still fell in sheets. At one hundred feet he could see the gun clearly.

He could just make out through the rain and dark the outline of the guard in the control chair. A smile spread across his face as he realized that the man was wearing large sound suppressors to protect his hearing from the guns' awful noise. There was no possibility the gunner could hear him approach.

Jim raised the left arm of his suit, selected the auto shotgun, and stopped ten feet below the gun. He didn't relish the idea of shooting the man in the back, so he considered ways to disable him. A plan was taking form when he remembered the fact that this man had been systematically sinking the balloons that he believed might support Abigail and the children. The auto shotgun discharged reflexively and the deed was done.

As if to confirm the righteousness of his act, two more storage chambers flew into the water beneath the silent barrels of the Gatling Guns and were quickly supported by giant yellow balloons. Jim didn't know if Abigail was in one of those chambers or not, but he had bought her more time. The guards were surely onto his position now and he had to move. He turned back the way he had come, mayhem his only thought.

The hundred-yard jog across the deck passed as if in a dream. The first light of morning broke far out to sea. The massive waves had softened to midsized rollers that were mostly absorbed by the giant tanker. Jim reached the mid-deck gun encampment and stopped short. The gun was unmanned, but if he moved any farther down the ship, he would expose his back and flanks to attack. If the attack came from the Gatling gun, it would be over. He would, likely, die on the deck of this ship, but he hoped to draw it out as long as possible.

With the dead gunner behind him, he had the advantage of keeping his potential attackers in front. Jim stepped to the nearest hatch and heard a sound that made his heart freeze: the telltale whoosh of a rocket-propelled grenade. He turned in the direction of the sound as the trail of white smoke snaked toward him in slow motion. The RPG struck the bulkhead next to him and exploded with a force that threw him sideways onto the deck. The suit flashed and beeped around him as it attempted to recalibrate itself, but it didn't appear to be damaged. Jim tried to stand, but only slipped on the wet deck; his fall was a stroke of dumb luck as a second RPG streaked over his head by inches and hissed its way out to sea.

He didn't wait for a third shot as he rolled to his side and extended his left arm. He aimed in the general direction of the RPG exhaust trail and fired. The suit stiffened around his arm and drew his fire slightly to the left. It took a second for him to realize that the suit was tracking the targets automatically. His shots had been zeroed in on a spot where a man had once stood fifty feet away. All that was left now were strewn body parts and a headless stump.

Jim struggled to his feet on the wet deck and began moving forward. He fired at the guards that appeared in the bulkhead behind the dead man, but they ducked quickly out of sight. His holographic screen blinked angrily at him until he looked back at it. It asked ENABLE LAUNCHER? Jim clicked the YES command and fired four grenades in rapid succession into the bulkhead. The explosions were disastrous to the men inside. Jim moved on but he knew that they were adjusting tactics, it's what he would do. A lone target, even one with superior firepower, can always be out flanked.

49 All Hands

Fawwaz al-Barq had seen and heard things aboard the *Pura Vida* that would never allow him a good night's sleep again. He stood at the far end of the deck and watched Lantana through the lens of a Barrett fifty-caliber sniper rifle. He took a long, slow breath, but still struggled to steady his aim. He had loaded the weapon with depleted uranium shells that would easily penetrate the armor blanketing the American.

Fawwaz clicked off the safety and held his breath. He had a perfect shot at the back of Lantana's head. It would be a mercy kill. The scope shook slightly with his concentration—and a thought that would not leave his mind. He was haunted by Mendelbaum's lie. He had told him that the cryo-chambers were in good working order and that there was nothing to worry about. Fawwaz had known it was a lie, but he had done nothing. Why? Why would he allow Mendelbaum to betray the sheik? Even now, Rafiqua's body was probably warming up. It was likely that Mendelbaum had never been able to treat her. He had manipulated the sheik for his money. The old fool was so completely taken in by this infidel ship that he had lost all sight of what was important. Fawwaz would not be judged harshly, he would enter the Kingdom.

Fawwaz took the telescope from his eye, laid the massive rifle on the deck, and climbed into the control chair of the ship's central Gatling gun. He took a breath and enjoyed the smell of the sea air. His stomach unknotted. He had endured the last indignity of this ship and its heretical crew. He would tolerate it no more.

Lantana could stop Mendelbaum but he would need help. Fawwaz swung the Gatling gun around and trained it on Lantana for a moment as he pondered his options. His mind wandered to his wife.

The crackle of his radio in his ear focused him back onto his hatred of this place.

"Wazzie," he heard a moronic American mercenary yell into his earpiece. "Do you have a clear shot? We can't get shit for penetration on that suit. Wazzie? Fire your fucking weapon!"

Fawwaz gripped the control handles and aimed the barrels of the weapon toward the cadre of mercenaries that continued to fire pot shots at Lantana. The pistol rounds glanced off him, but one man was firing an M-16 with armor piercing bullets, forcing Lantana to take cover. Fawwaz watched as three RPG-wielding guards took kneeling positions behind the shooter and lined up their shots. The suit would not survive a direct grenade attack.

Fawwaz found the middle of the six-man team and opened fire. The solid framework that housed the guns absorbed the recoil, but the shattering cacophony of six thousand rounds per minute ruptured his eardrums instantly. He heard none of the shrieks from the men below, but instead, saw only the spray of red that erupted in place of each man that the bullets found. It was over in less than fifteen seconds. The deck where the men had stood was a ruined mess of twisted metal; only the spattered remains of fabric, blood, and bone remained where the team had stood.

Lantana looked up at al-Barq in astonishment and yelled something. Fawwaz could hear none of what he said, so instead, he raised an arm in a wave and then pointed toward the hatch from which the rest of the security team would emerge. Jim seemed to grasp his meaning a moment before another team of men emerged from the lower deck. Fawwaz watched as Jim began running, jerkily at first, as if the suit were damaged, then gaining momentum until he looked like a rolling freight train.

The three-man team was surprised by the sudden burst of aggression from their quarry and was still searching for effective cover as Jim closed on them. At ten feet the first man began firing his pistol, rounds glancing off the carbon fiber shell in a smoky haze, and then Jim lowered his shoulder and connected with him. He drove him into the man behind him and crushed both into the bulkhead.

Fawwaz trained the guns on the spot they'd crumpled onto, but neither moved. The third man had raised his pistol and was firing at Jim from close range, but quickly ran out of ammo. Jim swung the right arm of the suit and caught the man in the top of the shoulder with a bloodstained scimitar. The guard fell to the ground and dropped something that Jim didn't see. Al-Barq screamed a warning, or at least felt like he did, and Jim looked up at him.

The grenade detonated noiselessly, but Fawwaz felt the concussion on his face and knew that Jim Lantana was probably done for. He had been blown into the hatch from which the guards had emerged and out of sight.

Fawwaz knew that his time was short. His betrayal had not been well-planned; he would have to improvise while he still had some time. He swung the multibarreled gun away from the dead guards and leveled it on the control bridge. He didn't hesitate as he squeezed the dual triggers this time.

Mendelbaum watched from the control bridge as his men finally pinned Lantana down. They had him with small arms fire for the moment and should have additional rocket-propelled grenades brought out any second. The pistol shots were doing no damage to Lantana, who returned fire with the auto shotgun.

Mendelbaum swallowed hard against the bile rising in his throat. Where was al-Barq to end this? Where was the fucking RPG team to blast this murderer to hell? A grim smile spread on Mendelbaum's face when he caught sight of his chief of security. He had taken the high ground on Lantana . . . he was training the Gatling gun on—

"No!" Mendelbaum screamed. But it was no use. Al-Barq, his trusted chief of security, had just saved Lantana. Nothing of the six-man team remained but a mess of gore that sloshed around the deck with the pitch of the ship. Mendelbaum was already moving through the lower emergency hatch, shotgun in hand, when the barrage of heavy shells tore into the bridge and turned the helmsman to pulp.

But Mendelbaum was unconcerned; the worst of the storm had broken. The autopilot would engage and continue steering the ship. He sprinted through the tunnel to the reloading chamber of the central Gatling gun; moments later, he stared at al-Barq's exposed legs above him. The roar of the gun made his hands shake, but he wasted no time aiming into al-Barq's stomach. He fired twice and the guns stopped. He stared at the carnage in wonder for a moment, but didn't allow himself to truly revel in it. Not yet. The fight with Lantana was still underway, and Lantana would most likely be hunting for him. Using Guillermo's suit must have given him access to the ship's cameras and schematics; that was the only way he could have navigated his way to the deck so easily. Mendelbaum could use that. He wanted to be with Jim at the end. The best place would be the Great Room. He clicked his microphone and said, "Meet me in the Great Room, Jim. It's the big one in the middle of the schematic."

Mendelbaum would not disappoint him, but he needed to make a final stop. It was time.

50 The Calm

Abigail stared at the LCD screen for several minutes after the deck gunner sank the last of the balloons. She took a deep breath, counted to sixty and released chambers seven and eight. There were only two chambers left, and she and the children needed to be in one of them. But she needed to give Jim enough time to disable the guns if he could.

The chambers ejected like all the others and their yellow support balloons inflated, but this time, no one fired on them. Abigail smiled as she ushered the children into the second-to-last storage chamber. If Mendelbaum were counting the chambers, he might think that they were still aboard, waiting until the last possible second to try an escape. It was now or never.

She sealed the door, strapped the children into the safety harnesses arranged along the wall of the chamber, and flipped the eject lever. The pod was thrown out into the ocean with frightening speed; stacks of gold bars shifted uncertainly in their steel cages in one direction and then crashed back the other way as the pod landed in the water.

Katarina screamed in fright, but Edvard laughed as if he were on an exciting roller coaster. Abigail tried to calm Katarina, but there was no consoling her. The pod sank for what seemed like an eternity. Abigail thought for a second that she had picked the one chamber with defective flotation balloons to try to escape in, then an explosion from the outer walls of the structure shook them hard and she caught a glimpse of an expanding yellow form outside the tiny viewing port. The pod felt like it was being kicked around like a soccer ball as it rocketed back to the surface and bobbed uncertainly.

Edvard smiled at her; Katarina was as white as a sheet, but unhurt. Abigail cradled Katarina until she stopped shaking and prayed silently that she didn't hear the horrible bumblebee hum of the deck guns.

51 The Longest Night

Jim shook his head to recover his senses and tried to stand up. There was more killing to be done before he could pass peacefully. The suit was not responding to him, and an angry red light flashed in front of his eyes. The help from the security chief had been unexpected and life-saving, at least temporarily. The Gatling guns had gone silent, which could only mean one thing: He was on his own. He blinked several times and realized that his vision was out of focus. Slowly the red lights materialized into words on the holographic screen before his eyes.

CRITICAL DAMAGE blinked angrily before him. He selected the icon that said REPORT and scanned the info. The suit's main offensive weapons were offline, the life support and medication systems were running at half capacity and the actuators in the right knee and hip were damaged.

He had heard Mendelbaum over the radio; he knew where he would find him.

Jim rolled to his side, grabbed the railing of the stairs and hauled himself up. He had been blown into the open hatch and had tumbled down a long flight of metal stairs. He took a step with his left leg and the suit responded normally. But when he tried to move his right foot forward, it felt as if his leg were stuck in half-dried cement. Instead of aiding his ability to walk, he was being forced to drag his body weight and the weight of the suit forward with each step. He looked at the damaged right side and saw the problem: the titanium hip bracket was crushed into the hydraulic actuator. Dull gray oil was leaking from the damaged components.

This would not do. He considered taking the suit off, but remembered the wound to his abdomen. He scrolled down the LCD screen and searched for a medical report. He found it and scanned it quickly. The suit had stopped the bleeding by applying a cauterizing gel patch and had started him on antibiotics, painkillers, stimulants, and fresh-frozen blood plasma. The suit listed his chance of recovery at 90% if his treatment were sustained.

The cauterizing gel was the only thing keeping his bleeding in check. Removing the suit was a death sentence unless he was treated within minutes, but trying to fight in the crippled walker without the weapons wasn't likely to deliver a better result. Hopefully, he had faced the worst of the security force already. He knew that the shotgun and grenade launcher on his left arm were disabled, so he clicked the small button in the palm of his right hand and was heartened to see the bloody scimitar snap into place. That was something.

Jim scanned the schematic and confirmed that the Great Room was directly ahead, no more than a hundred yards. He began a slow, limping journey to find Mendelbaum. He realized that he could do most of the walking with his one good leg. He would take a large step forward under the power of the suit, then drag his right leg and the ruined suit forward until his feet were together. Then he would take another long step with the good leg.

The trip was agonizingly slow. In ten minutes he had made it only half the distance to the Great Room. But no guards had appeared. His awkward stride was making his hip sore and for the first time in a while, he could feel the tear in his abdomen. He stopped to catch his breath and clicked on the LCD screen. He scrolled down to the available medication list and found that cocaine was the only thing left; the rest of the drugs were damaged in the explosion. No painkillers.

In another ten minutes of concerted effort, Jim stood in front of the doors to the Great Room. He didn't know what he hoped to find when he entered; he hadn't thought that far ahead. So when he entered it, he was surprised to see Mendelbaum standing at the polished ebony podium. He looked like he was getting ready to deliver a sermon. His face was calm, even serene. But Jim knew that he was anything but relaxed. He stopped just inside the hatch and stood still. Mendelbaum didn't need to see him dragging his leg. Jim slowly raised his left arm and pointed the barrels at Mendelbaum. It was a bluff, but it might work.

"Give it up, Doctor."

Mendelbaum kept his eyes focused on the podium. "Ah, Mr. Lantana. So good of you to join me here at the end of things."

Jim didn't answer. There was something deeply unsettling in Mendelbaum's mood. He was genuinely calm, relaxed even. As if he had won the day. But the ship was crippled and Jim had destroyed the security force. It was just him and Mendelbaum now. How could he possibly be so self-assured? Jim smiled inside the protection of the suit. "Help me radio for help so that we can evacuate the rest of the patients and medical staff."

Mendelbaum seemed amused by the request. He stepped away from the podium and walked toward Jim without a hint of fear. Jim tensed himself inside the suit and got ready for a strike. He couldn't use the gun, but he could swing the blade well enough. At four feet, Mendelbaum halted his approach and stood with his arms crossed over his chest. It was now or never. Jim squeezed the button in the palm of his right hand and nothing happened.

Jim stood frozen, unable to move the suit at all. It was locked. He was a fool to let Mendelbaum get close to him. Mendelbaum had never trusted Guillermo with a weapon like this. There had to be a secret override built into the suit. He had just needed Jim to get close and he had activated it. He probably had something in the podium that required a line of sight; otherwise he would have disabled him long ago. Jim focused on his breathing and waited for the death stroke, but Mendelbaum did nothing.

He just stared at Jim blankly for several long moments. He opened his mouth to speak but found no words, and this seemed to change something in him. His expression began to oscillate between pain and insanity. He opened his mouth to speak, but again said nothing. His green-tinted face flushed scarlet, and he just closed his mouth and glared. When he finally spoke, his voice was a whisper. "Why would she choose you?" It was not really a question, more a sad statement.

His next words were inaudible, he was so angry he couldn't form words. When he finally did speak it was in an effeminate shriek, "You defiled her!"

Jim gave him a long, toothy smile and Mendelbaum snapped his jaw shut. He was off balance even though he was in complete control. Jim pushed him. "You stole her life. You murdered her husband and held her child here; she'd have sacrificed herself in an instant to destroy you. But she had to protect Edvard."

Pale blotches appeared on Mendelbaum's face. "S-she sank my gold! Everything's ruined!"

"This place is pure evil. You had to be stopped."

"No, I saved your wife. That little girl has your wife locked inside her. She's a gift."

"A gift we never wanted!" Jim howled. But he knew that he was lying. He was as unhinged as Mendelbaum and was quickly losing any advantage he might have enjoyed. But he couldn't stop. "She wouldn't want this. My father didn't want this."

"Oh, but he did. You saw the video. You know that he wanted to save her more than anything in the world. That's why he killed himself."

"He's comatose, not dead."

"Semantics." Mendelbaum took a deep breath. "None of it matters now. There's no stopping what I've done. Even if she gets off the ship in a storage container, the fallout from the explosion will get them all. It's over, and you and I will spend our last moments together."

Jim felt as though he had been struck with a hammer. "What have you done?" he asked, but his mind had already made the connection. It had taken him too long to drag himself through the ship to confront Mendelbaum; he had given him the time he needed to overload the reactor. The reality of his blunder sent a wave of nausea through him. "How long do we have?"

"Not long now."

Jim closed his eyes and felt the solid armor of the suit around him. He flexed his arms and it was as if they were cast in iron. He tensed his right calf muscle and stopped when he felt movement. Mendelbaum could not know how badly damaged the suit was from the grenade attack. He had assumed that Jim was completely immobile, locked inside the suit. But Jim realized that the ruined actuators in his knee and hip were not holding him frozen in place, he could strike from close range. He would have one opportunity, and it needed to be perfect. He needed Mendelbaum to get in very close. He opened his eyes.

"She tastes like honey, you know."

"What?" Mendelbaum said. He was confused for a moment, and then his anger exploded back to the surface, just where Jim needed it.

"Her body," he said. "It tastes like honey poured on ripe nectarines."

"I-I—" Words had escaped Mendelbaum again. The look in his eyes confirmed what Jim wanted to see; he couldn't wait another second for Jim to die.

He pulled a short dagger from his belt with his right hand and reached around to the back of Jim's head to unhook the facemask with his left. As he drew the knife back, Jim tensed himself, but did not break eye contact. He winked at the green bastard and watched a fresh wave of rage sweep across his face. Jim struck out with his titanium-and-Kevlar-wrapped foot and heard a satisfying snap as he crushed Mendelbaum's left tibia and fibula bones.

The dagger never fell. Mendelbaum collapsed on the ruined leg and stared at it helplessly. It seemed to take him several seconds to remember to suck in a breath and scream in agony. He grabbed his ruined leg and rolled from shoulder to shoulder for several seconds. After a moment, still shrieking, he remembered to reach for his pistol. Jim watched as he struggled to train the pistol on his exposed face. He fired and missed as Jim used his one working leg to tip himself forward, still frozen in place like a statue. He landed on top of Mendelbaum with a heavy crunch—and lay immobile.

Mendelbaum howled with such pain and unspeakable rage that it sounded like his vocal cords ruptured. He was pinned beneath Jim Lantana, the violator of his one true love, and the thousand-pound suit he had stripped off his murdered brother. Jim could hear him wheeze for breath as he crushed down on him. Mendelbaum wriggled beneath him for several seconds before he finally freed his right arm and began to fire the pistol harmlessly off into the air above them. His shots found the chandelier, which now hung at an awkward angle, and Jim heard the tinkle of smashed Swarovski crystals a second before the shards rained down on them.

“Do you feel that?” Jim asked. There was no response, just a bit of flailing. “I think you’re turning me on, moving around like that and all,” he said. The wiggling stopped for a moment, and he thought

Mendelbaum might turn the pistol on himself. They lay like that, trapped together for what seemed like an eternity to both men. Mendelbaum stopped struggling, Jim hoped he had died, but feared he had come up with a new plan. He heard the gun clank against the wood paneled wall they were now sprawled upon, and sensed more than felt, Mendelbaum methodically probing the back of the suit. His hand stopped moving and there was a dull click. Jim felt the suit go slack around him and realized that Mendelbaum was worming his way out.

A second later, Mendelbaum was free; the suit remained deactivated, but Jim could move with great effort. He couldn't see Mendelbaum, but as an afterthought, he snapped the visor back into place. As he did so, two pistol rounds collided with the Kevlar mask, stunning him. He struggled to stand up under the weight of the suit and made it only to his knees as the next barrage of bullets bounced harmlessly off the armor. The exertion tore open his wound, and he cupped his hand ineffectually over the outside of the suit. There was no cooling gel to cauterize the wound or pain medication to calm him. He sagged beneath the weight of the horrible suit and made a feeble attempt to look for Mendelbaum. The suit's electronics and the heads-up display remained black; he could see almost nothing through the tiny visor. He felt like a preposterous medieval squire, crushed by the weight of his masters armor.

Jim squeezed his right hand and felt the spring-mounted scimitar click into place. He dug the tip into the soft wood paneling and used it as a crutch to hoist himself back to his feet. The effort was horrible. It felt like hot acid seeped into his wound, and the coppery taste of blood filled his mouth. But he was on his feet. He stood still, panting with the exertion, and finally got a fix on Mendelbaum—he had crawled back to the podium nearly twenty feet away; it was an insurmountable distance in Jim's condition.

Mendelbaum's leg was ruined and he was out of bullets, but Jim couldn't get within striking distance to finish him. So he chose to change tactics again. "How much longer?" he asked with little more than an exhausted whisper.

"Mmm, I estimate three minutes until the fuel rods around the core go critical; then there should be a multi-megaton detonation." Mendelbaum said. "You've lost her."

"How do you know Phineas didn't change or disable the reactor destruct parameters?" he asked earnestly. The horror reflected in Mendelbaum's face was wonderful, and Jim smiled in spite of all. Mendelbaum hadn't considered Phineas. He had assumed that the original guidelines they had perfected with Jacques were still in place. But why would they be? The clever fat man had thought of everything else.

"Son of a queer-baited bitch," Mendelbaum spat. He turned and began dragging himself the rest of the way to his ebony podium. When he reached it, he hauled himself up on his right leg, clicked the sequence of keys needed to access his LCD screen, and began scanning text. He read for several minutes, oblivious to Jim.

Jim had an idea.

The override that Mendelbaum had used to disable the suit moments earlier was hidden somewhere on his back. Perhaps the same switch would get the suit back online. He had to try.

Lifting his arms to his chest was like bench-pressing several hundred pounds after competing in a triathlon. Jim sucked in a ragged breath and held it as he labored to hold his hand steady. After a few agonizing seconds, he was able to unhook the chest straps. The suit fell open and slid off him down to his waist. He was exposed. If Mendelbaum had any bullets left he was an easy target, but Mendelbaum was engrossed and didn't give him any attention.

Jim glanced at the podium and then down at his semi-cauterized wound and nearly got sick. The tear was gaping open, partially covered by an oozing layer of bloody gel. He took a deep breath, reached around to the back of the suit, and realized that Mendelbaum had stopped typing. He glanced up, considered options, but didn't move.

"You were right," Mendelbaum said at last. "Phineas has prevented me from creating a nuclear detonation. He removed the explosive material from around the trigger. I won't get a proper nuclear bang; it'll be more akin to a massive dirty bomb." He smiled as he said, "We're going to get one hell of a meltdown!" He glanced back at the podium. "It'll overload right about . . . now."

There was a dull hiss from deep inside the ship and then an echoing BOOM. The entire ship pitched to starboard under the force of the blow and both men fell to their knees. Jim knew that Mendelbaum was right. To melt down a reactor, all you had to do was remove the uranium rods from their protective lead housings to allow for a rapid decay. Once the reaction became too hot, a meltdown occurred like the one at Three Mile Island.

The ship and everything aboard would be so irradiated that nothing would be able to survive on it for thousands of years. If Abigail and the kids weren't far away, they wouldn't survive, but at least they had a chance. Phineas had known that Mendelbaum would want this as a last option, and he had been clever enough to disable the ship's ability to create a massive detonation without affecting the ship's power needs.

The *Pura Vida* slowly rolled back to port and was level for a few seconds. Furniture, glass shards, and broken dishes tumbled past both men as the she began to list to starboard for her final journey.

"You know, Katarina's not the only one," Mendelbaum said from the floor. "The others will sink with us now."

Jim heard the words but ignored them. He guessed that the radiation levels throughout the ship were off the chart, spreading in an expanding arc away from the reactor beneath their feet. He thought he was past caring; there was really nothing more he could do, but Mendelbaum's words had energized his fingers. The hiss had grown to a high-pitched whine as the reactor failed, but he continued fumbling with the back of the suit.

Jim's pointer finger worked into a small indentation along the spine of the suit, and he found the tiny toggle switch hidden beneath a rubber flap. He flipped it and felt the suit come to life around him as he began sliding to the far side of the vast chamber with the roll of the ship. Their decline into the abyss was no doubt aided by the millions of gallons of water Mendelbaum had foolishly brought in, but the explosion must have ripped a massive hole in the side for the tanker to sink so fast.

Jim threaded his arms through the Kevlar straps and pulled the suit up around his torso. He struggled to fasten the heavy plastic clasps and didn't see Mendelbaum progressing toward him in a last, hobbled charge. He caught the glint of the falling blade a second too late, and the dagger found its mark in his upper chest. The blade sank to its hilt as he hurled Mendelbaum back with the added strength of the suit. Mendelbaum landed in a pile, the bloody dagger still clutched in his hand.

There was no pain at first. Jim was aware of the suit sealing around him and recognized the cooling sizzle of the cauterizing gel as it flowed into both wounds. He assumed that the blade had missed his heart because he was still conscious, but as he struggled to take a breath, he felt a gurgling in his chest that could mean only one thing. The pain swelled out from his punctured lung to the entry wound and back again like a wave trapped in a shallow pool. The small ragged gasp that he managed burned like super-heated air. He considered not breathing again as he sank to his knees.

The ship had rolled forty-five degrees to port and stopped as it took water; both men lay piled in the corner of the Great Room where the right hand wall met the floor. Jim watched as Mendelbaum dragged himself around behind him, presumably to disable the suit again.

With his last effort, Jim raised his right arm and squeezed the small button in his palm twice. He heard a pop as the titanium spring released and the scimitar spun away like a boomerang. A second later a cacophony of smashed crystals rang out over the banshee howl of rushing water and the gathering nuclear meltdown. Jim felt a sense of calm as the thousand pound chandelier crashed down on top of them. Mendelbaum screamed horribly and fell silent.

Jim sucked in another breath of fiery air and a curtain of red spots descended around him. He decided not to breathe at all for awhile. He felt his mind begin to drift and the sense of calm deepening. To his chagrin, only a few seconds passed before two thin plastic tubes snaked into his nostrils and shattered the calm drift. He became acutely aware of his pain, and he struggled to roll onto his side, but found he was pinned beneath the massive chandelier. He couldn't see Mendelbaum, but there was a deep, dead silence as the ship listed onto its side and lay still. The wail of the reactor had grown to an overwhelming scream from deep inside as a hundred tons of nuclear fuel went critical. It would be over soon.

The tubes that had once kept Guillermo alive tunneled deep into his chest and supplied oxygen to his one good lung. The spots cleared for a moment, and he could see the ocean rushing in through the smashed stained-glass skylight that had once adorned the ceiling above the chandelier. Far out on the horizon he caught a glimpse of the yellow sun rising over the water.

In a deluge of smashed furniture, glass, and silk drapery, the water overcame the Great Room, and Jim knew the ship was beneath the waves. The quiet of the ocean was deafening. He stared at the gaping hole in the sinking ship that seemed to grow larger and realized that he was drifting upward. Small rubber pockets in the suit were inflating around him. He gained momentum and an instant later drifted through the opening and out into the dark water.

It was black for a long time before he crashed through the roiling surface of the water and bobbed on his back. He squeezed his eyes shut against the blinding orb of the sun above him and turned his head. When he reopened his eyes it seemed as if the sun had seared his retina because, against the horizon, another serene yellow ball bobbed like a toy.

52 Arabs, Admirals, Toys

Christiana gripped the polished railing of the *Marquis* ocean liner but still felt unsteady. She used her free hand to pull Zakar closer, and he seemed to sense what she was thinking about. He pulled her head down to cradle her against his chest, and she felt the world stabilize. He smelled of fine Tabarome cologne, a scent she had come to cherish. She released the railing, wrapped her arms around him, and tried to let the gentle rock of the ocean calm her nerves. Her near rape by Jacques the Worm had been the most traumatic experience of her life. She had mentally prepared herself for the fact that she might be required to have sex while aboard the ship, but the memory of the encounter still sent a shock up her spine that made her want to be sick.

“Don’t think about it anymore, Love. Besides, you’re a spy. You should be used to this kinda thing.”

His teasing broke the mood and she released the memory, and him. “I’m not a ‘spy.’ I’m the deputy station chief of the NSA in Europe. I’m a spy *master*.”

Zakar said nothing. He returned his gaze to the sea. They had found nothing in the last three days of searching, and Christiana knew that Admiral Lantana was getting restless.

"You sure moved back into field work easily," Zakar said. It was her turn to remain silent.

She had been a news reporter for all intents and purposes for the last decade. Her cover had become part of her life, a part she enjoyed very much to be sure, but still only a veneer that masked the true nature of her work. Being a journalist was a clever ruse that kept her fingers on the pulse of Europe's radicals.

"You're not going to turn into a problem for me, are you?" she asked.

Zakar leaned away from her in a gesture of mock insult. After a second of thought, he said, "You got me off of that gawdawful ship. I'll do anything you want."

They hadn't spent more than a few minutes apart since their escape in the helicopter, and neither had brought up the ship. They had headed out of the storm on a course toward France and been able to limp along until they were in calmer weather. The helicopter ran out of fuel, but was equipped with utility floats like a seaplane. They had touched down one hundred miles off the southern French coast, and she had activated the back-up homing beacon the admiral had given her. The first beacon was still aboard the *Pura Vida*, broadcasting the ship's position on a secure frequency. It now indicated that the *Pura Vida* was resting on the ocean floor, nearly a mile beneath them.

Her objective had been to locate the ship, confirm Jim Lantana was alive, and bring in the rescue operation led by Admiral Lantana. Instead, she had narrowly escaped with her life and a disinherited Arab no one cared about but her. Zakar had confirmed Jim was aboard, but only after they were miles away from the *Pura Vida* and nearly out of fuel. To compound the situation, the families of the diplomats, heads of state, foreign dignitaries, and other assorted rich people who were aboard the *Pura Vida* were less than pleased with the ship's disappearance. In trying to bring the ship to justice, they had created a major international incident that was only growing worse with each hour they spent at the scene. The sooner they left the area the better, but Lawrence Lantana refused to budge.

"Did you love him?" Zakar asked her.

"Who?"

"Lantana, of course."

"I thought I did, but I realized that it was more the idea of him that I loved. Besides," she said, smiling, "I have a rich boyfriend now."

“Not so rich anymore, I’m afraid,” Zakar said.

They fell silent for a few moments as they both gazed out to sea.

Christiana finally said, “I agreed to locate Jim Lantana because his father asked me to.”

“I know, you told me about the letter that the Admiral gave you to open in the event he was killed or incapacitated.”

“I owed him my career. It was his recommendation that secured my promotion, and he never expected anything for it.”

“So when he asked for help, there was no saying no,” Zakar said.

She had told him most of the story of her interest in the *Pura Vida* moments after their escape. They hadn’t cared to speak of the ship again until this moment.

Christiana said, “I had no idea that Jim could get permission to stage a raid on the *Pura Vida* so quickly. He was already gone when I read the admiral’s letter. Director McHale wouldn’t put me in touch with him, so I had to improvise.”

“So the suicide was a ruse?”

"Yes, but a very dangerous one. He very nearly did kill himself with the amount of barbiturates he ingested."

Zakar leaned in and kissed her on the mouth. "I love it when you talk that way."

She kissed him back briefly then pushed him off the high-powered binoculars that lay in her lap. "We have work to do," she said seriously.

"We're going to need the whole U.S. Navy if we don't get out of here soon."

She knew he was right but ignored the comment. She had expected to be met by a Navy Destroyer and a team of SEALs. Instead, Lawrence Lantana had arrived aboard the *Marquis* with a terrified Owen Tiberius and a crew suited for a cruise ship.

Zakar picked up on her malaise, and added, "If any of the ships searching for the *Pura Vida* become hostile, we're sunk."

Christiana pulled away from him and raised the high-powered binoculars to her eyes. Seconds later she spotted the first man-made object she had seen in the last three days. It was far out on the horizon, and it reminded her of a child's toy. She lowered the binoculars and yelled over her shoulder to Admiral

Lantana, “I’ve got something!”

The yellow balls bobbed in the flat current, and she engaged the distance meter on her binoculars. She was shocked to see that they were nearly a mile out.

“What is it?” Lawrence asked from behind her.

“I don’t know, but they’re huge,” she said, passing over the binoculars.

The Admiral kept the lenses glued to his eyes as he gave the intercept orders.

53 Forty Days Later

Carmichael MacHale, the suspended assistant director of the CIA, stepped back from Jim's hospital bed and opened the curtains. Sunlight streamed in and Jim blinked rapidly. He had been in a coma for thirty-nine days. His awakening the day before was cause for celebration, but he hadn't found much to say. Carmichael had been his only visitor, and no one was allowed to see him until several facts had been verified. The facts had checked out, and Carmichael had been placed on leave. He had secured permission to talk to Jim, and it might be his last official meeting.

News had spread fast that Jim was allowed to have company, and visitors were on their way to see him today. Lawrence Lantana was the first scheduled, but Jim was on the verge of canceling the visit.

"Glad to see you awake," Carmichael said. Jim had no response, so Carmichael kept talking. "That suit was some piece of hardware; we've been going over it around the clock. If you hadn't thought to hang onto that balloon, you'd still be out there."

Jim managed a half smile, but he realized that would probably have suited the director just fine. In the last five minutes, Carmichael had filled him in on the events of the last month. With furious movements of his skinny arms, he had told Jim all about the rescue by his father and Christiana Facchinetti, and the progress that the kids were making in adjusting to life away from the ship.

Carmichael could tell Jim wasn't ready to talk, but he refused to leave. Instead, he pretended he knew how to read the heart rate monitor. The momentary silence was too much for him and he launched in again, "Anyway you look at it, the suit saved your ass. The levels of radiation that must have been released when the ship went critical would have cooked you, otherwise. You don't know how lucky you are. Did you know the suit had a back-up of the ship's log that confirms your story? We were able to access it using the override key Ms. Valquist took with her." Carmichael took a breath and looked at Jim. He still wasn't getting a response so he said, "It exonerates you and your father."

Carmichael sensed his discomfort and began running on at the mouth again. "The ship sank with lots of rich and powerful people aboard, but from what we can tell, they were all frozen in the cryonics chambers. It doesn't look like the ship had more than a few patients in the active hospital treatment facilities. The families of the rich popsicles seem too embarrassed to come forward. Something about spending that kind of cash to have your relatives frozen and floating in the middle of nowhere, I guess. Anyway, they don't seem to be aggressive about, well, you know . . . It looks like you and your dad are in the clear."

"They deserved a hell of a lot better than that," Jim said. "Some of them, anyway."

Carmichael snapped his head toward him, startled to finally hear his voice. Jim smiled briefly as he realized that his father was probably already here, waiting.

As if sensing his thought, Carmichael said, "He's outside, you ready to talk to him?"

Carmichael took Jim's silence as an affirmation and patted him on the leg as he left.

Lawrence Lantana walked into the room. When Jim didn't speak, Lawrence began as best he could by clearing his throat. The sound was awkward coming from Lawrence Lantana. His cheeks blushed slightly, and Jim couldn't help but smile.

It was only then that Lawrence said, "It looks like your old boss Carmichael is out of the CIA for his handling of the data you gave him. He never should have let you go in alone."

Jim stared at his father for a moment, then looked away. He should have canceled this visit.

Lawrence shuffled his feet, kicking at an unseen speck on the floor. “I’m sorry I couldn’t tell you about Sharon or the ship.” He paused, unsure of how to talk to his own son. “I wanted to tell you what had happened while you were away, the lengths to which I went to try to save her. But once she was gone, and I had failed you, it was just too much.” Lawrence stopped and searched Jim’s face.

Jim opened his mouth to speak but found no words.

“Once I saw the video Mendelbaum made of me, I knew that he would never stop. Owen had introduced me to the ship, but in reality, he knew very little of its inner workings. Mendelbaum had me. I had to either kill myself or do what he wanted. And he wanted too much.”

“Your suicide didn’t feel right,” Jim blurted. It was his turn to feel out of place. “If you wanted to die, you would have swallowed your .45, not a bunch of pills.”

“I hoped you’d react that way. I sent Christiana a detailed explanation of what to do to help you. My hope was that you’d start investigating the ship on your own, with her resources to aid you. A United States Senator with C.I.A. and media connections would have a real shot at taking the ship down." He smiled as he said, "I never guessed that you'd get the Agency's sanction in less than a day and head out for it alone."

Jim looked back at his father and said nothing. Lawrence sat down heavily in the room's one worn chair and began again, "I didn't know how to tell you what I'd done to try to save Sharon. We hadn't spoken," he said, searching Jim's face, "really *spoken*, in months." Jim studied his father, and caught the briefest grin before he said, "I thought it was even money you'd have me committed. I had no proof the treatment facility even existed. But if you dug into it yourself, if you found someone who couldn't lie about what they knew, you'd learn the truth."

"That was why you sent me out on the *Marquis* after Sharon died."

Lawrence nodded.

"Did you know they cloned her?"

Before Lawrence could answer, Abigail popped her head around the frame of the door. Edvard stood confidently next to his mother and smiled, Katarina held onto Abigail's long coat so tightly that her small knuckles were beginning to turn white. After a second's hesitation, the trio moved in on him for an embrace that tore his heart in two.

Jim made up his mind not to think about the *Pura Vida.* They would start a new life, a pure life.

Forthcoming by Benjamin C. Yablon

PURE DEATH

Lawrence Lantana arrived right on time. The pretty secretary escorted him back to the office where he was warmly greeted before the door was all the way open.

"Admiral Lantana, thank you for coming,"

Lawrence walked slowly into the lavish office. He had been summoned the day before by his friend George Thormopolis, the Under Secretary of the Navy. "Of course, George. What can I do for you?"

"I need to discuss the ongoing salvage operation. You know how much gold went down with that ship, yes?"

Lawrence nodded.

"Hello Admiral," Came a sweet female voice from behind him.

"Christiana?" He said turning toward the sound.

"It's good to see you," she said. This was odd. Christiana was the deputy station chief of the NSA. She didn't usually have any contact with the Navy.

The Under Secretary cleared his throat and continued, "There are interested parties at the highest levels."

"Understood. What does that have to do with me?"

"We need you to convince him to help us. We need him to review some chatter coming to us from the wreck,"

"Chatter?"

"Yeah, some of the systems of the ship are operational and broadcasting. We think it's a message Mendelbaum left for James."

"Get this through your head, George: it's over. The boat sank. She went critical, exploded, and drifted to one of the deepest, coldest places on the planet. It serves that bastard right."

The Under Secretary remained silent and calm, a fact that made Lawrence want to slug his old friend. "He owes us, Lawrence. You owe us. We supplied the finest team of doctors in the country to treat him. It's a miracle he lived even with their help."

"I'm not dragging Jim back into this. He's making a new life with Abigail. Besides, the wreck is too deep and too hot to salvage. That gold can't be touched for fifty years at least."

“Maybe.”

“Maybe? George, what the hell are you talking about? I’ve seen the report. It’s hotter than Three Mile Island down there.”

“The vaults were lined with lead. It’s likely that some of the material avoided the worst of the contamination. Anyhow, the wreck is in international water. The Kuminyaga Trench can be accessed by anyone with the desire and budget to make the attempt.”

“I know all of that. There’ve been what, six failed expeditions over the last ten months? It’s too deep for manned missions, and it’s going to take a manned mission to make a proper recovery. Only the Chinese are willing to sacrifice their divers over it. Let them have it. You’re not sending in Navy divers, are you? What aren’t you telling me? It’s the signal you’ve intercepted.”

“I can’t give details; it’s eyes only.”

“And you’re telling me that James has clearance?”

Christiana put her hand on Lawrence’s arm and said, “The message is for him. Make the call. Please.”

Made in the USA
Lexington, KY
15 September 2012